W9-BYC-272

White Lies and Other Half Truths

By

Barbara Tiller Cole

White Lies and Other Half Truths

Published by Createspace. Visit them at *www.createspace.com,* an Amazon.com company

Email address: BarbaraTillerCole@gmail.com

Blog: http://BarbaraTillerCole.tumblr.com

Dedication and Acknowledgements:

To Nina, Casey, Linda, Aimee, Linnea, Pat, Jane, Mischa, Debra Anne, Mary Anne, Katie, and Lynne for their help and assistance with this story.

To my Georgia Girls! You Rock!

To All Colin Firth and Matthew MacFadyen fans everywhere!
A special thanks to all those who participated in the Darcy Wars.

To all those who love the gift of books given us by Jane Austen.

To my Mom and Dad, I miss you!

To my dear friend, Shannon!

To my very special mentor, Ruth!

And especially to MY Mr. Darcy, Dick! I love you!

White Lies and Other Half Truths

Prologue

What did it matter; it was just a little white lie? I never thought it would get so out of hand. It seemed simple enough, as I did not choose to have a confrontation in a ballroom.

Elizabeth continued to contemplate the events during the ball at Netherfield that had so changed her life. *I thought that I hated Mr. Darcy then! He had caught me off guard. When he asked me to dance, saying no would have meant that I would have had to sit out the remainder of the evening; so I said yes.*

The dance started out simply; but Elizabeth's impertinence got the better of her. "We must have some conversation, Mr. Darcy."

He responded with a raised eyebrow, "Do you talk as a rule while dancing?" They traded small talk when they came together in the dance.

Mr. Darcy asked, "Do you often walk to Meryton?" This led to a brief discussion of Mr. Wickham. Elizabeth was disappointed that Mr. Wickham did not attend the ball, and she was sure that Mr. Darcy had something to do with it. The more they talked, the angrier Elizabeth became. Suddenly she knew that she could not dance the second of the set with him. Her creative thoughts concocted a plan of escape, but her impulsivity did not achieve her intended outcome.

Elizabeth faked a sprained ankle in order to quit the ballroom. She never, ever, thought that Mr. Darcy would follow her as she hobbled away; yet follow he did.

As Elizabeth entered the Netherfield library, Mr. Darcy caught up with her. Guiding her to a chair near the fire, he asked, "Miss Bennet, please let me help you sit down. Can I get you anything? May I get you some ice for your ankle? Or would a glass of wine help, perhaps?"

"No, Mr. Darcy. I assure you that I am quite all right. I just need to sit quietly. Please feel free to return to the ballroom, sir." But leave he did not. She contemplated why he did not recognize her desire to be rid of him.

"Are you sure that it is just a sprain and not a break? Let me see," he asked. With that he picked up her foot, took off her shoe, and examined her ankle moving her foot back and forth. Remembering the event, Elizabeth was sure he did not think of the impropriety of his actions at the time. She remembered the sensation when his bare hands first touched her foot. It was like warm water soothing it. The heat began in her foot, and shot all the way up to her cheeks within seconds.

Elizabeth was an innocent; the feelings she experienced were quite confusing. Mr. Darcy obviously felt something as well, as his eyes turned to Elizabeth in that same moment, and he said, "Ah, Miss Bennet, I believe your ankle is going to be fine..."

They glanced at each other tentatively. Elizabeth's glance more so than Mr. Darcy's, however. Mr. Darcy looked again at Elizabeth, and this time his eyes did not leave her face. Nor did he release her foot, but began to rub it. "While you rest your ankle for a few minutes, Miss Bennet, would you allow me to speak to you of Mr. Wickham, now that we are away from the others?"

"What? Ah, you may speak Mr. Darcy," she was distracted and breathless by his touch. Elizabeth was shocked, but could not help enjoying it; amazed that he did not seem to realize what he was doing. As he continued to rub her foot, she did not stop him. It felt too good.

Darcy told Elizabeth of his relationship with Mr. Wickham. "Miss Bennet, Mr. Wickham was the son of my late father's steward..."

Darcy continued to tell her of the history the Darcy family had with old Mr. Wickham. Darcy's father had trusted his steward, George's father, and depended on him. His father had been the godfather of the younger Mr. Wickham. He had supported him through Cambridge, intent on providing him a living as the rector at Kympton. After Darcy's father passed, George Wickham had requested and was given three thousand pounds in exchange for the living, along with the one thousand pounds designated in the will.

Darcy spoke of George Wickham's habits and of him returning to demand the living when his funds ran low. His discourse culminated with the story of Wickham's attempted elopement with Georgiana.

As Darcy's story concluded, Elizabeth found that she could no longer stop her tears. She had always prided herself on her ability to judge character. Realizing how wrong she was disturbed and humbled her. *Oh what must he think of me!*

With her embarrassment over her mistaking the nature and quality of both men, she responded, "Oh, Mr. Darcy, I believe I never knew myself. I have always prided myself in my ability to judge character. I could not have been more wrong. What must you think of me?"

"Miss Bennet, you must not blame yourself. Mr. Wickham appears all ease and friendliness; but he has fooled a great many people, including my father. Please do not cry. Mr. Wickham is not worth your pain," Darcy answered.

He stopped rubbing her foot long enough to pull out his handkerchief and hand it to her. She wiped her eyes, then stood and walked to the window and looked out. In her distracted state, she had forgotten her ankle was supposed to be sprained.

Mr. Darcy walked up behind her and put his hand on her shoulder. She turned around as he spoke to her in a surprised tone, "Ah, Miss Bennet your ankle seems to have healed."

She turned around to look him in the eyes. She was mortified. Her cheeks glowed bright red as she quickly dropped her eyes to the floor. "Mr. Darcy, I am quite embarrassed; I told you a white lie, sir. I just needed to get away, and only pretended to sprain my ankle. I am very sorry, sir. I truly have misjudged your character." With much more courage than she actually felt at the time, she turned her eyes towards him and said, "Can you ever forgive me for deceiving you?"

Mr. Darcy picked up her hand and looked deeply into her eyes. He had often noticed Elizabeth's fine eyes, but this was the first time that Elizabeth had ever noticed how expressive his eyes were. They were rich, dark ebony pools, and they captured her. He lifted her hand to his lips and kissed it. As Darcy's lips touched her hand, a sensation like a lightning bolt flew through her body, and her heart began to race. Darcy did not release her hand; and as he held it tenderly, he said in a voice as soft and warm as an embrace, "Miss Bennet, I am more than willing to forgive you, if you can find it within your heart to forgive my unthinkable and absolutely untrue comment. I believe you overheard a remark I most assuredly did not mean on the first night of our acquaintance. I should have asked for your forgiveness quite some time ago."

Her cheeks coloured again, and it was obvious to Darcy that she remembered the comment to which he referred. She found that she could not help herself. She locked eyes with him and smiled, "You are forgiven, sir."

Darcy then smiled a rich, warm smile, so wide that Elizabeth saw dimples in his cheeks she had never imagined existed. They just stood smiling at each other. Before she knew it, he began alternating his glance between her eyes and her mouth.

Neither knew how it happened, but they were drawn together. Elizabeth felt totally under his power; and she gazed at his mouth as well. Like a moth to a flame, she inched towards him as she sensed him moving closer to her, until their lips met in a soft, tentative kiss. She watched as he pulled back from her for a few seconds, to glance into her eyes for approval and then began again. This time she felt him deepen the kiss, as she lifted her arms to touch his shoulders. Elizabeth remembered the feeling of his lips, soft and firm, as well as the warm fluttery feeling that overtook her stomach. As she allowed him to pull her closer and deepen the kiss, she felt his arms wrap around her waist.

Just seconds later the door to the library opened.

"Elizabeth, Mr. Darcy! What is the meaning of this?"
Mr. Bennet entered the library and closed the door.
A white lie had just opened a rather large can of worms!!

Chapter 1

1 December 1811, Netherfield, Pre-Dawn

Fitzwilliam Darcy stood at the window of his bedroom, watching the first lights of dawn. It was early, but anxious to see his fiancée, he could no longer sleep. He enjoyed celebrating the awakening of each new day. Elizabeth was to meet him for a walk before they broke their fast at Longbourn. Darcy had acquired a special license and met with his solicitor regarding the settlement before returning from London the day before. He had had no time alone with Elizabeth as he arrived just before tea with her family. They had agreed to meet for a morning walk in order to talk privately.

Darcy did his best thinking while gazing from windows or pacing back and forth. Had it really only been five days since the ball at Netherfield? It had been a whirlwind. He shook his head; remembering the events of that evening.

~~*~*

"Elizabeth, Mr. Darcy! What is the meaning of this?"

Mr. Bennet entered the library and closed the door.

Elizabeth and Darcy pulled apart instantly; startled. With sheepish, embarrassed looks on their faces, they looked at Mr. Bennet. "Ah, so Mr. Darcy I take it that you no longer think my Elizabeth is not tolerable enough to tempt you?" The expression on his face was between a smirk and a leer. Neither could determine whether he was enraged or diverted. "Quite to your advantage that it was I who entered this door instead of another, is it not? Elizabeth, can you imagine the nerves and flutterings that would have resulted had it been your mother instead of me that entered this door? This has the makings of quite a scandal, do you not think?

Then he turned to Darcy, "Mr. Darcy, I expect you at Longbourn in the morning. Can I **tempt** you to arrive around ten o'clock?"

"Yes, sir," Darcy stuttered as he looked at the floor. He had not felt quite this embarrassed since his father had caught him red-handed, pleasuring himself at age fourteen. *Oh, I cannot think of that now.*

"Come along, Elizabeth," Mr. Bennet reached over to grab her hand. "I believe we will leave the library together. Mr. Darcy, you can leave in a few minutes. We do not want to give the gossips anything to ponder. It is possible that we may be able to avoid a scandal, is it not?"

"Mr. Bennet, would it be possible for me to speak to Miss Elizabeth for just a few more minutes?" Darcy asked.

"No, Mr. Darcy! I think that you and Elizabeth have done quite enough **talking**, as you say, for this one evening. Perhaps I will allow you an audience with her in the morning, after we meet. But for now, Elizabeth and I must take our leave. Come along, dear."

~~*~*~*

Darcy's recollection of that evening caused him to scratch the back of his head and stretch his neck as he recollected his cataclysm of feelings since then.

Darcy's mother taught him that his primary duty and honour was to his family. She encouraged him to believe that going against their expectations, such as marrying for love instead of connections and monetary gain, was not something he should contemplate.

However, his father had always encouraged him to marry for love. This conflict between his parents had often bewildered and intrigued him.

Oh, he knew that Elizabeth, for he could not think of her with any other name now that he had tasted her strawberry lips, had attracted him from the first time he saw her. His admiration had fostered a desire beyond any he had experienced. He had managed to mask that desire, even to himself, until her sister was sick and she came to Netherfield to attend her.
It was at that time that he began to pleasure himself each night as he remembered her exquisite eyes, her raised brow, her impertinent grin and joyous laugh, her bounteous breasts with ripe buds he had occasionally glimpsed through her gown when she talked with him, and her hips that swayed as she walked. He had dreamed of her every night since, waking each morning erect and straining, as his body responded to the desires of his dreams. He had struggled with the belief that he could not seek his true

desire, to claim Elizabeth as his own. Yet the events in the library had led him to give way to duty and honour, and to plan a future with the woman he knew that he now loved. Sitting and leaning back in the chair in his room, his mind returned to that meeting in Mr. Bennet's library the morning after the ball.

~~*~*~*

"So, Mr. Darcy, do take a seat," Mr. Bennet stated as Darcy entered the Longbourn library the morning after the ball. "Would you like some tea; or perhaps some of my fine brandy? I believe that I will have a small glass. Would you like some as well?"

"Thank you for asking, Mr. Bennet, but I do not need anything at present," Darcy responded. Darcy stood and began pacing the room. "Mr. Bennet, I understand completely why you have invited me here this morning. My actions, and my actions alone, led to the events of last evening. Please do not blame Miss Elizabeth. I alone am responsible, and I am more than willing to remedy this situation." Darcy stopped and returned to his chair and looked directly into Mr. Bennet's eyes.

"You see, sir; I am in love with your daughter. I believe I began to fall in love with her the first time I saw her. I respect her, I delight in her vast knowledge of literature, rejoice in her musical skills, am thrilled each time I hear her laugh as it is as light and carefree as a crystal bell. I would ask, sir, that you grant me permission to ask Miss Elizabeth for her hand in marriage."

Darcy was nervous and was rubbing his hands together, "I have been thinking about this all night. I know that your daughter's feelings for me may not be as strong as my feelings for her, but we cleared up many of our misunderstandings last evening. I believe that her feelings for me will grow. It is possible that someone other than you could have seen the events of last evening, and the consequences of that are too great. I believe we should marry soon, and I hope that you will see fit to grant us your blessing."

"You believe that my daughter would want to marry you, Mr. Darcy? I thought you found her only tolerable, and not handsome enough to tempt you," Mr. Bennet smirked. Darcy was startled to realize where Elizabeth had gotten much of her sense of humour.

Darcy stood again and resumed his pacing, running his hand through his curly locks, "Last night, I apologized to Miss Bennet for my most unkind and untrue statement the first night of our acquaintance at the Meryton Assembly, sir. I knew that it was highly likely she had heard me, because she walked by me very shortly afterwards and smirked at me. I believe it was in that moment that I began to fall in love with her. I had not even looked at her prior to that moment. I was in an ill humour that evening, and Bingley was trying to goad me into dancing. Please allow me to apologize to you for any ill humour I have displayed toward any member of your family. As a child I was quite shy, and over the years I fear my shyness is often misinterpreted as aloofness. I meant no slight on any member of your family, sir."

"Thank you, Mr. Darcy. You might do, you might do indeed. But I cannot speak for my daughter, sir. I agree that it would most likely be best for you to marry, and marry soon to avoid any potential scandal that could affect all of my daughters. But even with the fear of scandal, I will not force my daughter to marry you if she is unwilling. I will give you time for an audience with her this morning; and if she is less than sure at this time, I will allow you to court her and speak with her about the advantages of marriage over the possibility of scandal. But you will be your own man, sir. You will have to make your own request. Do we understand each other?"

"Yes, I believe we do, Mr. Bennet. If Miss Elizabeth does say yes, I would ask that we be allowed to marry within a fortnight. I will need to make a quick trip to London to procure a special license and work with my solicitor on the settlement. I need to return to Pemberley prior to Christmas, and would like a little time with my new bride before family arrive. I know that I am being presumptuous, but would the eleventh of December be enough time for you?"

Mr. Bennet chuckled, "Yes, you are a little presumptuous, but I have no problem with a wedding that soon, that is, if my daughter accepts you."

"Well, while I am being presumptuous, should all go well today, I would like to invite you and your family to come to Pemberley for Christmas. I want to assure you that if your daughter does accept me, I will consider your family as my family, sir."

"Even Mrs. Bennet, Mr. Darcy?" Mr. Bennet questioned.

"Yes, sir."

"You do know, of course, that Elizabeth is my favourite. I know that I should not favour one of my daughters over the others, but her extraordinary intelligence and keen wit were evident even as a child. She was too smart for her mother, and so inquisitive. I found that I spent a great amount of time conducting her education as a child. She has probably read most of the books in this library, and her memory for details is incredible. She will be quite a challenge to you. I assume that you honour these qualities in my Lizzy, for why else would you have fallen in love with a woman of no connections? I would have thought that you would have married a wealthy heiress, sir."

"If wealth and connections were what I was looking for, I could have chosen to marry long ago, but I did not. My father encouraged me to marry for love. Not everyone in my family will understand my decision, but I will not let anyone harm Elizabeth. If any of my family chooses not to accept my decision, then I will discontinue my communication with them."

"And Lady Catherine, I assume she will be the one most unhappy with your decision. As I understand it, she has long hoped for an alliance between you and her daughter, Anne? She will be quite disappointed with your decision."

"How do you know of that? Has Mr. Wickham shared this information with you?" Darcy felt his anger rising.

"No, I did not hear it from Mr. Wickham. You may be surprised to know that your father, George, and your Uncle Edward were good friends of mine at Eton and at Cambridge. I know much about your family."

Darcy sat down suddenly, stunned, "You are Tom?"

Mr. Bennet nodded his head.

"My father often spoke of you. This is unbelievable, sir. I had no idea."

"No, I would think not. But knowing your family has helped me decide to give you the chance to convince my daughter to marry you, instead of calling you out, eh? I have heard that you are an excellent man, Mr. Darcy. I spoke with Elizabeth this morning; and she has agreed to nothing, as I did not ask that of her. Believe me when I tell you that you have always inspired deep feelings in her. Certainly, they were not always kind thoughts, but she has never been indifferent to you. Lizzy has never acted as she did last night with anyone. I am quite sure that you were her first kiss. She would not have allowed it had she been disinterested. Your cheek does not seem to be injured today. I assure you, you would have been soundly slapped if you had made her unhappy. Might I suggest that I allow you that interview now?" Mr. Bennet said as he began to usher Darcy out the door.

"Perhaps we will talk more later. Her plan was to await you in the back parlour. I wish you good favour with my daughter, Mr. Darcy," Mr. Bennet offered.

"Thank you, Mr. Bennet. I hope to return to you within the hour."

"Very good, then." And with that Darcy walked out of the library.

~~*~*~*

As Darcy approached the back parlour, he heard a loud voice coming from the room. He instantly recognized it as Elizabeth's, and his stomach leapt into his chest as he moved to the door.

"No, sir! Do you understand the meaning of the word **no**, Mr. Collins? Nothing would cause me to reconsider my answer to you. No! You are the last man in the world that I could be ever be prevailed upon to marry!" Darcy heard her words and was incredulous. *Does that toad think he has sense enough to ask MY lovely Elizabeth for her hand? The very gall of the man!*

He then startled as Mr. Collins responded, "My dear, Cousin Elizabeth, I know you will reconsider. I know your parents will press my suit, and you and I will be married quite soon. It is highly unlikely that you will EVER receive another offer of marriage."

Upon hearing that statement, Darcy entered the room. "That statement, sir, is what is highly unlikely. You will excuse us, Mr. Collins," he stated as he entered the room and moved to stand between Elizabeth and Mr. Collins. Darcy glared at the man with an angry impenetrable stare, commanding him to leave the room. With such a look, Mr. Collins was so startled that he literally backed out of the room while bowing.

Chapter Two

1 *December 1811, Longbourn, Pre-dawn*

Elizabeth Bennet stood at her window, glimpsing the first light of dawn. She had hardly slept. Elizabeth was not made for unhappiness; yet on this day, this morning, she had never felt so insecure, or had so many unanswered questions on her mind.

So much had happened since *'the event.'* She struggled for the right analogy to explain how she felt. Perhaps she could explain her feelings by comparing them to the River Severn whose twists and turns, rises and falls were so numerous. It was the longest river in England. At times, like this morning, her feelings were coming to a waterfall. She could hear the roar of the falls crashing over the precipice onto the rocks below, yet not knowing how long or fast she would plummet as she traversed the crest. She did not know whether she would be crushed or buried beneath the rushing waters. Elizabeth was troubled indeed.

As she attempted yet again to find her courage, fears tempted her into near panic. She decided to sit down and reflect again on the events of that morning, the day after *'the event.'*

~~*~*~*

Elizabeth headed to the breakfast room early. She was hoping to speak to her father prior to his meeting with Mr. Darcy. She was in luck as her father was already there, while the rest of the family was still abed. "Good morning, Elizabeth. Will you join me in my library for a private conference over our morning repast, my dear?"

"Yes, Papa, let me quickly get a cup of tea and a pastry. I will gladly join you." He took her plate as they walked down the hall to his library.

Mr. Bennett closed the door behind him and locked it. Both knew that little was private at Longbourn. They had discovered long ago that if they wanted to be in each other's confidence, locking the door was necessary. With the exception of Jane, none of the ladies of the house ever knocked prior to entering a room.

"Sit, Lizzy, I believe we must have some conversation this morning."

"Yes, sir," Elizabeth said, looking at her lap. She did not know what her father would say, but dreaded his words of disgust and disappointment. Surprisingly, those words were not to come.

"Come, come, Elizabeth, I am not going to take you to task. It is quite evident you have already done that yourself. You look as though you have not slept well." Mr. Bennett watched Elizabeth startle a bit. "Oh, do not worry, your Mr. Darcy will not return to thinking you do not tempt him. It is just my habit to study you closely, and I know you have slept poorly."

"Yes, you are correct, Papa. I have been reviewing the events of last evening most of the night," Elizabeth said almost in a whisper.

"My dear, it is not your habit to be missish. I do not intend for you to become your mother. I already spend too much of my annual income on smelling salts for her," to which he chuckled softly.

"It is quite obvious that you and your Mr. Darcy have resolved much." He paused for effect, and then, with a smirk and a slight laugh, continued, "But I must know how you came to care for him enough to be caught in such a situation last evening? I must be sure he did not force himself upon..."

Elizabeth interrupted him, "Oh, no, Papa. The events of last evening were entirely and completely of my making. I am solely at fault for our... for the impropriety of being caught in a room alone. We were dancing, you see. I pretended to sprain my ankle to get away from him, and he followed to be sure I was well. We ended up talking, and clearing the air.

"Then I told Mr. Darcy of my white lie about my ankle. He then told me about his white lie, stating to Mr. Bingley that I was only tolerable, and we forgave each other. Then, we just ended up kissing. It would not have happened in the first place, if not for my lie.

"Papa, please do not be mean to him or call him out. He did nothing I did not allow, perhaps even encourage... I do not know... I have never experienced anything like this before. I fear that I hardly know myself..."

"Elizabeth, stop, you are running away with yourself. Slow down and catch your breath. I am not upset with you. I am actually not upset with Mr. Darcy, if you are happy. However, I do believe that due to the possibility of scandal, it might be provident that you marry.

"I have no intention of forcing you to accept him, or to force him if he is unwilling; unless, of course, a scandal does break out. But I sense you are not indifferent to him, are you? Your feelings for him have always been intense, if not always favourable. I know you well enough to believe you would not have allowed events to transpire the way they did last evening if you did not find HIM tolerable enough to tempt you, eh?"

"Papa, please do not force him..."

"Elizabeth, unless I am very, very wrong, Mr. Darcy is quite in love with you. I do not believe I will need to force him. I expect him to come here today to ask for your hand. You might not yet love him, but you should think seriously about whether you would be willing to accept him.

"Mr. Darcy is a good man, my dear. You are not aware of this, but I have known the Darcy family for quite some time. His father, George and his uncle, Edward, were friends of mine at Eton and later at Cambridge.

"I happen to know that Mr. Darcy has had a great deal of responsibility placed upon him at a young age. He is the master of a very grand estate and guardian of his sister.

"Now why do you not go and rest a bit in the back parlour, as Mr. Darcy arrives shortly. Do some serious thinking, my Lizzy. I will send him to you when we are finished. I love you, I hope you know that."

Elizabeth was flabbergasted with her father's attitude towards '*the event*' and Mr. Darcy, but she simply answered, "Yes Papa, I do."

~~*~*~*

Elizabeth smiled for a moment as she reflected on the events that led to that particular conversation with her father. So much had happened the night of the Netherfield Ball.

Several days ago, Elizabeth had spoken with Charlotte Lucas about the night of the Ball. Unfortunately, it appeared that her mother and sisters had not presented themselves to good advantage. Elizabeth was grateful that William had not witnessed any of it, for she was still insecure regarding what he thought of her family.

It was reported that Lydia had stolen Captain Denny's sword and ran around the ballroom, daring him to catch her. Lydia had always been a silly girl; and where Lydia went, Kitty usually followed. This was the first formal event Lydia and Kitty had been allowed to attend. This was not a formal introduction, but was the first time they were '*out*.' Elizabeth knew her father was concerned about the impropriety (of course who was she to talk about impropriety) of Lydia's public actions (at least Elizabeth's were witnessed only by her father).

Perhaps her father would rethink Lydia and Kitty being '*out*' so young. Elizabeth was aware this had caused a serious disagreement between her parents, and her father had given in to her mother, in order to re-establish order in their home. Elizabeth also knew that her father had let her mother know, as well as Lydia and Kitty, that should their behaviour reflect badly on the family, this would be the last occasion they would be allowed to attend for some time. Elizabeth believed he had threatened to send them to a finishing school if they could not act like young ladies.

Charlotte said that Mary sat in a corner the entire evening, her head buried in a book. Mary did not have any interest in socializing, as she was always either reading or practicing the pianoforte. Elizabeth also knew something about her that no one else knew; Mary was writing a novel. Even though Mary always seemed to carry around a copy of Fordyce's sermons, it was a ruse to keep hidden the books that she really preferred. She was currently reading a novel by Mrs. Radcliffe.

Elizabeth occasionally read new scenes when Mary needed input regarding her writing. She would help Mary clarify whether the scenes fit the period of time, some two hundred years prior. Elizabeth occasionally assisted her in research needed for her story, by studying books in her father's library. Just the week before, Mary told Elizabeth she had settled on a pen name. She was going to use '*Lady Mary Anne*.' Elizabeth was constantly surprised at Mary's creativity.

Then there was her mother. According to Charlotte, her mother must have been quite tipsy, talking too loudly about a possible match between Jane and Mr. Bingley. Charlotte said she saw her flirting, *how embarrassing*, with Sir William. Elizabeth felt a cold chill run through her body.

As she concluded her thoughts of the night of the ball, she thought again about the toad that was Mr. Collins. She was still horrified that the greasy excuse for a gentleman had approached her! *I truly think he must use lard to slick back his hair! He has a funny smell about him. It is horrid, pungent stench of wet socks and fried fish. That is it!'* She shivered.

Elizabeth continued to stand at the window, thinking of the enigma that was her fiancé. Her father was right. She had never been indifferent to him. She remembered the first time that she saw him.

I was out for my morning walk and sat upon the fence between Longbourn and Netherfield. Two unknown gentlemen, riding magnificent horses, galloped across the meadow. The blonde was handsome enough; but the brunette with the wind blowing through his hair, nearly took my breath away. He did not wear a hat that morning and was laughing. The sight had been so mesmerizing, that Elizabeth had been unable to move.

I had never had that kind of reaction to any man, much less a stranger. Questions ran through my head. Who is this man? Will I ever meet him? Is he real? Elizabeth remembered feeling warm and flushed seeing him for the first time. *Why it* ***was*** *Fitzwilliam I saw that morning. Extraordinary!*

Later when he walked into the Meryton Assembly, before he spoke, she stopped and grinned to herself. *I was again struck that this was the most handsome man I had ever seen. Albeit, he did not look very happy that night; but even frowning Fitzwilliam is a striking, devastatingly, handsome man.*

I guess that was why I was so offended and my pride so wounded when I heard him speak that 'now forgiven' offensive statement. Thinking back, his statement was probably as much of a white lie to get Mr. Bingley to leave him alone as my sprained ankle was a white lie to escape him.

And his kiss! His lips were so soft, so warm, and so firm all at the same time. And his scent! It was a combination of lime and musk, with a wildness about it... combined with exotic spices from the West Indies. Whenever Elizabeth found herself thinking about his kisses, she would discover that she was warm and flushed.

And Lord, I still cannot believe that toad, Mr. Collins, she giggled. *I do not think I will ever forget what a ridiculous sight he was as he backed out of the room. What ever possessed him to think that I was awaiting his addresses? What possessed my mother to think that I would consider saying yes to such a man?*

... yet, after Mr. Collins had left the room, Mr. Darcy had remained.

It was with a smile that she began to think about that particular interview.

Chapter 3

Darcy and Elizabeth reflect back to the proposal

After Mr. Collins backed out of the room, Elizabeth and Darcy glanced at each other. Elizabeth's cheeks were red, her heart racing. She walked to the picture window to calm herself. Darcy closed door, hoping he and Elizabeth would have an uninterrupted conversation.

Witnessing the interaction between Elizabeth and Mr. Collins had raised Darcy's ire. His righteous indignation at Collins' presumptiveness and idiocy had absolutely nothing to do with Elizabeth; he needed to get his feelings back under good regulation in order to successfully press his suit.

Darcy imagined that Elizabeth was also affected. He had seen the flushed red colour of her cheeks and the set of her jaw. He heard her quite loud, and substantially sound, rejection of the toad's addresses. As he looked over at her standing, gazing out the window, he knew he needed to give her time to compose herself.

What whimsical irony had joined forces in the universe to have him presenting a marriage proposal directly following his aunt's ridiculous parson? *Only one time in life does this situation present itself, and this is my lot.* Darcy determined that thinking of the humour of the situation would calm him. Perhaps this would be something they would learn to laugh about in its retelling. One could never tell.

With the kindest of thoughts, he walked to Elizabeth and stood to her right. He allowed enough space between them for a feeling of separation. Gazing at her, he saw her cheeks, still flushed; and her breasts rising and falling at a much faster than normal rate. *Good God, man, get yourself together. You absolutely cannot think of her breasts at this moment, or your fate will stand with Mr. Collins.*

Taking another breath, he turned slightly and said, "Miss Elizabeth, I imagine you are quite upset at the moment. Might I get you something? I could return to your father's library and get you a glass of wine if you like?"

Elizabeth turned towards him and answered. "It is considerate of you to ask, sir; but I have tea over there, already," she said as she pointed to the secretary. "You could bring me a cup?"

"I would be happy to do so, Miss Elizabeth. I believe you take your tea with two spoons of sugar, and a little cream?" Darcy said with a smile.

"You know how I take my tea?" Elizabeth's brow arched, as she was quite surprised. Darcy loved her quizzical expression. It warmed his heart, and it worked towards dispelling his anxious irritation. It also broke some of the tension that lingered in the room. She watched him as he went to the secretary that held the tea service.

"I believe you will discover that I know many things about you, Miss Elizabeth," he stated with conviction.

She arched her brow again and smiled, walking to a chair near the secretary and sat down to face the fire, still deep in thought. They both knew they needed to get beyond this very awkward situation.

Darcy walked to her, placed the cup on an end table to her left, and placed his own to the left of hers. Before sitting himself, he turned and asked, "Miss Elizabeth, do you mind?" He directed his hand towards the chair.

"Oh, Mr. Darcy, how rude of me. Please do sit down. I fear I am not yet myself."

"Please, Miss Elizabeth, do not make yourself uncomfortable. I am perfectly willing for you to take as much time as you need to calm yourself." With this he paused. "I...ah...I take it you were not expecting your previous guest to join you?" He had a small, friendly, open smile on his face. He wanted her to know that he was more than willing to hear her speak of whatever she wished. He also thought it might help her to speak of the lingering ghost of the toad in the room.

Elizabeth dropped her head into her hands before removing them to look over at Darcy. He intently watched her as she sighed before she started. "Mr. Darcy, I wish I could say I was completely unaware of the possibility of such an interview. I knew there was a slight possibility, particularly after Mr. Collins procured my first set at the ball. But I certainly never contemplated it happening in this fashion. I am perhaps more embarrassed than I have ever been in my entire life; and still full of ire at the *gall* of that man for considering that I would be happy as '*the companion of his future life,*' as he so inelegantly stated.

"Mr. Darcy, you may not know this, but Mr. Collins came to Longbourn a week ago. At the direction of your aunt Lady Catherine de Bourgh, of whom he speaks incessantly, he came to offer us an '*olive branch*' he says. Longbourn is entailed away from the female line, and as I have no brothers. It appears that Mr. Collins will inherit, should my father pass away prior to him. He came to choose one of us — let me remember how he said it — *to honour one of Mr. Bennet's daughters by taking her as my bride, allowing her to rejoice for a lifetime in the condescension of Lady Catherine de Bourgh, my magnificent benefactress.*"

"My mother has been speaking with him, apparently, and told him that Jane... Well... ah... you know, Mr. Darcy, that my sister has deep feelings for your friend. It might be quite imprudent for me to mention it at this point. But my mother, though quite ridiculous at times, does care for her favourite daughters... Jane and Lydia. Since she knows, as well as I, that Jane's heart is quite spoken for she apparently told Mr. Collins that Jane was spoken for. She then went on to tell him that I was *not nearly as attractive as Jane, but as the second daughter in the family I would accept my family duty and honour his petition.*"

"He said that in a marriage proposal? That is ridiculous!" Darcy exclaimed as looked over at her to gauge her reaction.

"Yes, quite. You are being most kind, sir. But certainly you do not want to hear all the disingenuous words that ridiculous toad of a man spoke in his rejected proposal!" Elizabeth exclaimed as she smiled a weak smile in his direction.

"Miss Elizabeth, believe me, this must be the most unusual situation in which I have ever found myself. I would imagine that the same could be said of you?" Darcy looked to her and she nodded her head.

"I believe that if we are able to look at peculiar, ironic levity of the position in which we find ourselves, it will allow us to find enough composure to have the conversation that was predestined for this '*interview,*' as your father called it." Darcy lightly chuckled and found that his comments had produced what he had hoped. Elizabeth lightly laughed as well, bringing a smile to her face.

She took a sip of her tea and said, "Yes, I believe you are right. Irony might be helpful. Perhaps Shakespeare said it best, *'*All the world's a stage, and all the men and women merely players: they have their exits and their entrances,*'" shared Elizabeth.

"Ah, yes, from As You Like it. You must admit Mr. Collins' exit was something of that. It could have come right from one of Shakespeare's comedies," he chuckled and stretched out his leg a bit as he sat in the chair.

"Perhaps, Mr. Darcy, but your entrance was sheer poetry itself," she said as she joined him in laughter.

"* *'A little foolery that wise men have makes quite a show'*, also from As You Like It and I believe that it has been quite a show so far today'," Darcy laughed a bit louder.

"Yes, Mr. Darcy, *'*A fool thinks himself to be wise, but a wise man knows himself to be a fool'* therefore it is quite clear that Mr. Collins is a fool, while you are quite wise, think you not?" Elizabeth said as she continued to laugh.

Darcy laughed whole-heartedly then, and Elizabeth found herself joining him. They laughed harder as the laughter of the other infected their spirits. Occasionally, they would glance at each other, and it reignited their mirth. Darcy was holding his abdomen, as his stomach muscles were sore from his deep belly chortle. At some point, they did not remember why they laughed; but they laughed so hard they were both in tears. As their laughter came to an end, Darcy pulled out his handkerchief and moved to Elizabeth in order to wipe the tears that were sliding down her face. Then he wiped his own and placed it again into his pocket.

He then moved to his knees on the floor in front of her, and taking both of her hands in his, he smiled into her eyes. "Miss Elizabeth, I know that the events of the last day may have slightly rushed the timing of the words I say to you now. But they have been in my heart for so long, I have no problem whatsoever in voicing them. From the very beginning of our acquaintance, I have had a passionate regard for you. Your expressive, emerald green eyes caught me in their lure the first time you turned to me, which was unfortunately after I had made that comment we have discussed last evening," he paused, and they both chuckled.

"The level of your love, kindness and care for your sister while you were both at Netherfield is something I have never seen before. Your quick mind, clever words and definitive opinions have captured my mind. Your beauty is unsurpassed, as you are by far, the most beautiful woman of my acquaintance. And, I have rarely heard anything that has brought me more joy than to hear you sing and play, other than perhaps the sound of your laughter."

"I know beyond a shadow of a doubt, that there will never be another woman with whom I wish to share my life. I love you with all my mind, body and soul. I also know at this moment, your feelings for me may not be what mine are for you; but alas, that worries me not. I know you have some passionate regard for me, as I have witnessed last evening," he stopped and raised her hand to his lips and paused for just a few seconds and smiled.

"I have witnessed first hand your ability to love those you care about. I will commit to spending the rest of my life making myself worthy enough for you to care about me."

"Elizabeth Bennett, will you consider allowing this imperfect; not always well articulated, passionate man, to make you his wife? Will you marry me?" Darcy stopped and continued to look into her eyes. His heart was beating faster than he ever remembered. This was the moment. He had lived the last six years, since his father's death, not caring if he ever married. That is, until the spirit of Elizabeth Bennet had captured him. His breath caught as he prayed that she would accept him, as he did not know if he could live without her.

Elizabeth looked deeply into his eyes. Their warm, gentleness pierced her soul. His proposal was unlike anything she had ever dreamed, even when she HAD dreamed of a knight in shining armour sweeping her off of her feet, and asking for her hand in marriage. His words were the most beautiful she had ever heard. And while she did not know if she yet loved him, she KNEW that she was FAR from indifferent to him; she knew that she never wanted another to kiss her lips. The memory of their kiss was firmly in her thoughts as she voiced the words he longed to hear, "Yes, Fitzwilliam, I will be happy to marry you."

Darcy took both of her hands, kissing the back of one and then the other, over and over. He was grinning from ear to ear. Then he began to laugh again; a deep, rich, full laugh. He stood and lifted her to her feet. He pulled her into his arms and hugged her to him as she put her arms around his waist. He lifted her off the floor and spun her around and around. They both were laughing and smiling at each other. Finally, he stopped and placed her feet back on the floor.

He gazed at her eyes and then her lips, and dipped in to softly kiss her bottom lip. He suckled it as she slightly opened her mouth. And as they began to deepen their kiss, they heard a horrible screech.

Out in the hall they could hear, "Mr. Bennet, Mr. Bennet, you must come and make Lizzy marry Mr. Collins. Mr. Bennet, do you hear me! Lizzy must marry Mr. Collins or I will never speak to you or your Elizabeth again," screeched Mrs. Bennet. Darcy and Elizabeth stopped their kiss. They looked at each other and began to laugh again.

*Quotes are from the works of William Shakespeare.

Chapter 4

1 December 1811, Just after Dawn, near Longbourn

Darcy slowly paced the front boundary of Longbourn. He had dressed and walked from Netherfield with eager anticipation of seeing Elizabeth. After returning from London two days ago, he had lunch with the entire Bennet clan yesterday. But he and Elizabeth had remained in the company of her family. They had briefly discussed what he accomplished in London, but they had not had any time alone.

Darcy had asked her if there was a possibility of spending time together this day. Stating that she had a habit of walking before breaking her fast each day they had agreed to walk together to Oakham Mount. He had been so anxious to see her that he arrived shortly after dawn.

As he paced back and forth he remembered, *she looked so lovely yesterday. I do believe that she has never worn a dress in which her assets were so prominently displayed. When I complimented her on the dress, I could not but help but look at her lovely breasts, so voluptuously exposed by the décolleté neckline. When she caught my eyes looking, she blushed a lovely bright colour of pink.*

He ran his hand through his hair and smiled. *How I enjoy making her blush. She told me the gown was new, that her mother insisted she purchase it. I must thank Mrs. Bennet for her good taste! Luscious Lizzy, indeed. Good God, I have never had to retreat to so many windows in my life. Just the thought of her breasts and I find myself aroused. I do believe that I have been up more than down in the last five days.* As he thought it, he began feeling the first stirrings of his arousal. He stopped walking a minute and took a couple deep breaths.

Elizabeth is a maiden and I doubt she is acquainted with such things. What would she think if she saw me? I must calm myself before she arrives. It will not do for me to be erect before we even begin our walk. I wonder if I have time to relieve myself. Oh God, how could I even think of such a thing out in full view of the road. Darcy began his slow pace again, but periodically ran his hand through his hair.

I will think of Aunt Catherine. She was horrible when she visited... something about Mr. Bennet... not believing that I would consider being a part of his family. Perhaps I will talk more with him. He did say that he was a friend of my father and uncle. Perhaps I can learn more when I go over the settlement papers with him. There, I am calmer. Ah... I see her now.

Darcy watched as she approached. She was wearing a lavender muslin gown with a much higher neckline than the one she had worn the day prior, but he still thought she was lovely. Her hair was pulled up, concealed under a lavender bonnet. The closer she got to him, the more he noticed that her body language did not appear open and inviting. She was plodding along in her steps, her arms crossed in front of her chest, and she was looking at the ground. As she got even closer, he realized that she was definitely not smiling; in fact it looked as if she had a scowl on her face. He knew he could lift her mood as he had done that the day he proposed, and he could certainly do it again.

"Good morning, my dear. You look quite lovely this morning," he said with cheer.

Her response was not what he wanted. Not what he wanted at all as she whispered, eyes fixed to the ground, "Thank you, Mr. Darcy".

Oh dear, I know I have done something wrong. But what is it? Is she angry with me? Did I do something yesterday that was insensitive? Why is she angry? Darcy's thoughts were a jumble as he caught up with her stride. She had not even paused for him to join her, but continued walking.

With as much cheer as possible, he said, "Oh, are we back to Mr. Darcy? I thought you agreed to call me William when we were alone." He offered her his arm but she did not take it.

Good God, what have I done now? She must be angry with me. Should I ask her? Maybe we should just walk for a while as the walk may calm her spirits. Perhaps she did not sleep well.

"It is a lovely day, is it not? I watched the sunrise from my window at Netherfield, anxious to see you. I am glad you agreed to this walk as it has been so long since we have had time alone. Perhaps we can walk each morning until the wedding. It seems as soon as we break our fast each morning others take over our lives, and there is no time to spend together. Do you not agree?" Darcy said lightly.

Anticipating a pleasant retort, all she said was, "Yes, sir."

Ah, it must be much worse than I even imagined. I am back to sir. Is she regretting her agreement to marry me? Oh Lord, what would I do if that were the case? I do not believe I can live without Elizabeth now. She is just so lovely, so precious to me.

Darcy continued to contemplate what could be wrong. "Elizabeth, have I offended you in some way? Are you angry with me for some reason?" he cautiously and pleadingly asked.

"No, sir," was all she would say. She continued to walk and avoid his eyes.

I wonder if, maybe that is it. I know that Georgiana has a time each month where she is ill at ease, and often irritable, her monthly courses is what she calls it. Could that be it? I cannot ask her. I know that it happens monthly when a woman is not pregnant, but to be honest I do not even completely understand it myself. So I certainly cannot ask her if that is it, but at least that could be it.

They continued to walk, "Are you unwell, Elizabeth?" Darcy was truly trying to understand. But he felt like he was failing badly. They had reached Oakham Mount.

Elizabeth suddenly stopped and turned towards him, answering sharply, "No, I am not unwell. I fear I am poor company, as I am feeling quite taciturn and disagreeable. Perhaps you would find your own company preferable to mine, sir." As she ended her statement, she walked away.

Darcy caught up with her and quickly stated, "I am content to be in your company no matter your state, and am more than willing to remain silent if you prefer." With that, Darcy said not another word the entire way back.

His mind, however, was not quiet. *I do not believe that I have ever heard her with such an edge to her voice, well, with me. There was her interaction with Mr. Collins. Ah, Elizabeth, please tell me what troubles you? If only thoughts could transcend a soul.*

They continued to walk. Her pace slowed just a bit, and she allowed him to walk beside her; but no other direct communication was to be had.

Darcy continued to muse, *Maybe I should show her the letter from my Uncle Edward. Receiving it was a quite a surprise yesterday. Uncle Edward said when he heard of my engagement that he laughed out loud, so strong and so long that my aunt, and even Richard, wondered what was wrong with him. I know that he knew Mr. Bennet, but I do not know anything of that history. They must have been close.* There was a rough patch of ground and Darcy offered his arm to Elizabeth and she took it this time.

Oh, my Elizabeth, what troubles you so? They continued to walk. This encounter had not progressed as he had hoped. As much as Darcy had enjoyed their two past kisses, they were not enough for his impatient ardour. He had hoped to be able to have some intimate time with his fiancée today, but it was not to be. In fact, they seemed farther apart than ever before.

Elizabeth stumbled over a root in the ground, but before she could fall Darcy caught her. She looked at him quite briefly and blushed. He brought her arm up and placed it around his and guided her on in their walk. They did not speak, but she did not pull away from him. They glanced at each other briefly from time to time. Only once or twice during the remainder of their return to Longbourn did they catch, even for a second, the other looking.

At least she has not turned me away and no angry words have passed through her lips—luscious, strawberry, ruby lips. Oh, stop it Darcy. You are not going to taste those lips today. Be grateful that she has not run from you completely

Minutes later they arrived back at the path to Longbourn.

They stopped walking and Darcy turned to her. "Elizabeth, I know you may have preferred to be on your own today, but thank you for walking with me. I believe that I will return to Netherfield as I have business that requires my attention. Accomplishing such tasks now will allow me to be able to spend uninterrupted time with you after our wedding. Please get some rest, and please tell me you will be willing to walk with me tomorrow morning. Even if you still do not wish to speak, just being in your presence gives me joy and calms my spirit. Shall I see you in the morning?" He smiled at her.

She chanced a brief look at Darcy and saw his smile and his dimples, "Yes William, I shall see you in the morning." She did not smile. The look was short. But she called him William. For Darcy it was enough.

Darcy walked back to Netherfield and was greeted by Miss Bingley. "Ah, Mr. Darcy, where have you been so early in the morning?" Darcy had been doing everything possible to avoid Miss Bingley. She was bad before in her pandering, but since his engagement she was outrageously inappropriate. He was sure she desperately clung to the thought that she might change his mind. He was also much on his guard, because if there was a way she could disrupt this wedding, he had no doubt she would.

She was desperate, clingy and horridly rude to anyone deemed no benefit to her small world. She was quickly approaching spinsterhood. For the life of him Darcy had no idea why Miss Bingley had, somehow or other, believed that she would eventually be Mistress of Pemberley. Charles had been telling her for years that it was futile. Darcy had repeatedly hinted that he was not interested, but she would not relent. The true fact was that Caroline Bingley was the last woman in the world that he could ever have been prevailed upon to marry. She was almost as ridiculous to him as Mr. Collins was to Elizabeth.

Ah, maybe we could speak about the hilarity of Miss Bingley's ridiculous attempts to catch my notice. Elizabeth would like that, would she not? I could tell her of the time she decided to impress me with her fashion sense by wearing the most horrid orange ball gown to the Stanhope's ball last season.

Darcy had returned to his room by now and was sitting at the small desk flipping through some correspondence. *The gown made her look like a pumpkin. The headpiece she wore included a dead parrot, mostly orange in colour with plumes or such coming out in all directions from the dead bird.* Darcy separated out personal correspondence he desired to read later after completing some business matters.

Did she actually think that such a foolish sight would impress me? Her shoes were orange, her gloves were orange, and she was even wearing an orange fur, so orange that it could not have actually come from a real animal. Richard had been there that evening and had dubbed her 'Lady Parrott of the Island of Orange-a-tangs'. Hilarious! Yes, I will tell Elizabeth that story sometime soon.

Darcy worked the majority of the day on his correspondence. He and Elizabeth had written letters to tell of their pending nuptials prior to leaving for London. Having caught up on business, he opened a letter from his cousin, Richard. Darcy had written of his engagement, but also to relate the presence of one George Wickham in the neighbourhood and request help:

~~*~*~*

30 November 1811, Matlock House

Dear Darcy:

You dog! You are getting married! It is hard to believe. I take it that you met your beloved in the wilds of Hertfordshire while there with Charles.

We had heard in an express from Lady Catherine that a *hussy with nothing to commend her other than her arts and allurements, with little or no wealth or connections*, had trapped you. I have to tell you when the old man read that, he laughed so hard I did not think he would be able to stop. I have never seen him like that, Darcy.

He kept saying things like, *That old dog. He and George won. Oh, this is precious. I cannot wait to see Tom.*

Tom who, Darcy? Do you know of what he speaks? I know that your father had a friend named Tom, and that the two of them and my father knew each other at Eton and at Cambridge. I also know that my father continues to write to a Tom on a regular basis, but I do not think they have seen each other in years and do not really remember who he is. Do you? Is there some connection between Tom and your Elizabeth?

Father has been no help at all, he keeps saying it is not his story to tell, and then he starts laughing again.

We are all coming to the wedding, by the way. Dad insists and he has written to Aunt Catherine, telling her he expects her to either come to the wedding or be silent in regards to her objections. He is still the trustee of Rosings, you know. He told her he would not put up with her disrespecting you, or creating problems for the family.

Now, to that other matter. I have made some inquiries and found out a transfer for Ensign Wickham was already in the making. By the time you get this letter, Wickham should be bound for Newcastle. Someone has already bought up all of his debts, so I was unable to assist you. The only further information that Colonel Forster would tell me is that a local gentleman now owns them.

Well, enough for me, Darcy. Enjoy the bewitching eyes of your fiancée. I look forward to meeting the future Mrs. Darcy quite soon. We will arrive three days prior to the wedding, and are grateful for Bingley's invitation to stay at Netherfield.

Till then...yours, etc...R.F.

~~*~*~*

2 December 1811

Darcy woke early with a determination to discover what was bothering Elizabeth. He had left her to her own thoughts for the remainder of the day yesterday, hoping and praying that she would be back to her old self when he saw her this morning. Part of him feared that she might not come to meet him today. But he hoped that she would hold to her promise. He had a plan.

As he stood at his window in the pre-dawn light he worked out the last details of his plan. He would continue to question her until he determined what the problem was. Even if he angered her, it would be preferable to what happened the day before. At least if he angered her, she would talk to him; and hopefully she would tell him what was wrong. Darcy was certain that if he knew what was wrong, he could do something about it. Powerlessness was not something that Darcy could tolerate for long.

The last time he felt truly powerless was when Georgiana had almost eloped with Wickham. Darcy would not fail Elizabeth. He could not fail this time. If he knew the problem, he could fix it. He was sure of it.

Chapter 5

Just before Dawn, Longbourn

Elizabeth was troubled. Quite troubled; and she just could not shake the feeling of panic. Oh, she knew that she had been completely unfair to Darcy the day before. She imagined that by now, he had worked himself into an apprehension that she had somehow changed her mind about marrying him. It was not that. She thought that, I have no idea how to tell him what is wrong. But I am sure, very sure, that he will not let the subject drop until I tell him all.

Part of her wished that she could avoid this talk for another day, but she had promised him. She had promised to meet him this morning. So she prepared herself for the day and left the house.

As soon as Elizabeth crossed over the bridge departing from Longbourn, she saw Darcy leaning against a fence rail. His back was slightly bent, and he was looking out at the field instead of her direction. As she looked, she thought, *Ah, he is so handsome and tall. I love his curly hair, and his eyes are loving and kind to me since our engagement, so why do I feel so troubled? I have to be able to speak of this; but I cannot!* She continued to contemplate as she approached him, *I, I just cannot! But he did ask me to be honest... no more white lies. I will have to try and let it go. I must. I cannot make him miserable all morning as I did yesterday. I must attempt conversation. Oh, but how? I am mortified*, mused Elizabeth.

Just before Elizabeth reached him, Darcy shook himself out of his reverie long enough to see her approaching. He turned towards her, the smile on his face was like sunshine glowing on his entire countenance, and it reached her. She felt his smile deep within her soul. Elizabeth tentatively smiled back at him, and looked again at the ground. She was attempting to look more open, more receptive today. Her arms were at her side, she was walking slower and she stopped in front of him.

"Good morning, Elizabeth," he said with a hopeful lift in his voice. She still appeared to be quite troubled, but she looked to be in at least slightly better spirits today.

"Good morning, sir," she looked at him quickly and then diverted her eyes yet again. She really was trying.

"Ah...so I am still 'sir' today?" Darcy smiled at her and lifted his brow in question. She glanced at him.

"I guess, sir, I mean William," she said in almost a whisper.

He reached out and lifted her hand and kissed the back of it, contemplating for a minute that she was going to resist even that, but she allowed it. He released her hand quickly, not wanting to push her too much. He was intent upon getting to the bottom of what was disturbing her today.

He offered her his arm and said as he began to turn, "Come, and let us walk."

Elizabeth did place her arm through his, but her hand was so tentatively placed, that it only touched his sleeve. Darcy was content for the moment, as she was not rejecting him outright. His determination began to rise to the surface as they began to walk.

"Elizabeth, I know you were very upset about something yesterday. Are you feeling better today?"

"A little, sir."

"Can you tell me what is troubling you?" he continued.

"No, sir," she responded softly.

"Can not, or will not, tell me?"

"Either, both..."

"Are you unwell?"

"I am well, sir," but she continued to stare at the ground as they walked.

"Is someone in your family unwell?"

"They are well, sir."

"Have I said something to upset you, Elizabeth?"

"No, sir, although I would prefer it if you could let this go."

"I cannot, Elizabeth. Do you not see how much I care about you?"

"I do, sir," she said and they continued to walk slowly.

"So you will not tell me?"

"No, sir."

"What if I guess it?" He was trying to be creative in his attempts to get to the bottom of this.

"Guess what, sir?"

"If I guess what is troubling you?" Darcy smiled as he responded.

"I do not know that you can, sir."

"Has someone in my family upset you? Did my Aunt disturb you?"

"My father talked with her, sir, not me."

"You did not speak with Lady Catherine?"

"No, I did not, sir."

"Are you overwhelmed with plans for the wedding, Elizabeth?"

"No, I am fine." She stopped for a moment and looked up at him, "I am fine, William."

"I do not believe you, Elizabeth! Remember you told me no more lies, not even little white ones? You remember, do you not?" He reached out and touched the side of her cheek with the back of his hand.

"I remember you asking me. I do not remember agreeing."

And then she began to walk again. Darcy, turned and walked with her and said, "Elizabeth, do you not trust me?"

"I want to, William."

"But you do not yet trust me?"

"Yes. No. Ah... Oh... I don't know."

"Can you truly not tell me what is bothering you?"

"No," was all she said. Ah, thought Darcy this is progress. At least she has admitted that something is bothering her, even though she will not trust me enough to reveal it.

"Someone has said something that has disturbed you?"

Elizabeth said nothing. Darcy proceeded to go through all of her family members asking if one of them disturbed her, until he asked her, "Was it your mother?"

Again there was silence. It appeared that William was on the right track now.

"Your mother has spoken unkindly to you, Elizabeth. Is that what has disturbed you?"

"No."

"But your mother said something to you that has upset you?"

"Not directly... not exactly..." and she breathed heavily. "William I cannot tell you this. Do not ask it of me. Please let this go. It will benefit nothing. It is not proper..." and she caught herself quickly as she was afraid that she had said too much.

Darcy contemplated what she had just said. *She thinks she cannot speak of it. She has heard something from her mother. She thinks it is not proper to tell me... ah...* Darcy suddenly relaxed. He had an idea of the topic that had disturbed her. *We are to be married in a little over a week. She does not believe that she can speak of this with me. Ah, her mother may have spoken to her about marital duties.*

Elizabeth sensed that he might have guessed the subject of her distress. *But what should I tell him if he insists. Can I speak with him? I know not how.*

"Elizabeth, do you know of a bench or a place where we might sit for a few minutes, my dear."

"Yes, William, there is nice quiet place off this upcoming path. There is a bench that my father once carved out of a log. We can go there, I suppose. But I do not promise that being off the open road will cause me to speak to you, sir."

They walked in companionable silence for a bit. Both were full of anxiety regarding whether a conversation would be forthcoming. What or how much would be revealed? As they reached the bench, Darcy motioned for Elizabeth to sit, and then he sat next to her. He reached out and took one of her hands into both of us.

"Elizabeth, look at me for a moment," and she turned towards him to look at him. "We are alone, just you and me. We are to be married in little more than a week. God will bind us together for the remainder of our lives. There should be nothing between us. Please talk with me. What did your mother say to you?"

Elizabeth found she could not maintain the intensity of his look, but she found the courage to say, "William, she did not speak to me directly, I overheard a conversation."

"Were you eavesdropping, my love?" He smiled teasingly at her, and it broke the tension a little for her.

Glancing at him, she shook her head and gave a tentative smile back, "I assure you kind sir, if I had realized what I was going to hear, I would have been anywhere else. Oh, how I wish I had never heard what they said."

"They, Elizabeth?" he said with a question in his voice.

"My mother and her friends." She took a deep breath and looked at her hand clasped in his. "They were in the back parlour, where we were the day of your proposal. I was behind the pocket door in the small sewing room."

"What did they speak of, Elizabeth? Please tell me! We cannot start our marriage with anything between us. Please trust me! I want to hear everything and anything you want to say to me. I will not love you less. I promise." He paused just a minute and asked in a very quiet voice, "Did they speak of ah... marital duties, Elizabeth?"

Too strongly, she gasped in surprise, "How did you..." Then Elizabeth stood up and began to pace back and forth—short strides, not fast, back and forth in front of the log. She rubbed her brow, she wrung her hands, she hugged herself, and then she stopped and looked at him.

"William, I will tell you if you insist. But before I start, you need to know that I am mortified. If I tell you, however, sir, you must agree to remain seated. You cannot touch me or hold my hand while I tell you this," she started pacing again.

"You cannot interrupt me. I fear an angry reaction from you, and believe that you will have one to at least to part of what I heard. I can only tell you this if you promise to agree to these things. Will you agree to this?" She stopped and looked at him again.

"Yes, my dear, I will agree to all you have asked." Little did he know how hard it would be to hold to his agreement!

"It would perhaps be best if I just told you about the whole of the interchange that I overheard..."

~~*~*~*

Two Days Previously (Subtitle: The Frigid Witty Bitty Sisterhood)

Elizabeth had entered the sewing room in preparation to do some mending. Darcy had left after luncheon with her family, as he had just returned from London and had correspondence that demanded his attention.

When she entered the sewing room, she realized that she could overhear her mother and her friends in the back parlour. She sat down to mend the hem in one of her dresses, but she was arrested by the first words that she heard.

"Fanny, what a good match your Elizabeth has made," it was Mrs. Long.

"Yes, indeed, although Mr. Darcy appears to be quite disagreeable and slighted her in the past, she will want for nothing. He has 10,000 a year I understand," stated her Aunt Phillips.

"Most likely more. He has a house in town and a very large estate in Derbyshire. Oh, the pin money she will have, the carriages, the jewellery and the gowns. My Lizzy will want for nothing. Nothing indeed," gloated her mother.

Lady Lucas joined in, "He is such a tall and imposing gentleman. I am sure he is quite used to getting exactly what he wants. I fear your Elizabeth will be in for rude awakenings come her wedding night."

"Ah yes, Lucy, and I imagine he will demand an heir right away. He is seven or eight and twenty, I believe. He has waited long enough to get married after all," declared Aunt Philips with sound conviction, responding to Lady Lucas. She laughed, causing the other three to join in.

"Yes, indeed, he is most likely quite eager to join with my Lizzy. You should see the way he looks at her since their engagement. I would imagine he would be quite a demanding husband from the passionate looks I have seen on his face. I certainly never saw such a look on Mr. Bennet's face. When men have their carnal needs, they usually just come raise your skirt or gown and in three minutes they are gone." Mrs. Bennet laughed heartily.

"It has never been a problem for me to lie still and let Mr. Long lift my gown. He was always in and out quite quickly, thank God."

"Fanny, have you spoken to Elizabeth of her duties yet? She needs a warning. He is such a tall and large man; she needs time to prepare herself. She is so small and so slight. I hope she can manage the first time. I would suppose it would be quite, quite painful for her. I wonder if she is even big enough to fit him in," Aunt Phillips cackled.

"Oh my, he may just split her open. I hope they don't have to call for the apothecary after their first time," added Mrs. Long.

"Linda, you know Fanny does not need to completely terrify the poor girl. I remember on my honeymoon, the first time I saw Sir William's manhood, I was so shocked I passed out. He just had his way with me anyway. Probably easier that way, I was just sore the next day. I did not have to remember the moment of pain when he entered me for the first time!"

"You must also tell her as many ways as possible to avoid marital duties. I know I have become quite efficient in fending off Mr. Phillips over the years. Why, even last night I told him that I had a stomach ache and just could not bear to have his weight upon me."

"Oh, Mr. Bennet truly believes that I have so many flutterings and tremblings that he avoids me most of the time. I must admit that it was very creative of me to come up with a nervous condition that would last my entire life. It can always be depended on as an excuse to avoid my husband visiting my bed," Fanny laughed.

And then she continued, "Little does anyone know that I have been faking my nerves for years! Of course, I end up having to smell those nasty smelling salts when I do not even need them. But I get to escape to my bedroom for my nerves. Sometimes I use them as an excuse to miss other things. I could have been an actress, you know!"

"Fanny Bennet, you mean that all of these years, you do not suffer from your nerves," Aunt Phillips exclaimed, and they all began to laugh. Their laughter escalated to cackles, and ended up with all of them pulling out their handkerchiefs to wipe their eyes.

"I do not think she can use nerves as her excuse. She is too like her father for that. Perhaps I should encourage her to have arguments with her husband m and keep him so mad at her that he will want to avoid her bed, "Fanny pondered creatively.

"Yes, her impertinent mouth has always been a problem for her. I still cannot imagine a man such as Mr. Darcy choosing your Elizabeth," Lady Lucas shared.

"Perhaps he thinks with all of her walking, she will have long endurance. I imagine a man like that would like to come to her over and over all night long," Aunt Philips announced.

"Beatrice... oh... I must help her with excuses. She cannot have to bear him over and over. Even Lizzy does not deserve that," Fanny responded to her sister Phillips as she rose from her seat and walked to the window for a bit.

"Well, the best thing for her to do is to encourage him to get a mistress, or maybe two. He is so rich; making such an arrangement will be no problem for him. Then she can just enjoy his riches and avoid his company," Mrs. Long stated.

"Oh, I would imagine a man such as he already has a mistress. He has probably had one since he first came of age. He looks like a man who would need a way to complete his desires on a regular basis." It was Lady Lucas this time.

"I wonder what it is these paid mistresses and courtesans do to keep men so comforted and occupied. Do you think they really enjoy relations? I know I have never enjoyed them in all of these many years," said Mrs. Philips.

"Nor I, Beatrice, but it is a burden we wives must bear." Mrs. Long agreed.

"I once talked with a courtesan while visiting a modiste in London for over an hour. She told me it has a lot to do with whether a man is willing to arouse a woman prior to actually entering her. She shared with me tips about how I could encourage Sir William to touch me on my breasts and in my private area before entering me. To be honest; I have never had the courage to ask him to do so. It just seemed too improper. This woman told me she was very satisfied, and she thoroughly enjoyed relations. She said women could have as much enjoyment from them as men, but I have never believed that could be so," Lady Lucas admitted.

"Well," Mrs. Bennet giggled and blushed. "Once, when we were newly married, Mr. Bennet took my gown all the way off and actually, well let us just say that he acted like he was a hungry baby. I must say that I enjoyed it quite well; but I never encouraged him to continue. I was always told that I was to remain still and quiet. I was not to let my husband know I found any enjoyment in anything, or he would think me wanton. So it ended up being just that once. But I find myself thinking back on it from time to time."

"Well, you were wise, Fanny. If you had encouraged him even once, I dare say he would have become insatiable. He may not have let you leave his bed, repeatedly ravishing you until you could no longer stand," Mrs. Long giggled as she finished and they all joined in.

"Well, all I have to say is I pray Elizabeth can bear him a child quite quickly after marriage, with any luck on the first try. As soon as she is sure she is with child, I am sure she can convince him to leave her alone. If it is a male child, perhaps he would be happy to avoid her bed for the remainder of their lives," announced Fanny.

"As if she could be so lucky," stated Mrs. Philips. And they all agreed.

~~*~*~*

Elizabeth finished recounting her tale, but continued to pace. She did not hazard a look at William for several minutes. When she could look at him, he was looking down and running his hand through his curls. She could tell that he was breathing heavily. It was apparent to her that he was trying to calm himself.

She knew that he would be angry about what her mother and friends had said about him. She just prayed that he would not be angry with her. She could not believe she had told him all of this. She did not even know what it all meant. She, in the deepest corners of her heart, hoped he would be willing to explain some of it to her.

She had no one she trusted to talk to, except, perhaps her Aunt Gardiner. But Aunt Gardiner was not scheduled to arrive for a few more days due to her Uncle Gardiner's business. She needed to believe that marital relationships were not as horrible as her mother and her friends had said.

A few more minutes passed, and Darcy said quietly, "Come, my dear. Sit by me, please." He said it as gently and with as much love as he could allow himself at that moment. He motioned for her to sit on the log next to him.

Elizabeth was not expecting him to be calm and gentle; but she could not have been more grateful. She returned to the log, and he took her into his arms and hugged her tightly to himself. It was what they both needed to calm themselves, at least enough to speak of her confession. It was several minutes before Darcy spoke again, as he lifted her head to look into his eyes.

"Elizabeth, do you know of what they speak? Did you understand all of what they said? Was this the first time you had heard talk of such things?" Darcy asked.

Darcy thought, *Good God, no wonder she was terrified and so reticent to speak with me! Would she believe any of it was true? That I would have a mistress! I know now why she had been so apprehensive to speak with me. But I promised her I would not be angry with her. Even if I feel anger at the presumption of her mother and her friends, saying what they did of me, I will not show my anger. At the same time, I am grateful I can help her overcome this.* Darcy's thoughts were having the desired effect, helping him to calm down. She said she would trust him. He could not fail her.

"I know very little, William. Oh, I am a country girl and I have seen our sheep and cattle mate. I have changed the nappies of my boy cousins, but I fear that I do not know much else. I know that men are built differently than women, but I have never seen a man. You are the first man to kiss me."

"Will you trust me, Elizabeth? Will you trust me to talk with you more over the next few days, and try to calm your spirit? This has been a very difficult revelation for you. We have been gone for some time and should go back soon, but I would like to help calm your fears. I believe that our marital relations can bring you as much pleasure as they will bring me, but it will not be so unless you trust me to guide you in this matter. I promise not to force anything upon you that you do not wish. Will you try, my sweet Lizzy?"

"Yes, I will try to trust you, William," she whispered to him. And after a deep breath, she said, "I am so grateful for your reaction to this. I was so afraid that you would only hear the unkind words they said of you, and not how they affected me. You know not what it means to me for you to comfort me and not share your anger; for I know that you must be angry. I know you that well, you know. You must have been affected by part of what they said," she chanced a glance into his eyes.

"Yes Elizabeth, I was angered by part of it. I want to assure you that I have NEVER had a mistress, nor will I EVER choose to have one. You have my promise on that. One by one, we will speak of these things over the next few days. If you will permit me, I will be your teacher. I will do all I can to relieve your fears, my love."

"Thank you, William," she said as she nestled her head under his chin.

"Good! Now today I do want to ask of you one thing. Think of it as your lesson, can you do that?"

She smiled up at him and simply said, "Yes."

"What did you feel when we kissed? The two times that we have kissed, what did you feel? Can you describe it to me?"

Elizabeth was blushing and she looked down at his chest, but he immediately lifted her eyes back to his. "Tell me, my love, what you felt. I know you felt something."

"I felt warmth. It started in my lips but it spread quickly and I felt warm all over," she stopped.

"That is a good start, now what else did you feel? What did you experience?"

"My heart felt like it would burst out of my chest. It was like I felt full and trembling at the same time. My legs started to quiver, and I thought I might fall down. My stomach was fluttering but it was like, I do not know how to describe it, it was like rushing water."

Darcy smiled at her, "Elizabeth, I believe God gives us those feelings in our body to allow us to enjoy each other. Believe me when I tell you, I believe you will feel even better when we join as man and wife. There is much I will tell you before our wedding, a few things I can show you, but more I can teach you after we are wed. Right now, however, I would like to kiss you again. Is that all right, my dear? May I kiss you?"

"Why, Mr. Darcy, you have never asked before," she said with a grin, a small giggle and a raised brow.

Thank God for this woman. My Luscious Lizzy is back! Darcy thought.

"Minx!" he exclaimed as he pulled her onto his lap and then kissed her. It was a full mouth, soft, warm, slightly wet kiss. He kissed her again and again. Then he alternated between kissing her top lip and her bottom lip, instilling her with his love. He moved to kiss the right corner of her mouth, and then the left corner, and then he kissed along her jawbone and down her neck to the pulse point where he kissed her long and deeply, conscious not to do leave a mark. Then he returned up the same path. When he reached her mouth again, he paused.

He looked deeply into her eyes, and he saw an emotion there that he had not seen before. He would not yet ask her to speak of what she felt. But it looked like adoration, gratitude and if he was lucky... perhaps, just perhaps, trust. He kissed her long and deeply on her mouth one last time. Then he stopped and rested his forehead against hers.

"I believe that was enough of a lesson for today, my dear. Let us get you home." They rose and walked again towards Longbourn. This time she did not hesitate to walk arm in arm with him.

Chapter 6

2 December 1811, Longbourn

Tom Bennet sat at his desk, still laughing over the letter he had received from his friend, Edward Fitzwilliam. He decided to read that one line again:

If only George were still here to realize that you and he had won and not Catherine and Anne.

Yes, Edward, George and I won indeed. To you, Fitzwilliam! He laughed quietly to himself and downed a shot of his favourite port.

As Tom Bennet continued to sit and meditate on his good fortune in having won a son-in-law such as Fitzwilliam Darcy, that same gentleman knocked on his door, requesting admittance.

"Come in, come in, Mr. Darcy," exclaimed Mr. Bennet. "To what do I owe the pleasure of your company in my private abode this afternoon? Have you tired of my Lizzy's company already and come to re-negotiate?"

Darcy laughed, "No, Mr. Bennet, I fear that I will never tire of your daughter's lively company," and then he smiled. "I just received the settlement papers from my attorney in London and wanted to review them with you, sir, if you have time. If you have any suggestions or improvements, they would be most welcome. Plus I need a little information from you before they can be finalized."

"Have a seat, have a seat," Mr. Bennet exclaimed with a smile. "May I offer you a taste of my best port? Care for a little celebration with your soon to be father-in-law, son?"

"That sounds very good indeed." With that, Mr. Bennett poured Darcy a drink, and another for himself. He pointed towards a chair in front of his desk and Darcy sat down.

"Now, Mr. Darcy, how do you wish to proceed? Do you want me to look over what you brought and then talk about it, or the other way around?" Mr. Bennet questioned.

Darcy handed him the sheaf of papers and said, "Why do you not review the papers, sir. I will look over the shelves of your library as you do, if you do not mind, sir."

"Fine, fine," Mr. Bennet said distractedly, as he was already looking at the papers.

After some time passed, Mr. Bennet said, "This is very thorough, Mr. Darcy, but I do not think you have taken Lizzy's dowry into consideration."

"I was unaware that there was a dowry. It has been said that the Bennet sisters are dowerless..."

Mr. Bennet quickly interrupted him, "Yes, yes, as it has been said that you are worth ten thousand pounds per annum. I dare say you are worth at least three times that from what I see in these documents."

Darcy blushed slightly and said, "As you see, sir."

"Well, well, you see Mr. Darcy; we all have our secrets, do we not? Actually, not even my daughters are aware of their dowry. I hoped they would marry for love, and I never wanted them to be placed on the marketplace of the *ton* with a price tag on their heads. I dare say you know what that is like. Do you not hear ten thousand pounds a year as you enter ballrooms?" He raised his brow at Darcy with a smirk. Darcy was reminded of his favourite expression on Lizzy's face.

"I have grown accustomed to it over the years, sir. But I do understand what you say. So Lizzy has a dowry, we can just add that to her settlement," stated Darcy rather matter of factly.

"Do you not have any curiosity of what the dowry entails, Mr. Darcy?"

"If you would tell me, I would be happy to know, sir. It makes little difference. I love your daughter, and am perfectly prepared to marry her with no dowry at all."

"That gives me great comfort, Mr. Darcy, great comfort indeed. But what say you to twenty thousand pounds, sir?"

Darcy was astonished. Both his eyebrows rose and his mouth hung open in amazement. He had to shake himself before he could say anything at all. "Then, Mr. Bennet, I would imagine there are other things you keep in secret, such as **your** annual income?"

All Mr. Bennet could do was laugh.

"Mr. Bennet, to say I am surprised is an understatement. All of your daughters have a dowry of twenty thousand pounds?"

"Well Mr. Darcy, Jane and Lizzy do, that is true. My other daughters' dowries are somewhat less, though more than what is bandied around as YOUR annual income. But please, sir, I really do not care for my family to know any of this. You may, of course, tell Elizabeth in private if you like. But request her silence as well. If my wife became aware of my true income, she would drive me to distraction with her financial demands. I am certain she would insist I move by the end of the week to a finer estate, and there would be no dowry for any of my daughters by the end of three months," he said as he let out a warm chuckle.

"Mr. Bennet, this may be a very improper question, but how, I mean in what manner are your funds invested to acquire such wealth?"

"Ah, you come to the crux of the matter. I have been rather sly with you, son. You and I have many investments in common, sir. The Royal Exchange Assurance, South Seas Company, West Indies Company and the Bank of England. Most recently, your Uncle Edward had me invest with the railroad scheme of which you are aware. I also have my own investments, many with my brother Gardiner."

"You will like him; by the way, they will arrive three days before the wedding. Lizzy's Aunt and Uncle Gardner allowed her to spend much time in town, pursuing educational and cultural activities that have given her benefits she would not have had if she had always remained here at Longbourn. You may want to become familiar with some of his investment projects, as they have netted me quite a substantial sum of late."

"I will look forward to meeting them. Elizabeth has talked enthusiastically about the Gardiners. Now I understand more of how you made your money, sir, but how did..."

"How did I come to learn about the investments in the first place, you ask?" Mr. Bennet interrupted...

"Yes sir," Darcy replied.

"Mr. Darcy, your father was my best friend. When young men, he and your Uncle Edward and I were inseparable. We met at Eton, and later attended Cambridge together. In fact, I accompanied your father on his Grand Tour. Your father and I were very close. There will never be as true a friend as your father. Your Uncle Edward and I still correspond; in fact, I just received a letter from him today. He is quite happy about your engagement, by the way."

Mr. Bennet paused for a moment and then continued. "The three of us were involved in many investment schemes together. I will always be grateful for his, as well as your uncle's, financial guidance. It has proven quite helpful over the years. I could live on a much larger estate and provide poorly for my family. But Longbourn has been in my family for many generations. I had hoped to be able to leave it to my son. Alas, that was not to be, but at least I am able to do well by my daughters. Mrs. Bennet, for all her nerves, will be quite surprised by the fortune she will have at my demise. Her foretelling of being turned out into the hedgerows will never come true, I assure you."

"Mr. Bennet, there is one more thing that I need to discuss with you today. Since I now know of your friendship with my father, I know you must be familiar with Mr. Wickham."

With a disgusted snarl, Mr. Bennet said, "I assume you want to discuss how that snake has been attempting to blemish your name in the neighbourhood." Darcy started slightly and Bennet continued, "Do not think me unable to tell true character, Mr. Darcy. I have heard some of the same stories I imagine you have over the years. While you may have more first hand knowledge, I knew which man to stand by."

He reached over and picked up the decanter of port and refreshed both of their glasses. "When my Lizzy came to me with Wickham's tale of woe after he spouted his poison to her, I told her to be careful judging either you or Wickham before knowing you both well."

Mr. Bennet lifted his arms up and placed his hands behind his head. "The reality, Mr. Darcy, is that I do know you. I have followed your life. I have kept up with you through your uncle, and I knew there had to be a reason for any decision you would make. I decided to speak with Colonel Forster. I discovered that Mr. Wickham had accumulated quite a bit of debt for just two weeks in one neighbourhood. I purchased the debt, by the way. Call it a future guarantee I could send him to debtors prison should he impose himself on any of the young women of my acquaintance," Mr. Bennet put his arms back no his desk." After speaking with Colonel Forster, he agreed to assist me in having him transferred elsewhere, and I will gladly tell you that he was transferred to Newcastle while you were in London."

Mr. Bennet concluded, "Mr. Darcy, you should also know none of my family, with the exception of Mrs. Bennet, knows of my history with your family. You may tell Lizzy if you like. She should know just how highly I hold you and your family. I did tell her that I knew your family, but nothing further."

Darcy said with gratitude, "Mr. Bennet, I am truly grateful you took such prodigious care of this matter regarding Wickham. I had written to Colonel Fitzwilliam... ah, Richard, as you are friends with his father, to see if he would help me affect a transfer. He wrote back to say it had already been accomplished. I did not initially think it to be you, Mr. Bennet, but I thank you."

"Glad to be of assistance, and glad to get the scoundrel out of Meryton. He could cause nothing but trouble for you now that you are to marry Lizzy. I could not chance him trying to take vengeance on you through one of my daughters. I did it to protect my family. Speaking of family William, I was so sorry for your loss, or should I say losses. Lady Anne was a wonderful woman, and I know you miss her still. And my friend George, well, the world is less bright because of his passing," Mr. Bennet shared, bringing his arms back to his desk.

Darcy saw that Mr. Bennet's eyes were wet, though the tears did not fall. Suddenly with dawning comprehension, Darcy said, "My father often talked of you, Mr. Bennet."

Mr. Bennet laughed and held out his hand, "Ah... Yes... son," and then he, as an after thought extended his hand and said, "Mr. Darcy, it is quite good to meet you, my name is Thomas Bennet, but your father called me Tom."

Darcy shook his hand heartedly, as he smiled and said, "He never gave me many details regarding your friendship, Mr. Bennet. But, one of the last things he said was *Fitzwilliam, if you ever have the good fortune to meet my friend Tom, tell him I love him and I have missed him.* I should have tried to find you, Mr. Bennet..." and Darcy trailed off as he looked regretfully.

"Well, well, we are to be family now are we not, son?" One of the warmest smiles that ever graced Tom Bennet's face was bestowed on his soon to be son-in-law.

"We are indeed. I dare say my father would be pleased?"

"Oh, I dare say your father would be ecstatic, as we often discussed a hopeful match between our children. I dare say you are grateful that our hopes have been realized instead of those of your Aunt Catherine, eh, Mr. Darcy?"

"Grateful indeed, Mr. Bennet," and Darcy chuckled, then his eyes widen in comprehension. "Wait, if you are..."

"Yes, it does indeed, it does indeed," Bennet said as he shook his head and grinned.

~~*~*~*

Tom was sitting at his desk and smiling. His elbows were on the desk and his hands were under his chin with his index fingers up to his nose. He was tapping his nose without even realizing it, to the rhythm of the music playing in his head.

~~*~*~*

Tom Bennet was at a ball and the most beautiful creature he had ever beheld had just entered the ballroom. He was three and twenty, and it was her coming out ball. He was struck, love struck, at first sight. He had managed to ask her to dance, and when he first touched her hand, it was like fireflies dancing through his body.

~~*~*~*

Tom shook his head, sighed and came back to the room. As he thought of his time spent with Mr. Darcy, he realized that if this was what it was going to be like to have sons-in-law, he was going to enjoy it indeed. Well, it might be unlikely any of them will be as clever as Elizabeth's Darcy. It had been a fine day indeed.

~~*~*~*

As the day came to an end, Lizzy and Jane sat upon her bed. It had been their habit for many years to sit together and review the day in one or the other's bedrooms. Since Lizzy's engagement, this pattern had been broken. Lizzy had not come to Jane's room, and as Jane had decided that Lizzy had chosen to keep to her own counsel had not approached her. But tonight, Jane was determined to make sure her dearest sister was not making a mistake. When she entered Elizabeth's bedroom she found Lizzy sitting on her bed, looking off into space and smiling. She was so far off in her own thoughts; she did not hear Jane enter the room.

Jane entered the room and sat on Lizzy's bed. "Lizzy, you seem much more peaceful tonight. Are you happy, dearest sister? Please tell me you are. I so want to be sure you are content. I could not bear it if you did not respect your husband. You have seemed so upset the last couple days I was afraid you were angry with him? Did he hurt you?"

"Oh no, Jane, it is much the opposite I dare say." Elizabeth's smile grew a bit wider.

"Oh... really... now you have aroused my curiosity. Pray; tell me what you mean, Lizzy."

"Jane, oh Jane," Elizabeth took Jane's hands in her own. "Has... ah... has any man ever kissed you?" Lizzy blushed and looked at the bed when she spoke and then back up at Jane with a blush and a raised brow.

Jane giggled, "So that is what this smile is all about. No, but I dare say I would not push Mr. Bingley away should he try," Jane said with a giggle. "He is so wonderful. I think he is the most perfect man in the world, well, at least for me." Jane stopped and looked at Elizabeth with almost the same impertinent grin and raised brow.

"Yes, Mr. Bingley does seem to be quite perfect for you. Has he not spoken of marriage yet, Jane? I thought he would have made an offer by now."

"Oh, Lizzy, I do hope so. He is so considerate. Perhaps he does not want to detract from your and Mr. Darcy's wedding. He told me today he could not imagine being happy with anyone but me in his life. I do so want that to mean he intends to offer for me. Do you think that is what he was saying? I confess I want to believe it to be so."

"Oh, Jane, I believe he loves you very much. William told me the other day he had never seen Mr. Bingley as deeply in love as he is with you. He also asked me what I thought about having Mr. Bingley as a brother. I believe he wanted to make sure your feelings were as strong as his friend's. Without breaking any confidences, dear sister, I assured him that I believed your heart to be deeply engaged. Do you not think Mr. Bingley's best friend would know something of his feelings? So there!"

They both laughed. "Lizzy, what are your feelings for Mr. Darcy? Do you love him? We always agreed to only marry for love. What has changed so suddenly? Why, it was not two weeks ago that I thought you hated the man."

"Oh, Jane, my heart is so full of William. As my father has suggested to me, I have NEVER been indifferent to him. I have always had very strong feelings for him. Did I tell you of the first time I saw him and Mr. Bingley riding across the field of Netherfield at a breakneck pace? Something stirred in me at that moment. I hardly knew what to call it then, but I think I may have fallen in love with him at first sight. Then there was his comment at the Meryton Assembly, and many misunderstandings after that. But when he kissed me at the ball..." and then she stopped. She had never told her sister about '*the event.*'

Lizzy then spent time telling Jane about her and William's rather unique courtship. She did not tell her of the conversation she had overheard between her mother and her friends. There was no use in having Jane become terrified of marital duties as well. And after this morning, Lizzy did not think she was fearful anymore. Her time in the glen with William that day, as well as his kisses, had awakened something in her she could not name. But she knew that she looked forward to seeing him in the morning. After Jane left for her bed, she realized she never answered her sister's question. *Do I love William?* However the more important question to her now, as she drifted off to sleep was, *Do I tell him that I love him?*

Chapter 7

3 December 1811

Darcy awoke at Netherfield realizing he had slept better than he had in over a week. He contemplated all the revelations of the previous day as he readied himself for his walk to Longbourn in the morning's first light. As he left and began to walk, he gathered his thoughts, as he wanted to have a plan.

Amidst the revelations of the Darcy, Fitzwilliam and Bennet families' connections – Darcy did not forget his early meeting with Elizabeth the day before. He was so grateful she had been willing to tell him what had upset her. He was quite angry that Mrs. Bennet and her friends would think such things about him, but the only thing that mattered was what Lizzy, his Lizzy, thought about him. She had become *Luscious Lizzy* in his thoughts. He could not shake the inappropriate pet name. He was not sure when, if ever he would use it with her, very likely not until they were married for some time; but luscious she was.

Thinking over their kiss, when he had pulled her onto his lap, it had only been seconds before he had become erect. That was one of the problems he had to face. He had to move slowly. Her fears would quickly overwhelm her if he did not take his time; savour each moment, each step forward. He needed to talk with her, explain things to her, alleviate all her fears, or at least as many as he could.

Recently married men of his acquaintance had told him, perhaps when they were in their cups, so many different stories of maidens on their wedding nights. There were stories of horrified young brides, or young brides coming into the flower of youth. But there were also tales of young wives bringing to their young husbands hours on end of wantonness. Darcy knew there were probably many levels in the middle, but he desired the latter. He wanted, needed, and desired his *Luscious Lizzy*. His hope and wish was for her to enjoy the marital bed as much as he. That would require fortitude, it would require patience, and it would require him to remember constantly his love for her—not just his lust.

Darcy thought back to when his father caught him pleasuring himself when he was fourteen. His father made a decision at that time to educate him in such matters. He did not want his son to be found in a compromising situation, forced to live his life regretting his choices. He did for Fitzwilliam what his father had done for him. He made an arrangement with a courtesan, who had a reputation for being quite discrete, to spend a weekend with his son.

He had told William at the time that he needed to learn how to keep himself under good regulation, while being able to release his desires in a non-compromising manner. Darcy Sr. told him he did not mind him relieving himself, but he needed to be discrete. His father instructed that most assuredly he could not allow someone to walk in on him, as he had done.

William's mother had been furious when she learned of it. George later told William that he did not regret the decision. But, thinking back on it now, Darcy remembered the hormonal young boy that was taught the arts of pleasuring a woman. He did not regret having that education when he was a teenage boy. When he thought of Elizabeth, part of him wished that he could come to their marriage bed as innocent as she. He did not want any son of his to learn lessons in such a way.

Oh, yes, he had been prepared well in the arts of pleasuring a woman. He had been taught ways of bringing a woman to a level of arousal in which she would welcome his carnal ministrations, and not simply tolerate or attempt to avoid them; although it had certainly been a while since he had practiced this knowledge. To be honest, other than the time with the courtesan, there had only been two other courtesans, and they while on his grand tour.

Darcy had never wanted to toy with an innocent. His father had instilled in him the responsibility of avoiding a compromising situation. Pemberley and his family reputation were too important to him.

He learned as a teenager how to keep himself in good regulation amongst company when aroused. When he was young his family and friends often teased him about how much time he spent gazing out of windows, but this was what worked for him. Exposing his arousal to an innocent was simply not done in polite company. But not even in his teenage years had Darcy been as aroused as he was around one Elizabeth Bennet.

He had also learned how to prolong an erection for longer than he had ever imagined, so he could assure his lady of being thoroughly aroused and finding her pleasure once, if not several times, before he took his own.

Darcy had spent the majority of his evening the night before, improving his own mind and refreshing his own skills by the extensive reading of a text his cousin Richard had sent him with his recent letter. Richard had sent him the English translation of a book written in India. It was also illustrated. Richard had inscribed the inside cover with 'May your truly ENJOY marriage, dear cousin. Richard'

Truth be known, Darcy was quite grateful for the gift. He had a little less than a week to slowly initiate Elizabeth into the joy of intimacy. He would have to go slowly, just a little step each day; but he had a plan. He was thoroughly looking forward to moving forward with a carefully planned strategy this very morning.

As he was approaching the bounds of Longbourn, he saw that Elizabeth was already there.

"Good morning, dearest, you look quite stunning this morning," stated Darcy with utter conviction.

"Good morning to you, William. You are looking quite handsome yourself." She smiled so sweetly it filled his heart with utter joy.

"I take it you are better this morning than the last two," as he took hold of both of her hands. He lifted one hand and then the other to place a kiss on the back of each. Then he turned them over to kiss the inside wrist on one hand and then the other. And then, to her amazement and shock, he took one hand and kissed the inside of her hand and then lightly traced a circle in her palm with his tongue. He then repeated it on the other hand.

Her breathing increased, and her countenance flushed bright pink so quickly, it took her by surprise. She cocked her head slightly to the side and raised her eyebrow, and with the quietest of voices but a smile on her face she said, "Was this part of today's lesson, sir?"

Darcy gazed deep into her eyes, "Most assuredly, my dear." His ebony pools bored into her emerald depths. They just gazed at each other. Their smiles started small, but grew and grew until Darcy laughed and Elizabeth giggled. "Let us walk, my Lizzy."

As he began to escort her down the path, Darcy stated rather than asked, "I thought we would return to our glen today."

"Very well, kind sir." They talked of nothing and everything that might be important to the other as they walked. Darcy ended up telling her of her dowry, as well as their fathers' friendship. Elizabeth, while very surprised, found herself beginning to understand why her father had handled their impropriety the way that he had.

He had accomplished what he had intended. She was relaxed; no tension seemed present in her body. She was laughing, and her countenance was oh, so bright. She appeared happier in his presence than he could have ever dared hope. When they came to the glen, she assured him that she had never happened upon anyone there. They sat upon the log, Elizabeth quite close to him as she gazed up into his eyes.

Darcy moved the back of his fingers down her cheek, looking into her eyes, "My love, I have thought a great deal about what you revealed to me yesterday, and as we have seven days before our wedding, I hope to be able to answer most of your questions and lessen as many of your fears as I can. I want you to know I have heard from some of my friends after they married, that while some of their wives do experience pain, many others do not. The secret, I will tell you, appears to lie with the husband; so it will be my job to bring YOU pleasure. It can be a wonderful experience for both of us; and I want you to trust me when I say my greatest hope is that you feel an immense sense of joy and delight."

"What did you feel when I kissed your wrist and your palm this morning? I particularly noted a strong reaction when I did this." He took her hand in his and began to draw circles with his tongue in her palm. Almost immediately, Elizabeth started breathing deeply. He stopped a moment. "Talk to me, Elizabeth, tell me what you are feeling, or I will stop." He then began again.

"Oh, I feel like I have been running. My heart is beating faster, and my blood runs up to my cheeks," Elizabeth stopped speaking when his tongue began moving up to her wrist, up the inside of her arm, to the bend in her elbow, where he changed to kisses and continued up her arm to the edge of her capped sleeve. He stopped and looked at her.

"Oh, William, I do not even know how to describe it. What am I feeling? Can you tell me? I feel like I want more. You are not stopping, are you?"

Darcy lighted chuckled. "Oh, my sweet Elizabeth, no I am not stopping, at least not yet. But to answer your other question, I believe that what you are feeling is the first flush of passion. It is what a man and woman feel for each other, preparing them for marital relations."

"But do not all men and women feel this, William? I do not understand why my mother and her friends would want to avoid anything that would make you feel so giddy. "

"I do not believe most men take the time and attention to insure a woman experiences passion. I can assure you, I consider it a responsibility and a joy to help you find passion with me, Elizabeth. You are only just beginning to feel it, my love. There is more, much more. We have time, and we are going to go quite slow. There is no need to rush. I will not actually make you my wife in body until you are no longer afraid, even if it is not by the time we reach our marital bed. I love you too much to just 'take you' as is often crudely spoken."

"When you and I join, we will be making love. I will show you my love for you with my body. But it will not be a good experience for you, unless you are able to let go of your fear absolutely," Darcy said as he pulled her closer and gave her a brief kiss on her lips.

"I would expect that sometime in the next few days, your mother will want to have an audience with you. From what you have already told me of the conversation you overheard, I imagine that she is going to tell you something like this. I am going to speak as though I am your mother," he said as Elizabeth smirked at him. "Now do not laugh at me, my love, I am trying to ease your fear."

"Yes, sir, you are my mother. I am all ears," she giggled.

He decided if he could make her laugh as he talked about this, it would ease her mind further.

"Now, Elizabeth, I need to talk with you about your duty to Mr. Darcy, about your duties in the marital bed. Do not smirk at me, girl, you will be the death of me," William said in a high octave, pausing for a moment as Elizabeth hit him on the arm playfully. "You are to be married in just a few days, and as your husband is so quiet and disagreeable, and tall and big and quite demanding, he is most likely going to want to take you to his bed right after the wedding. Know that you must submit to him. You will lie on your back and he will just lift your gown a bit, and he will put his manhood into your secret place. It will hurt a great deal, but it will hurt less if you think of something pleasant, maybe like gallivanting off in the woods somewhere. Just be still, and close your eyes and think of something else, and soon it will be all over. Now, you must remember you are not to move, and you are not to make a sound. If you make sounds or appear to enjoy his attentions, he will think you wanton, and may even think you have not been faithful to him."

"Afterwards, there will be blood and you will be in some pain, so he will most likely leave you alone for a few days. He is going to want an heir quite soon, so he may want to come to you every day. If he does, you will get pregnant even sooner. When you are with child, you can tell him he cannot come to you. If you bear him a male child on your first time; then he will perhaps be willing to let you alone, and you will have your child and his money and will be quite happy. Now after you have borne him a child, we will talk more, my child. I will then tell you of creative ways to let him know he can no longer come to your bed, like having a headache or your nerves. Mr. Darcy is so rich he will probably just find a mistress, and then you will not have to worry about it at all anymore."

Elizabeth gasped, "William, you really think she will say something like that to me? What should I do if she wants to talk with me?"

"Well Elizabeth, if it were me I would tell her that you have already talked with your Aunt Gardiner, or some other woman that you know that is married', and that you know everything you need to know."

"I want to tell you a couple things you need to know. Almost nothing I said AS YOU MOTHER is true. It is what society wishes women to know about relations. I believe, and I hope you will come to believe that nothing is improper in our marital bed," he said as he kissed her softly and then continued.

"I fully intend on taking your gown completely off when I make love to you." Elizabeth blushed almost crimson as he spoke, but Darcy continued, "You know you are quite beautiful when you blush, my Lizzy? Back to the lesson – it is my hope that you will move, and that you will make sounds, and that you will let me know exactly how happy you are in my bed."

Elizabeth's cheeks were scarlet red, but she did look him in the eyes. Then she did something that truly surprised him when she said with her head cocked, raising her brow, "If you are to completely remove my gown, will I be allowed to remove your clothes as well, William?"

He lifted her onto his lap and pulled her around the waist towards him with one hand, as the other lifted her chin so she looked directly into his eyes. With a bright smile, he said, "Ah, my impertinent minx," and he lowered his lips to hers.

He kissed her deep and long. His lips were firm and strong, but the soft wetness was something Elizabeth could not explain. His lips caressed one lip and then the other as he coaxed her lips to open. He nibbled just slightly on her lower lips, and then ran his tongue along the crease of her lips, as she slowly found her mouth opening of its own accord. Somewhere in her, a moan began. It startled her, but delighted William as he deepened the kiss.

As she felt his tongue invade her mouth, she thought she would faint. It was startling, but his tongue seemed to have a mind of its own. It ran along the length of her teeth, it circled around the inner edges of her mouth, and then it began to do war with her tongue. Tentatively her tongue began its duel with his. She just lightly moved it back and forth to touch his and then pull back. She found her tongue circling his as their tongues waltzed a Pas de deux.

A gasp escaped from Elizabeth, and Darcy pulled back to look at her. Her eyes looked drunk with passion. He was utterly delighted. Her kisses were sheer ecstasy. He gazed at her with such tenderness, that tears began to slip from the corners of her eyes.

"Lizzy, are you all right?" he asked with concern as he witnessed her tears.

"Oh William, these are tears of joy. I... ah... I just never imagined that I could feel this way. Such joy," she said as she gazed into his eyes and a couple tears slipped from her eyes.

He reached up to wipe them away with his finger, and then brought his finger to his lips and licked it, "Ah, tears like honeysuckle." He paused and brought his hand up; allowing the back of his fingers to gently stroke the side of her face. Elizabeth, I love you. I have something for you. It arrived from Pemberley late yesterday."

He reached into his pocket and brought out a blue velvet box. They had their arms around each other gazing into each other's eyes, and alternating to the box. He pulled back slightly to open the box, and pulled the ring out. "Elizabeth, this ring was my mother's and my grandmother's before her, and my great grandmother's. I never imagined I could love another as I love you, and I vow to do everything I can to make you happy one day at a time, for the rest of our days. I have already asked before, but I ask again. Will you marry me, my dearest love, my precious Lizzy?" And Darcy slipped the ring over the fourth finger of her left hand.

Elizabeth looked down at a square cut ruby surrounded by diamonds and looked back up at him. He thought that he would drown in her adoring eyes. "Oh yes, William. Yes, I will marry you," and in a quieter, almost shy voice she whispered the words he had been longing to hear. "I love you, William." She reached up to kiss him, initiating the kiss this time.

As their interlude in the glen came to an end, Darcy and Elizabeth walked back to Longbourn. While they were off the main road, they walked with their fingers intertwined, occasionally glancing at each other. They enjoyed small talk; discussed when different guests were arriving for the wedding, and talked about the service itself. Significant details perhaps, but neither was really attending to them in earnest as they were both too entranced with their growing intimacy.

Darcy knew they would be back at Longbourn all too soon and knew, just knew he had to taste her lips once more. Spontaneously, he veered off the path, and laughingly pulled Elizabeth with him. As soon as he was sure they were far enough off the road, he pulled Elizabeth towards him once more and placed a hand on each of her cheeks, staring longingly into her eyes.

"My love, I just have to kiss you once more before I return you to your house." He rang a finger along the very light crease in her forehead and said, "I love your forehead," and kissed it. "And I love your brows, particularly when they are impertinently raised in my direction," and he kissed one brow and then the other. "I love your eyes. They are what first bewitched me, you know, deep and rich emerald pools," and he kissed one eye and then the other.

Elizabeth opened her eyes to look into his as he continued his journey. "I love this sweet button of a nose," and he kissed her nose. "And oh, how I love your lips," and he kissed her lips once, twice, three times; intense and deep kisses, but not prolonged. "And I love your cheekbones, high cheekbones like a Grecian goddess," and he kissed her cheekbones, first the one and then the other.

Then he slightly turned her head and whispered into her ear as he touched her lobe, "I believe that I have love this part, right here, since you first turned your head after requesting that I take you to your sister when you came to Netherfield." With that, he took her lobe into his mouth.

He suckled and nibbled as she softly moaned, "Oh, William, yes, William, oh that feels heavenly." Then he stopped and dropped again to her mouth. He kissed her lightly and gazing into her eyes, smiling a deep rich smile. She could see his dimples and his teeth.

"Elizabeth, tomorrow I would like to take you for a breakfast picnic. Would you like that?" Darcy asked.

"A breakfast picnic? You mean bring our breakfast with us on our walk?" Elizabeth questioned.

"Something like that. Would that be acceptable to you, my love?

"Yes, I would like that."

"Then you should mention to your father later that we plan to be gone a little longer than our normal walk, and that you will not be back for breakfast. It would not do to have him worry after you. I know you are his favourite. He would be quite upset with me if he thought you had come to any harm."

Elizabeth giggled lightly, "Yes, my father has always thought me the most sensible of his daughters. I am not so sure, however, I have been sensible lately."

"Sensible enough for me, my dear. Now let us return to Longbourn. I believe we are to join your family for breakfast."

Chapter 8

4 December 1811

Darcy and Elizabeth walked arm in arm, enjoying the morning conversation on the way to their glen. They were both rejoicing in their increasing intimacy, and the comfort they had with each other.

"William, tell me about your adventures as a young boy. Did the young Fitzwilliam get into any mischief?" Elizabeth entreated him to share with a bright smile.

"Mischief, hmmm. Well, one of my earliest memories was a time I got angry with my parents and attempted to escape the house on my pony, Sunburst. I was but four or five years of age at the time. Father saw me trying to saddle him myself, and he came out to ask if he could help. When he asked where I was going, I told him I was running away. His friend was with him, and they asked if they could run away with me. I thought it sounded like fun for all of us to run away! We went riding for probably only a couple hours, and I was so tired when we returned that I went straight to bed. The next day he told me to let him know anytime I wanted to run away, as he would be glad to go with me," Darcy chuckled and suddenly stopped speaking, smiling at her, a little in shock. "Elizabeth, I believe the friend was your father. We will have to ask him if he happens to remember the time I ran away."

"Oh, if it was him, I am certain that he will recall it. He has a very keen memory, and he has often teased me about the time I ran away because I did not want to take a bath," Elizabeth smirked at Darcy.

Darcy laughed, "How old were you?"

"Oh, I believe I was also around four or five. I hid in a tree, and my family continued to call me. I could see them down below, but I was determined not to let them know where I was. Father must have seen me though, because he came out and sat below my tree with some of my favourite lemon tarts. He sat there eating them, knowing that my stomach would eventually lead me home," Elizabeth laughed.

"I believe I would have liked you as a child, Lizzy," he said as he turned to her and kissed her on the cheek.

Lizzy smiled up at him, "I believe I would have liked five year-old Fitzwilliam as well." Then she reached up and kissed him on the cheek.

They continued to talk of their childhoods, and then began to talk about whether their children would inherit their tendency to run away, until they reached their destination. Darcy and Elizabeth pleasantly relaxed on a blanket spread out in front of a log in what they now called *their glen*. Darcy had brought a picnic basket that Bingley's cook had prepared for him. It was filled with three different cheeses, some crusty bread, a couple of scones, some rare fruit he had brought back from London, and a bottle of wine.

They were seated with their backs against the log, enjoying their meal. Darcy was teasing her with little bites of food he served with his fingers. He had begun to play a game lovers often play, using cuisine as a part of his seduction. Elizabeth had no idea what effect she had on him. Her innocence, in addition to her playful and carefree nature, had returned. She found that she liked Darcy's reaction when she caught, and either licked or nibbled his fingers as he fed her.

For Darcy, there was nothing about what he was doing that morning that was innocent. In fact, it was quite the opposite. In his determination to allay her fears about marital relations, he had been quite calculating. He had planned the agenda for this morning's repast, and today's "lesson", before he left Netherfield. He was slowly advancing his attentions to his fiancée.

Part of him, the proper and restrained gentlemen, was a little shocked by his calculations; but the lover inside him was concerned for Elizabeth. She had asked him to help her understand the conversation she had overheard. He knew if he desired a free and open level of intimacy, he had to educate her in the ways of love.

Darcy was no rake. The end goal was not to conquer and abandon. His goal was to make Elizabeth his wife in every way within the next week. He believed there should be nothing but openness and honesty between them as a married couple. His heart's desire was for propriety and societal notions to have no place in the Master or the Mistress' chambers. Darcy had been alone all his life. Now that he was to marry, he intended to sleep with his wife each night, whether it included physical intimacies or not.

He had chosen carefully when he planned this breakfast picnic, as he had picked only food that could be eaten by hand. It was always his intention to feed her. He delighted in kissing crumbs away from her lips. And he was thrilled with her improvisation, particularly kissing or nibbling his fingers as he fed her. She had even surprised him by feeding him as well.

He had plans for the blanket. Every time he lifted the wine glass to his lips and then hers. He gave her a long, deep kiss. The sweetness of tasting the very essence of her mouth – strawberry lips – and duelling with her nimble tongue enthralled him. It did not take them long before they abandoned their meal in pursuit of more delightful activity.

Elizabeth took it upon herself to move to his lap. In her innocence she did not hesitate to straddle his legs. She was thrilled with being even with his mouth. Remembering Darcy's lesson from the day before, she cupped his cheeks and kissed all the way down his face; beginning with his forehead and ending with his mouth. He was thrilled, and his erection jolted to life when she suckled his tongue.

With a husky, slightly breathless voice, he said, "Ah, I see that my bride is a most excellent student."

With a giggle, she said, "It is my goal to graduate with honours, sir." Then she moved forward to suckle his ear lobe.

"Well, you most assuredly are becoming quite a proficient in this particular lesson," and he groaned as her tongue explored the contours of his ear. "It is definitely to the advantage of your professor that you desire to be a true proficient. Even better that you are willing to practice quite diligently." Her neck was in his sights as she was delightfully exploring his ear, and he began kissing the stretch of her neck.

She slid even higher onto his lap, and he knew the moment her womanhood came in touch with his erection. His groan grew to an intensity that it caused her to stop and ask breathlessly, "William are you all right? Am I doing something wrong?"

Barely able to speak, Darcy remembered the lessons from the courtesan so long ago; how to control his breathing and his muscle tension, and even his thoughts in order to prolong his erection. He knew it would require every element of restraint he could garner to be able to continue in this endeavour without taking her innocence. But he was determined to only move a step or two at a time.

"I am fine, my love," he said with quiet restraint.

Elizabeth did not realize what she was doing as she gently rocked back and forth against his manhood. She became more and more breathless, and with a quiet, embarrassed voice she stopped kissing long enough to ask, "William, what is this? It seems to have sprung up suddenly?" She reached down and touched his manhood through his breeches.

"Oh, God, Lizzy. Give me just a moment." He pulled away slightly and took a calming breath as he pulled her against his chest and tucked her head into his neck. After a short time, he pulled back and looked deeply into her eyes, "You wished to learn, so I will tell you. What you feel is my manhood. As I get more... ah... excited, as passion begins to effect me, it gets harder and becomes more upright. Passion prepares that part of my body so it will more easily enter your secret place when we join as man and wife. Do you know of your secret place?"

Elizabeth blushed and nodded her head.

"Does this help you understand a little?" Darcy asked.

"Yes, a little. But, does that mean you wish for us to join as man and wife now?" She quietly asked.

"Oh, my love, I so look forward to our joining as man and wife. And yes, my body is prepared for that, but it will not happen now. You are not ready for that. You deserve for your first time to be in a bedchamber, in which there is every comfort and absolutely no chance of discovery," Darcy explained.

Elizabeth shyly cocked her eye towards him and asked, "Can I see it?"

Both of his eyebrows rose as he thought, *Good God, it is going to be delightful to be married to this woman. My plan is most assuredly working.* He calmed his thoughts and said, "Not today, my love, but know that I am quite delighted by your curiosity," and he very lightly chuckled. They gazed adoringly at each other.

He slowly negotiated their recline from leaning against the log to lying supine on the blanket. Darcy adoringly ran his finger along her face and then along her lips, while from time to time, she would attempt to nip his finger.

"Sweet Elizabeth, are you quite well?" he asked.

She smiled a smile that filled his heart so full it brought tears to his eyes. "Oh yes, William. I am very well, indeed."

He rolled them over so she was on her back and he was on his side, propped up on his elbow. He began moving his fingers from the side of her face and along her neck, and slowly along the edge of her gown, down along the precious skin towards her breast, and then back up again. Each trip down brought his hand a little closer to those creamy, luscious mounds that he longed to taste.

With a deep, seductive voice, he said, "If at any point you feel fear, you must stop me, my love. I wish only to bring you pleasure today. I intend to do so without you or me having to disrobe. Please ask any questions you might have. Also, if there is something you really like, please tell me as well. If you cannot ask me in words, then your body's reactions will tell me what you like. You are not to hold them back, do you understand? I delight in knowing I can raise your passion. Is that all right with you, Lizzy?"

"Oh, yes, William." She relaxed a bit and let herself give into his ministrations.

On the next trip, Darcy's fingers moved all the way down her neckline, very lightly dipping into the valley between her two mounds. He was entranced as he traced along her bounteous breasts. If he was being honest with himself, he had first noted her breasts, even before her eyes.

When Darcy's hand had first crossed the fabric, inching towards her breast, for just a second, Lizzy had a moment of panic. But she managed to push it down. He had told her he would stop should she wish it. He had told her he would give her pleasure without either of them disrobing. Yes, she would trust him.

Darcy flattened his hand and cupped her breast. For both of them, it was a sensational experience. Darcy knew he was getting closer and closer to accomplishing his desire. For Elizabeth, it was the awakening of the next step in her passion.

Darcy ministered to her breast through her clothes. His fingers traced circles around and around her breast, and alternated with squeezing lightly. He came closer and closer to her nipple on each circle, and Elizabeth's body involuntarily arched as a low moan escaped her throat. As soon as he reached what he thought was the edge of her nipple, he traced very light circles around the edge of her aureole, and watched as her ripe bud bloomed into hardness through her gown.

In reality, he was salivating. It took everything in him not to lower her gown and suckle the pert tip he had caused to ripen. That was not the lesson for today. He had promised to go slow. He had told her they would remain clothed, and he intended to honour his promise.

When he began to pinch her nipples, her moans became gasps. William rejoiced in her blooming arousal! He leaned down to kiss her, fully and deeply, as he moved his hand to her other breast. His tongue slowly began to mimic the motions that his manhood was yet restraining. She arched against him again as his fingers pinched her other ripe bud, and her arms wrapped around his neck as her fingers slid up into his hair.

Elizabeth's excitement was so great that she moved her arms down to his waist and pulled him towards her. Involuntarily, he found himself rolling on top of her. Both of them knew the moment his manhood pressed against her apex. Her instincts had already taught her to open her thighs wider to allow him atop of her.

To say Darcy was shocked was an understatement! This was not his plan, and things were spiraling out of his control as he felt Elizabeth arch towards him.

Elizabeth experienced a rush through her entire body. She felt dampness within her secret place, and a surge of heat from her head to her toes. She had never imagined that she could experience such sensual joy.

Darcy was near ecstasy, but he knew he could not allow himself to find release. He could not compromise her. He would not. Yet he could not stop. His hand traced a path down between their bodies from her breast, down her stomach to her bellybutton, dipping his finger into the hollow and tracing around the edge. Then his journey resumed, a journey with a most particular destination.

When he arrived at her mound, he cupped her sex through her dress and small clothes. Her moans and gasps were increasing as he approximated the location of her pearl. Their hips began to move of their own volition. This was for her. This became a meditative thought as his rhythmic pressing against her apex increased. Words flowed from his mouth that he could not control. "This is for you my love, all for you, for you my love. Let go, Lizzy, my Luscious Lizzy. Let go, let go."

Elizabeth did not really know what he meant by letting go, but she felt like she was flying. Soaring toward new heights, higher and higher, she was being carried on the wings of an eagle. And as the eagle reached its highest heights, it swooped with her towards the ground as she reached her pleasure, and a voice she had never heard before screamed, "Oh! William!"

Darcy had not allowed himself to find his pleasure. He knew that he needed to get himself under good regulation. He turned over onto his back and pulled her to his side. He was disturbed with himself and thought, *Things are moving too fast! Good God, how did I ever think that I could control passion, could meticulously plan these lessons. I was out of my depth from the start!*

As he often did when he needed to cool his ardour, he thought through his catalogue of thoughts guaranteed to cool his arousal. He thought of his parents' deaths, his loneliness and Georgiana's face crying, his Aunt Catherine and his friend's ridiculous sister, even his wife-to-be's mother. It served his purpose. His desire flagged, and his love for Elizabeth swelled.

Their breathing and heartbeats slowed, and Elizabeth turned towards Darcy with a joy-filled smile lighting her entire face.

Darcy spoke first. "Elizabeth, I am sorry, my love. I did not mean for things to go so far."

"Do I look like I am complaining, sir?"

"No, you look like you have experienced your first full bloom of passion. Are you all right, my love?" He asked as the back of his fingers moved along her cheek.

"Oh, William, I am wonderful. But was that what I felt, the bloom of passion as you called it?"

"Yes, I believe it was. You have felt a pinnacle of pleasure, of passion. It is a release that is given to us as a gift from God, as a part of the act of marriage," Darcy said frankly as he pulled her tight against his chest, and again tucked her head into his neck.

"Well, if that is the gift in the act of marriage, I cannot understand why my mother and her friends complain about it so."

"Well, my love, all women do not experience it when the act is performed. As I said before, it is up to the man whether the woman has as pleasurable experience as he does."

"But, you did not have that same experience? Did you William?"

"It matters not, Lizzy. I rejoice in your experience. I love you very much."

"And I love you, William." With a raised brow, she asked, "Did you call me Luscious Lizzy, sir?"

"Oh, did I say that out loud?" Darcy countered, looking away, a little embarrassed.

"Yes, you did, William."

"Then my answer is, most certainly, my love, luscious indeed. Luscious Lizzy." He kissed her again.

"Am I allowed to come up with a nickname for you as well?" she inquired in between kisses.

"You may call me anything you like, my love," as he kissed her again.

Chapter 9

4 December 1811

Fitzwilliam Darcy returned to Netherfield after his morning with Lizzy. The post had arrived in his absence. He took it and decided to return to his chambers to review his mail and, if he was honest, to be sure that he avoided Miss Bingley. He was suspicious of her, but he could not really point his finger at any particularly event or reason for his suspicion. As she was Charles Bingley's sister, he was attempting to deal with her in a civil manner, but his patience was beginning to wear thin.

So it was that he settled in to review his mail. As he separated his business correspondence from his personal, he found a letter from his sister.

Darcy House
2 December 1811

Dear Brother,

I hope you made it back to Netherfield safely, and that your reunion with Miss Bennet was all you anticipated. I wanted to tell you again how happy I am you are to marry.

William, I have been worried about you for so long. You had so much responsibility put on you when Father died, and have handled it admirably. I could not be prouder to call you brother. But I have sensed that you were lonely, and had no one to turn to when you needed help and comfort. I am grateful that you no longer have to be alone.

I know that I have been a trial to you, and I want to again ask for your forgiveness. I know you deserve every happiness. I am grateful you have found a woman that you love. I know that has always been your wish. I am grateful that by waiting, and avoiding all the match-making mamas of the *ton*, you have managed to find what you wholeheartedly desired. I know that Mother and Father would have been happy for you as well.

Please give Miss Bennet my regards, and let her know how grateful I am to soon have a sister. I will be travelling with Richard and his parents to Netherfield three days prior to your wedding. I long to see you. I am,

Sincerely yours, etc.
G. D.

Darcy thoughts drifted to contemplating how his Lizzy's liveliness had helped lift him out of a heaviness of spirit. How he hoped that it would help Georgiana as well! He looked forward to introducing the two of them.

If anyone could have seen him at that exact moment, with the exception of his family and Lizzy, they would not have recognized him. His face was relaxed, a smile of complete joy accentuating his dimples. He looked like a young man of eighteen again.

Darcy had never anticipated feeling this much contentment and happiness. He now believed he had never been happy before, not truly happy, for he was near giddiness with his love for Lizzy. He was in love. *Me! Fitzwilliam Darcy!* Only two weeks before he had been stuck in a life of loneliness and emptiness, and (in an instant) Lizzy had changed all of that.

Darcy contemplated, *Hmmm, what a joyful morning. But why did I ever think I could control the progress of passion?* While Darcy was thrilled with his progress in educating the pert Miss Bennet, he was also quite disturbed. His behaviour had not been that of a gentleman. He knew that. His plan did not include joining as man and wife prior to their wedding. He knew he could not trust himself if Lizzy again took the initiative as she had today.

He lay back on his bed, remembering the morning. Without realizing it, his musing caused him to become erect.

She is more beautiful each time I see her. I wonder if she is truly growing more beautiful, or if in my knowing her more intimately she is more beautiful to me. Her blooming passion is a wonder. To have been able to move her from fear to release in such a short time... oh... she is indeed a most worthy student. After we are married, I will let her borrow the book I received from Richard. After all, she is proficient at improving her mind by extensive reading. Perhaps we will look at the book together, and discover new positions we would like to try. Hmm, I believe I will enjoy that indeed. Darcy had not found release earlier, and could no longer stop from taking matters into his own hands.

Today, her eyes were wide and aglow as she came to her pleasure. Her breasts were swelling, and the sounds she allowed to escape... her gasps and moans as she got closer and closer. Her skin grew warmer and brighter as she took her pleasure. Her scent, yes I love her scent. She smelled of lavender today. Sometimes she smells of roses, but today it was lavender.

His breathing became faster and his face flushed. He moaned in memory and as the sounds were leaving his lips, he continued to think of Lizzy.

To think, I touched and teased her breasts until her ripe buds were protruding, hard and erect through her light muslin gown. Oh, how I wanted to take each nipple into my mouth and suckle. Ah, yes indeed. And her moans and gasps of pleasure as I teased her nipples. The flush upon her chest as her pleasure grew. Darcy was back on top of her in his mind, rubbing against her, mimicking the process of mating. All the while, he continued to stroke himself. He lost all rational thought as he increased his strokes to a frenzied pace as his release began spiralling upon him. He groaned quite loudly in his pleasure, and gasped her name, "Lizzy."

~~*~*~*

At almost the same time, Elizabeth entered her chambers at Longbourn and locked the door. She wanted some time to herself, wanted to be able to think over her breakfast picnic and her growing intimacy with William.

On the way home from their glen, they had spoken of wedding details. Lizzy told him her mother had insisted on her spending the next day with the family as she had fittings to attend to, as well as a need to spend some time with her family before the wedding.

William told her when the members of his family were to arrive, and mentioned how anxious he was for Lizzy to get to know Georgiana. Lizzy had questioned him about the other members of his family, and was pleased to hear that thus far all had been pleased for him, except for Lady Catherine.

Darcy told her more of the wish of his aunt and his mother for him to marry his cousin Anne. Lizzy had learned about the financial considerations, as well as familial reasons, that the two matriarchs formulated this plan. She had also learned that in no way had William ever considered the match, and that his cousin had never been inclined to marry him either. Lizzy found herself quite grateful that this plan had not resulted in a marriage, for she could no longer imagine herself ever being happy with another.

She could see her fiancé in her mind's eye. And remembered the events of the morning. *Oh, my word, I never imagined I could feel such pleasure, such excitement, and such ecstasy! And William tells me that it will get better! I shall die indeed! Oh, God! I believe William is truly the most handsome man that I have ever seen. His eyes, his lips, oh, and his mouth so warm and wet! I could get lost in the sensations of his mouth. And when he was pressing against me, I had no idea that I could experience such excitement. He said that our passion was what prepares us to join as man and wife.* She giggled a little; *I cannot believe I asked if I could see him!! I am mortified, but he did not seem upset. I wonder what he really thought when I said that?*

He seems to quite like my curiosity. But I still wonder what it looks like. I have changed nappies for my Aunt Gardiner's son, Harold, but he was only a little boy... William said that his becomes engorged and gets hard to prepare him to enter me.

Lizzy began to contemplate all that she did not yet know... and better yet, what she would soon experience. *Maybe there is something in father's library that will tell me more. Why am I so curious? It is only a matter of days before we wed. I have never had such thoughts as these in my life! Yet I long to know more.* In truth, Lizzy had always enjoyed reading. Broadening her understanding was something she had always sought. She reckoned her desire for learning all she could of marital relations should not have been any different. It was with that thought that she began to prepare for dinner, in hopes of arriving at her father's library before he returned from his chambers.

~~*~*~*

That afternoon, Fanny Bennet had taken the opportunity to retreat to her chambers. She had been quite busy with the furious pace that she had kept in order to prepare Elizabeth's wedding in less than a week's time. However, this afternoon, Fanny had begun to contemplate what it would mean for Elizabeth to become a part of the Darcy family.

Her daughter, *Mistress of Pemberley*! She would never have believed it could have been so! She had met the former *Mistress of Pemberley*, Lady Anne Darcy, when she raveled with Mr. Bennet to Pemberley to visit his friend George. Lady Anne was everything that Fanny was not. She was blonde, she was titled, came from a noble family, and she was very rich.

For too many years now, Fanny had compared herself to rich women of the *ton*. She would never measure up to the ideal she had created in her own mind. She knew that.

But on this day, she began to contemplate how her life might have been different if she had not denied her husband her bed for so many years. Theirs had eventually evolved into little more than a marriage of convenience. It was quite sad, for Fanny Gardiner had been very much in love with Tom Bennet. Had she discovered this regret too late? Was there a way to change the sad state of her marriage as it was today? Did she even want to try?

~~*~*~*

Tom Bennet sat at his desk and thought over the events of the last fortnight. After all these years, he would be connected to the Darcys as family. He knew George would have been ecstatic with the match—Tom's favourite daughter and George's only son. George had never wanted to give in to the machinations of Catherine and her desire to connect the Darcys to the de Bourghs.

It had been a delight to put Lady Catherine in her place when she had recently visited Longbourn. She had come to visit with the intent of intimidating Elizabeth, hoping that she would renounce her plan to marry Fitzwilliam. She had not realized who Elizabeth was, or more importantly who her *father* was, until arriving at Longbourn.

~~*~*~*

29 November 1811

Tom had been in his library when Lady Catherine was announced. Elizabeth had gone visiting the neighbours with her mother. Thus, Hill had come to inform him that Lady Catherine insisted on speaking with one of Miss Elizabeth's parents.

Tom entered the front parlour and saw that she had made herself comfortable in his favourite chair. As he entered the room, she rose to her feet.

"Ah, Catherine, what a pleasure it is for you to come to visit me at Longbourn. Why, I had a letter from your brother just today! He did not mention anything about your intentions to call on my family. How good it is you see you!" Tom Bennet smirked as he spoke.

With great surprise, Lady Catherine endeavoured to maintain her haughty air. "Thomas Bennet, what are *you* doing here?"

"I live here, Catherine. It might be more appropriate for me to ask you, what you are doing here?"

"You! You are behind this outrage! I should have known! Miss Elizabeth Bennet is your daughter?"

"Catherine, I have no idea what outrage you refer to! But yes, Elizabeth is indeed the second of my five daughters. What is that to you? Why are you here?" Tom Bennet of course knew why she would have come, but he would not give her the satisfaction.

"I am here to refute a rumour of an intended marriage between your... your... daughter and **my** nephew!"

Mr. Bennet continued, "I assure you Catherine, that if a rumour so exists, your presence here will do nothing but substantiate it."

"This is not to be borne, Thomas Bennet! I demand you tell me once and for all! Is your daughter *insisting* that she is engaged to my nephew?"

"She is indeed, Catherine, as is your nephew! By the way, he is currently in London obtaining a special license. He plans on returning the day after tomorrow. I know your nephew well enough to know he will not appreciate your interference."

"This marriage, which you delude yourself in to believing shall occur, will never take place! Darcy is engaged to *my* daughter!"

"Catherine, do you not **know** who you are speaking to? No agreement has ever existed! It was a presumptuous design you tried to impose upon Anne. You and I both know George never agreed to it. Your brother knows this to be the truth as well, and honours your nephew's match. In fact, he and his entire family plan to arrive in the late afternoon three days before the wedding!" exclaimed Mr. Bennet.

"You of course, are welcome to attend, Catherine." The last was said more calmly as he attempted to compose himself.

"Is this to be borne? Pray, attend to this, Thomas Bennet! Your daughter shall *never* be a part of my family!"

"Well, Catherine. You are speaking the truth in your last sentence, at least. For my Elizabeth will be a Darcy, not a de Bourgh or even a Fitzwilliam. Your nephew has asked her to become his bride and she has accepted. Why the notices have already been published, as they are in the paper today! Would you care to see for yourself, madam?

Lady Catherine scoffed at the suggestion, puffing her breast out like a proud bird. "Believe you me, Mr. Thomas Bennet, I shall know how to act! A woman of no connections and no fortune, who is determined to trap my nephew with her art and allurements; a woman bent upon exposing him to ridicule and censure! It shall not be borne! Oh, yes, I will know how to act!"

"Catherine, we both know all you speak of is intentional exaggeration. In regards to connections and fortune, as well as any threat you might try to make, this is just not true! I am aware that your brother Edward is the trustee of Rosings. In truth, you have a great deal to lose should you decide to turn on your family. You could find yourself displaced from your home, could you not?" Tom's gaze peered deeply into hers, his arms crossed in front of him.

"I am not accustomed to such language as this! You cannot threaten me! I knew that the Darcys would rue the day they connected themselves to the likes of you! I take no leave of you. I send no greetings to anyone in your family. You may inform your daughter that I am most seriously displeased," huffed Lady Catherine.

"Frankly, Lady Catherine, I care not if you are displeased. Now if you do not mind, my man will see you out," Mr. Bennet stated with finality.

~~*~*~*

Tom Bennet continued to contemplate his soon to be son-in-law and Lizzy's upcoming marriage. He thought of all of Mr. Darcy's relations. It was not long before he found himself reliving a ball he attended some twenty-five years previous.

~~*~*~*

20 October 1787

Tom Bennet entered the Stanhope's Ball that evening with anticipation. Would there be anyone there he would fancy this night? It seemed too soon for the season to draw to a close, and he had only seen one young lady he would consider as a future bride. He saw her standing across the dance floor, and moved in a determined manner across the room to approach her.

"May I have the next dance, my lady?" asked Tom Bennet.

"Of course you can, Mr. Bennet," a lovely pair of fine eyes and an impertinent grin smiled back at him.

He had led her to the dance.

As they had moved down the line, his partner said, "I believe we should have some conversation, Mr. Bennet."

Tom Bennet answered, "Do you talk as a rule while dancing then, my lady?"

"Oh, no, I would rather remain taciturn and silent. Like you, sir, I am often unwilling to speak unless I can say something that will amaze the room..."

The conversation continued with such twists and turns, and Tom Bennet was bewitched indeed. She was incredible. He began to consider that perhaps love at first sight did exist. As their dance came to an end, he escorted her back to her family.

~~*~*~*

Tom Bennet remembered that evening with fondness, but also with regret. What was love, he really did not know. Perhaps he never would know. Had he been telling himself a lie all of his life? It was not until he saw true love demonstrated between his daughter and Fitzwilliam Darcy that he began to believe he had.

Chapter 10

5 December 1811

Elizabeth had promised her mother and father that she would spend this day at Longbourn. She had broken her fast with her family, had her final fitting for her trousseau with the Modesto, and had taken a walk in the gardens with Jane.

Luncheon was with the family. They talked and laughed as they recalled happy memories of their childhood. Elizabeth was aware time was short before she became Mrs. Darcy, and she was grateful for a quiet day in this hectic time before her wedding.

However, she also found herself overwhelmed with a steady ache for William. She missed him. He had become such a part of her daily life, and of her happiness, that it was hard to have a day without him. She was grateful he was scheduled to come for dinner that evening.

She had promised to spend time with her father after lunch. So, she approached his library about an hour after completing their lunch, and knocked on the door.

"Come in, my Lizzy. Come and talk to your papa while you still can," Mr. Bennet said with a sigh.

"Oh, Papa, you know you are not losing a daughter! You are only gaining a son, are you not?" Elizabeth answered.

"Perhaps, but have a seat my dear. I want to speak to you about your Mr. Darcy, and let you know a little more of my history with his family," began Mr. Bennet.

"I know that you said that you were friends with William's father. But I would like to know more, as I will soon be a part of his family," Elizabeth returned.

"Well, I was not just friends with George Darcy, he was my best friend, Lizzy. I was also very good friend with Edward Fitzwilliam. He is your Mr. Darcy's uncle, and the current Lord Matlock. The three of us were almost inseparable both at Eton and then at Cambridge. We stayed in the same large suite of rooms at Cambridge, spent holidays in each others company, and stayed in each other's homes." Mr. Bennet stood up and walked to the window, lost in his thoughts.

"George and I went on our Grand Tour together. We visited France, Italy, Greece, Spain and even parts of the Mediterranean while we were away.

"I was best man at George's wedding to Anne. And, while I have not spoken of it with Fitzwilliam, I believe he may have made the connection. You see Edward and Amelia Fitzwilliam, Lord and Lady Matlock, were godmother and godfather for your betrothed. I am his second godfather."

Elizabeth was in shock at first, but finally said, "You are William's godfather? That is, that is unbelievable Papa. You have never spoken of it with him? I do not understand..."

"I thought it was important that you know some of my history with Fitzwilliam. He will be dining here tonight, and your mother knows of my history with his family—in case she should say something. I did not want this to be a shock to you," explained Mr. Bennet.

Elizabeth rubbed her forehead and continued to listen to her father in amazement.

"I was at Pemberley when Fitzwilliam was born, Lizzy. I was at his christening. I have followed him all of his life. I have kept up with his life through Edward. Though I have not seen Edward since George's funeral, we have continued to write. Edward is thrilled that you are to be his niece. He wrote recently that he believes George would have been thrilled as well."

Her father gathered his courage together to share what he meant to say next, "There is one other thing of which I wish to speak with you. This is something I have discussed with Fitzwilliam. It is about my financial situation, and yours as well.

"You see, George and Edward assisted me in my financial education. My financial situation is much different than I would have most people think. I made some very wise investments with my friends' assistance. Later, I was able to trust my own expertise, and I have amassed quite a fortune, Lizzy. You will now be the only one in the family to know of it. I trust you and want you to know, because despite what you may have thought, you actually have a dowry of twenty thousand pounds."

Elizabeth was stunned and had trouble forming her thoughts to speak, but eventually she exclaimed, "Goodness! But, how father? I do not understand!"

Mr. Bennet continued, "You see, my dear, I am aware that Longbourn is entailed to the silliest man in the universe. I wanted to make certain that things were in place for my daughters and my wife in the event of my demise. You and Jane both have twenty thousand pounds for your dowries. Hopefully—Mary, Kitty and Lydia will have the same by the time their suitors begin to call.

"One of the reasons I wanted to speak to you is I also have plans to keep your mother from being 'turned out into the hedgerows', as she is rather fond of complaining. I have provided for her and your sisters, should I depart this earth prior to her death. I purchased the Great House at Stoke a couple years ago, Lizzy. It is in good condition, and I have a servant in my employ that provides housekeeping once a week. I do not keep a staff as it is currently without a tenant, but my steward addresses have problems as they arise. It does not have the income that Longbourn does, but with the tenant cottages that are on the property, the income pays for upkeep and I have a little left over each year."

"Mama knows nothing of this?"

"That is one of the reasons I wanted to speak with you, Lizzy. You have always been the smartest of my daughters, and you know your mother's nerves as well as I. I have long believed that if your mother were aware of our true wealth, she would find a way for us to exceed our income. I have concealed the truth from her, as I wanted to be sure there would be a legacy to pass on to my family. "

"Papa, you know, I am not sure mother's nerves are as severe as we think. Have you ever thought she might use them as an excuse?" Elizabeth asked, with the knowledge gained from overhearing her mother's conversation earlier in the week.

"I do not know, Elizabeth. But it is such behaviour that persuades me to suspect she would exceed my income if she knew what it was. My dearest child, I have an income of over twenty thousand a year. Can you imagine how she would react? How soon every fortune hunter in the area would converge on this house to try and win my daughters for their fortunes alone? I would not have you marry for the funds you can give another, my dear. I have always desired for you to marry for love. Elizabeth, I hope I am not wrong. I believe that you have come to love your William, am I right?" He smiled a warm smile at her.

"Yes, Papa, you are quite right. He is truly the best of men," Elizabeth honestly answered him.

"Then I am very, very happy for you, my dear. That my dearest girl and my godson have made a match has made me exceedingly happy!"

"Now, I want to mention an errand I would like for you and Fitzwilliam to attend to for me before you leave the area for Derbyshire. Perhaps the day after tomorrow would work, as I believe that the Matlocks and Darcy's sister will not arrive until late that day. I would like for you and William to go and see the Great House at Stoke. I want you to look it over, and consider what your mother and your younger sisters would need to see to their comfort if they lived there. I would like to take advantage of Fitzwilliam's expertise in estate management, and have him look at the land. I am not sure what needs to be done to improve the property— if I should consider leasing it until it is needed, or if I should seek another estate altogether."

"Do you think the two of you would be willing to take a picnic, and visit the family's other estate, my dear?" He winked at her.

"If you are sure you support us being alone to do that, Papa," she laughed. "I am more than willing. You may discuss it with William tonight."

"Well, it has been unseasonably warm. I will loan you my curricle for the trip. It should not be a problem for you to travel there in an open curricle. I will be sure you have some heavy rugs included in case it gets a little cold. The two of you cannot get into too much trouble in that manner, can you?"

Elizabeth slightly blushed, which caused a Mr. Bennet's curiosity to rise slightly, but decided to let it go for now.

"Well, now you may run along my dear," Mr. Bennet finished and Elizabeth left the library.

~~*~*~*

Later in the afternoon, Elizabeth left the house and walked to Longbourn's stables, internally laughing at herself. She knew that Darcy applauded her curiosity, but she was also aware that her intended mission for the day was quite unusual. As William Shakespeare had said in Much Ado About Nothing, *curiosity could kill a cat*. Thank God she had gotten over her childhood fear of horses. She was grateful her father had insisted on riding lessons, as William had told her the best way to see Pemberley was on horseback. If she were still afraid of horses she would never have been capable of attempting her planned action.

Elizabeth approached Sampson's stall, feeding him pieces of an apple she had brought with her. "Hello there, Boy," she said as she patted him on the head. Sampson was her father's horse, and was a beautiful stallion. She had ridden enough with her father that she was quite familiar with the horse. As is often true with stallions, he would not allow many people to approach him.

Elizabeth had searched her father's library the day before, and had *not* found what she was looking for. So here she was in the stable. She had excused Stephen, the stable hand, by assuring him that she was not going to ride. He was told she only wanted to visit with the horses, so she was quite alone there.

She opened his stall and entered, continuing to maintain physical contact with Sampson in order not to spook him.

Little did she know as she entered Sampson's stall, that Darcy was entering the stable with Apollo. He watched her from afar as she greeted the horse, wondering what she was about.

He quietly secured Apollo and began to carefully approach Sampson's stall, as he did not want to startle Elizabeth or the horse. As Darcy approached them he held some sugar cubes in his hand to keep Sampson in check. He watched Elizabeth.

What on earth is she doing? He thought.

Elizabeth was squatting down and appeared to be rubbing the horses belly as if she were looking for something.

Darcy was gently stroking the horse's muzzle and cleared his throat to see if it would attract her attention.

Elizabeth pulled away from Sampson, standing up abruptly. "William! What a surprise to see you." She blushed profusely.

"I was invited to dinner, my love. I just came a bit early in hopes of spending some time alone with you. Though I have to admit I had not thought to find you in the stable, Lizzy. Can you tell me what you are doing?"

"No... I... William, I cannot."

"Cannot or will not?" Darcy questioned.

"Please William, please just let this be!" Elizabeth begged him.

"Elizabeth, you know you have promised not to lie to me," Darcy exclaimed.

She dusted off her clothes and approached him. "I did promise not to lie to you. However, I did not promise to always answer your questions. We ladies must keep an air of mystery about us, sir," she said with a raised brow and a slight smirk as she opened and closed the stall door, exiting Sampson's stall.

Darcy reached out and ran the back of his fingers along her jaw line, "I believe you are attempting to change the subject, my love. I will have you to tell me, you know."

But he did not press the point. He pulled her to him and gave her a chaste kiss, wrapped her hand around his arm and led her out of the stable.

They talked a little about what they had accomplished that day, agreed that had missed each other, and planned another breakfast picnic for the following day as they approached the house.

But just before they entered the house, Darcy drew her close and whispered in her ear, "While I do not claim to resemble your horse, my love, I *do* believe that you have selected your lesson for the morning."

And with that he entered the house, leaving behind a blushing fiancée with a gaping mouth.

~~*~*~*

Darcy sat at the Longbourn dinner table, determined to present himself in the best light. It was his desire to avoid focusing on Elizabeth's mother and her younger sisters, as he was determined not to concentrate on any behaviour that might be less than proper. If he saw things that would once have shocked him in the past, this night he would allow them to divert him. He had spent enough time amongst the Bennets to know that while Mrs. Bennet and Elizabeth's sisters were not always sensible, they all loved each other. He knew this was not always true in families. He also knew that Mr. Bennet was now planning on sending the youngest two girls to school.

During the afternoon, the Gardiners had arrived from London. Darcy had met them upon returning to the house with his fiancée, and he found them to be quite sensible individuals. It was also obvious they had a deep love for Elizabeth. Darcy remembered Mr. Bennet had mentioned their involvement in Elizabeth and Jane's education in London.

"Mr. Darcy, do you not think our Elizabeth looks quite beautiful tonight? She is wearing one of her new gowns. I helped her pick it out from the Modesto for her trousseau!" Mrs. Bennet exclaimed over dinner.

Darcy gazed at Elizabeth who was sitting opposite from him, "Yes, madam, very beautiful indeed." And then he smiled.

Everyone at the table, with the exception of Elizabeth and Mr. Bennet, were intrigued as they had never seen Mr. Darcy smile. In return, they all smiled back at him.

Darcy had a wonderful conversation with the Gardiners. Mrs. Gardiner had grown up in Lambton, not five miles from Pemberley. They had much in common as they spoke of their memories of Derbyshire. As Mr. Bennet had suggested, Mr. Gardiner appeared to be a very shrewd businessman. As they discussed a new business venture, Darcy found he was quite interested in making an investment.

"Mr. Darcy, you have such a handsome smile. You should smile more often!" Lydia exclaimed, and Darcy blushed.

Mrs. Bennet continued to talk to him, "Well, I have been doing my best to make sure Elizabeth is prepared to be your wife. We have ordered her clothing to insure she will be warm enough for the Derbyshire winters. I have been talking with Elizabeth about proper behaviour for a married woman. She is to be Mistress of Pemberley, no less, so I have continued to remind her she must not continue to wander about the countryside. Why only yesterday she missed breakfast and was gone almost the entire morning. I assure you, sir, I am attempting to curtail such behaviour in her. It will not be appropriate once she has become your wife. She cannot continue to run wild," Mrs. Bennet said shrilly. Elizabeth blushed and looked at the table. Darcy frowned slightly. Mr. Bennet glanced at Elizabeth with a slight smile, as he had a feeling that such behaviour was part of what attracted Darcy to his Lizzy in the first place.

Darcy's improper thoughts briefly focused on the words *'running wild'* for just a moment, and knew he would encourage her wildness. *Oh, it is not a time to think of this! I cannot go to the window during dinner. Thank heavens for the tablecloth!* Darcy decided he must re-attend to the conversation.

Mr. Bennet interrupted his wife, "My dear, Elizabeth was with Mr. Darcy yesterday morning. I believe they went for a walk and a picnic. I am certain that Elizabeth will continue to walk quite frequently, as I am sure there are many lovely paths to explore around Pemberley."

"Oh, Mr. Bennet, you need not be secretive with your family any more! I know you know *all* about the paths at Pemberley. In fact, Mr. Darcy, I once spent a holiday at your home when Mr. Bennet and I were first married!" exclaimed Mrs. Bennet. Elizabeth looked at her plate. Mary, Kitty and Lydia looked like they were in shock. Darcy was not sure what to say or where to even look. He ended looking towards Mr. Bennet.

"Mrs. Bennet, this has not been common knowledge of the family, but you state the truth," Mr. Bennet said.

Darcy decided it would be to the best advantage of this situation to encourage talk of Pemberley, rather than point out the impropriety of Mrs. Bennet's revealing a long held secret. Curiosity seemed to be the way of this day anyway. So he said, "Mr. and Mrs. Bennet why do tell us of your memories of Pemberley." And then to room in general he said, "Mr. Bennet was telling me just this week that he and my father were very good friends. I would like to hear more of your memories of Pemberley, and the time you had in company with my parents."

Mr. Bennet spent some time telling what he remembered of Pemberley. He told them some humerous stories of times with George Darcy. He also spoke of Darcy's uncle, and the company learned that Lord Matlock would be arriving three days prior to the wedding.

Mary discussed books with Darcy. She was very interested in the fact that he had met Lord Byron. They also talked about a book discussion group in which he participated. Mary asked if she could come and visit while they were in town in the spring, possibly for the season. Darcy looked to Elizabeth who nodded, and then indicated to Mary that she would be very welcome to come and spend some time with them, if she so desired.

Mr. Bennet shared over dinner that he was considering sending Lydia and Kitty to a new ladies finishing school near London in the spring. While Lydia and Kitty initially protested, Darcy suggested that they could come and spend any holiday they may be granted at the Darcy townhouse in town. They readily agreed they would look forward to seeing the Darcys while they were in town.

Darcy shared an amused glance with Mr. Bennet. "Mr. and Mrs. Gardiner, Mr. and Mrs. Bennet, and my new sisters to be—it would be my great pleasure, no, I should say *our* great pleasure if you would come to Pemberley for Christmas and celebrate the holiday with Elizabeth and myself. Please do say you will come?"

A chorus of agreement emanated from the table. "Will there be dancing while we are there, Mr. Darcy?" Lydia asked hopefully.

"Why, Miss Lydia, that will be something you must discuss with the new Mistress of Pemberley. What do you think, Miss Elizabeth?" Darcy smiled.

"Why, Mr. Darcy, I would be happy to plan for dancing at my new home. But only if you will find me handsome enough to tempt you to dance," Elizabeth coyly teased with love in her eyes; smiling at him.

Darcy released a deep, hearty laugh. All at the table were amazed. "I would be quite happy to dance with you, my dear Elizabeth," he said with a wide grin on his face.

With that, any doubts her family had regarding their upcoming marital felicity melted away. They were very well matched indeed.

While dinner had been quite nice, Darcy and Elizabeth were struggling to think of anything but finding a way to be able to spend time in each others' sole company. After dinner the men separated, but prior to returning to the ladies, Mr. Bennet asked Mr. Gardiner to give him a couple minutes to speak alone with Darcy.

Mr. Bennet spoke with Darcy and they had agreed to a plan of visiting the Great House at Stoke, two days from hence. They rejoined the ladies as soon as propriety would allow, and Darcy asked, "Mr. and Mrs. Bennet, it is such a lovely evening I wonder if you would allow me to escort Miss Elizabeth for a walk in the garden? I wish to speak with her about something."

"Yes, Mr. Darcy. Lizzy, my dear, go have a lovely walk. You have been in our company quite long enough this evening," Mr. Bennet answered with a light chuckle.

As Darcy and Elizabeth left the parlour for the garden, Darcy took Elizabeth's hand, kissed it and tucked it under his arm, "Oh, my Lizzy, you look quite lovely in the moonlight. *J'aime la façon dont le clair de lune brille dans tes yeux verts, leur faisant ressembler à des diamants rares.* (I love how the moonlight shines in your emerald eyes, making them look like rare diamonds.)

Elizabeth followed with, "And the moonlight makes your eyes look like deep ebony pools, William." She smiled into his eyes.

"You speak French, my Lizzy?"

"Yes, I do my love. *Tu es mon plus cher trésor,*" Elizabeth sighed. (You are my dearest treasure.)

"I love you, my treasure, my very accomplished woman. Why you did not let on that you have such language skills when you were at Netherfield? Perhaps it was due to the fact that you have more taste and tact than Miss Bingley? Let us walk out around the back garden path, my dear, as I desire to hold you in my arms without being seen."

William maneuvered her behind the garden wall, out of sight of Longbourn and the road. He backed her up against the garden wall and moved in towards her, putting his hands on each side of her head as he leaned in and kissed her. It was a deep and thorough kiss; first—full on the mouth, second—kissing and slightly sucking her lower lip, and then her upper as she opened her lips. He stopped, "Oh, how I have missed you."

"Tes lèvres sont délicieuses comme des fraises et rouge comme des rubis," he said during a brief pause before deepening the kiss. (Your lips are sweet like strawberries and red like rubies.)

He pressed his body into hers, and moved his hands to pull her hips toward him and said, *"Ta peau est comme du velours et ton odeur intoxiquant de lavande."* (Your skin is like velvet, and your intoxicating smell of lavender.)

She reached around his body, placing her hands on his hips as she pulled him towards her returning his kisses, duelling with his tongue as she instinctively began to rock her hips slightly against his. Breathlessly she said, *"J'adore, William. Et j'aime ton parfum épicé, tes lèvres douces et fermes."* (I love you, William. And I love your spicy scent, your firm, soft lips.) Their breathing increased in volume, their heart rates began to rise, and their temperature began to soar.

He began to kiss down her neck and one of his hands moved from her hip up to slip beneath the edge of her dress to capture her luscious breast, and then onward till he reached the centre where he began to rub the hardening ripe berry that was her nipple, *"Tes mamelons fermes se dressent comme des baies mures prêtes à être cueillies."* (Your hard nipples stand like ripe berries for me to pluck.)

Elizabeth's reaction to feeling his hand directly upon her breast was feverish. She gasped and said, "*Je désire ton contact, mon William, mon amour.*" (I long for your touch, my William, my love.)

They began to kiss at a frenzied pace. He returned his hands to her hips, and took hold of her bottom. Elizabeth found herself rocking her hips forward and back, bringing her closer and closer to the point of no return. Their pace was furious, and it spun out of control as she crested and gasped in her release against him.

Darcy, never expecting things to spiral out of control so quickly, followed her, breathing her name into her ear, "*Ma succulente Lizzy,*" as he was unable to control himself and released his seed.

They held each other tight and whispered words of love to each other. William placed soft kisses in her hair, on her cheeks, eyes, nose and then her mouth. He pulled back to gaze adoringly into her eyes, trying to sense if there was any fear or concern there, as he had not meant for things to go this far. But finding none, he tucked her head into his neck and hugged her tightly again saying, "My luscious Lizzy, *Ma succulente,* Lizzy."

Elizabeth rubbed her hands softly up and down his spine and leaned into him as she attempted to calm herself.

"Oh, Lizzy, I hope I did not scare you, I... I did not expect that to happen. I am usually in better control of myself... I... I would not wish to dishonour you."

"Oh Lord, William, do not worry! I am quite all right. It is just so startling to discover so many intense feelings. This is all so new, yet it feels so right. We are to be married in less than a week. We are already bound together. Do not worry so! It is important for you to know that I love you very much." She touched his lips as she spoke.

"I love you very much as well, and it is fitting that it is time for me to return to Netherfield." They looked into each other's eyes, touched each others cheeks, resting their foreheads together.

"Oh, my Luscious Lizzy, you truly know not what you do to me."

A short time later, Darcy returned to Netherfield, entering the back door and up the stairs so no one would be alerted to his "accident." *Good God, I have lost all rational thought and judgment. I cannot be married to her fast enough!* he thought as he entered his room to retire for the evening.

Chapter 11

6 December 1811

The next day Darcy and Elizabeth were again in their secluded glen, sharing another breakfast picnic. For today's lesson the professor sat leaning back against a tree and Elizabeth sat cuddled next to him. They were feeding each other little bites of food, nibbling on fingers and each other's lips, occasionally taking a break for a longer kiss. While they giggled and chuckled and grinned with one other, both were aware that a "lesson" had been declared for this day.

Darcy was trying to calm his ardour and his anticipation, as well as wrestling within himself in where he wanted this particular lesson to end. He settled back, and she moved until she was sitting between his legs, leaning against his chest. He had determined what Elizabeth had been trying to do the day before when he happened upon her in the stable, but he could not for the life of him, figure what had possessed her to look at her stallion's equipment. He found himself chuckling with the memory of it, and as he believed they both had satiated their *food* hunger, he attempted to hazard a discussion.

"My love, will you now tell me how you came to be examining your horse," Darcy asked and was grateful she currently could not look him in the face.

"I do believe that all of the truly mortifying events of my life have been observed by you, sir," Elizabeth covered her face and groaned. "I was hoping you had forgotten about that."

"Sweet Elizabeth, do not be embarrassed! Have I not told you your curiosity does you credit?" Darcy assured her as his fingers began to trail down her bare arms and back up.

"Ah, but, dear sir, did not Shakespeare himself say that curiosity killed the cat?"

"Why did you choose a horse, my dear?" he said somewhat amused.

"William, please do not make me speak of this!"

"I know you wish not to speak of it. Torturing you is not my intent, but teaching you has become my most privileged responsibility. I want to hear any thoughts you have had in the last two days regarding our increasing intimacy. Did we not promise each other to be completely honest and open? I dare say that our openness will greatly add to our marital felicity, will it not?"

"I am mortified," she almost whispered it.

"Elizabeth, please my love, I am thrilled at your adventurous nature. Please talk to me. Did you enjoy our picnic here last time?"

"William, you know that I enjoyed our time here, very well indeed. As well, I enjoyed our manner of parting last evening. I am simply not comfortable with speaking of it. Must I?"

"Of course. I will never force you to do anything against your will. But is this not lesson time? If the professor is unaware of the concerns of his favourite student, he cannot properly plan for any future teachings, now can he?"

"All right, William. I know my courage will continue to rise as we talk. What is it that you wish to know?"

Elizabeth relaxed into his chest as he kissed the top of her head and then her neck.

Darcy asked, "I want you to tell me what you felt when you found your pleasure, both here in the glen and yesterday evening before I returned to Netherfield."

"William, you call it finding my pleasure? Is that what I am supposed to call it? I did not know."

"Elizabeth, have you ever felt such before?"

"No." She said the next so quietly that he had to strain to hear her. "I never imagined that I could feel anything so exquisite. I found myself back in my room remembering our time together, and desiring to feel your touch again."

"Lizzy, I do not know if this will help you or not. But maybe if I am honest with you, it will make it easier for you to be honest with me. I have often found a release while thinking of you and touching myself."

"Can I watch you... so I might learn what pleases you, William?"

A little overcome by her question, William laughed as he said, "Oh, my dear, your enthusiasm will be my greatest joy, I do believe. But let us not rush our lesson, my Luscious Lizzy. You are distracting me... You have yet to explain the mystery behind the horse."

"Oh, but William the two things are related... All right," she said as she picked up his hand and intertwined fingers with his, "I will tell you, but you may think me very silly indeed."

Elizabeth continued, "When I returned to my chambers after our last picnic, my mind wanted to know more. I wanted to understand what I had felt. I wanted to know more about what our coming together will be like and I, well, I..." And she paused...

"Yes Elizabeth?"

"I wanted to know what your manhood looked like. So I went down to father's library to see if he had any books hidden there. I found though that if he has any of those types of books, he keeps them well hidden. The only book I could find was about animal husbandry. Yesterday, I decided I could at least learn something by going to the stable. I thought that my father's stallion's size would approximate yours the closest! So that was what I was doing when you came upon me. If you wish to call off the wedding because you will have the silliest of wives, I will understand."

Darcy was grateful he was holding Elizabeth in a way in which she could not see his face. He truly had to hold his breathe not to burst out in hysterical laughter, but he knew that would not help in his quest to keep her whole trust. "Oh, love, I do not think you silly. I think you are quite beautiful and quite desirable. I actually find your interest in such things refreshing." With that, he skillfully turned her around to face him and kissed her fully on the lips.

The reality was that all this talk of pleasure and her spirited curiosity had raised his ardour, and he found himself quite hard. He knew he needed to continue to move slowly and deliberately, but with any luck he might allow himself to find his own release in Elizabeth's presence today. He reckoned her curiosity almost demanded it.

Darcy deepened the kiss and was thrilled at his eager student's attempts to demonstrate she was benefiting from her lessons. While they were participating in a thrilling duel with their tongues, both of their hands began to wander.

For Elizabeth, she parted his coat and began to unbutton the buttons of his vest. Her hands moved onto the planes of his chest through his thin shirt. As she reached his nipples, he began to groan. Liking the power she had over him, she stimulated them and found him moaning in satisfaction. Her mouth left his as she kissed her way down his face. She reached his neck and then continued to kiss down his chest until she reached his nipples and began to suckle them through his shirt.

Darcy's moans grew, as his hands had also been quite busy. He had moved his hands down the sides of her body, and had grabbed the twin globes of her bottom, pulling her hard against his manhood. He was quite pleased when he heard her moan "William," against his chest.

"Oh, my Luscious Lizzy, I see you have anticipated your next lesson," he gasped, as his hands moved up her back until he found the buttons at the back of her neck and began to unbutton the small buttons to allow him to lower the top of her gown. He pulled her back up to look at him and his eyes, darkened in their passion, seemed to burn a hole into her soul. "Love, will you allow me to take your hair down? I long to see it wild and free."

"Let me do it, I can do it quicker and easier," and she quickly removed all the pins from her hair and shook it free.

"Oh, sweet Lizzy, you are so, so beautiful," and he buried his hands into the back of her hair, kissing her along the hairline until he shifted and gave her a long, deep passion-filled kiss on her mouth.

He then stopped and lowered the top of her gown. Both of them found their breath catch, as he revelled in the first viewing of her breasts beneath her chemise.

"No stays today, love?" he asked breathlessly.

"No, as I believe I was longing for you to touch my breasts," she was equally breathless.

Darcy lowered one side and then the other of her chemise. "Oh, no, I do not want to just touch them. I wish to taste them."

He then lowered his tongue to lave the edges of her aureoles and round and round until he came closer to the tip of her hardened ripe bud. Her aureoles were like light milk chocolate; and the tips hardened into a tight, red, hard berry.

He teased the tip by circling it with the tip his tongue. Then when he felt he could stand it no longer, he suckled her entire nipple into his mouth; hot and salivating, he tasted sweet nectar, the essence of his Luscious Lizzy's strawberry essence. It was pure ecstasy.

Elizabeth found she could no longer focus on anything but the feel of her nipple in his hot mouth. He kissed across one breast down into the deep valley in between, and over to the other ripe bud. He laved and suckled her other tip until she arched her back, pushing herself harder against him. By the time he began to nip at the tight berry at the centre, neither had conscious thought as she rocked harder and faster against him. His teeth grazed her tip a bit harder as he suckled, it sent her over the edge, and she gasped his name and hugged him to her trembling body.

They both gathered their thoughts, as Darcy moved her head so he could gaze into her eyes. So aroused, he was having a difficult time thinking clearly.

"Oh, yes, Lizzy! Your enthusiasm does you credit indeed. However, that was not the end of the lesson I had planned for today--but we can stop for the day, if you desire."

"Oh, William, I am more than willing to learn more. In fact, I long for you to touch me... touch me..."

"Will you allow me to lay you back on the blanket, my sweet, Luscious Lizzy?"

Elizabeth lay back against the blanket.

Darcy's breath caught as he beheld her. Her hair splayed out in all directions, her breasts bared to him, her lips swollen and engorged. He realized this next step could prove his undoing if he did not keep himself under tight regulation. He could never remember a time when he had desired *anything* more. But he could do this for Elizabeth...

He smiled at her, and his hand began to trace a path from her ankle slowly and steadily up her calf. When he reached the bend in her leg, he lightly drew circles around the back of her knee before continuing the journey upward along the inside of her thigh. They gazed deeply into each other's eyes. A small smile was exchanged—it communicated the depth of emotions they were experiencing.

As he continued his journey upwards, she found her legs quite naturally parted in anticipation. As he approached her centre with his hand, she moaned deeply as she slowly began undulating her hips in anticipation... Darcy opened one side of her small clothes and cupped her sex.

When his finger first touched her small pearl, this alone was nearly enough to send her over the edge. She rocked against his hand and their eyes locked, exchanging a gaze of pure desire. He moved one finger to separate her folds. She was so wet Darcy gasped as he began to touch her. He added another finger, simulating the motion of mating.

Darcy's thoughts were many. It took every lesson of restraint he had been taught, every thought of his deep love for her, and his rational brain to remind him of her innocence, not take her right there and then. His nostrils caught a scent of her sex, mixed with the lavender essence that meant Elizabeth to him, and he literally prayed that God would help restrain him. As her breath quickened, he sensed her release was near, and he leaned down kissing her deeply. His tongue mimicked the actions of his fingers, and within a minute her release sparked and burst into flames as she cried his name against his lips. Her trembling was so intense that it literally lifted her shoulders off the ground. He continued his ministrations, slower, with less intensity until she calmed herself.

He raised his head to look at her, and what he saw was pure erotic desire. She wanted, *needed* him to find such a release as well.

Elizabeth ran her hand along his face and gazed at him with love and gratitude, "William, please lay back on the blanket now." He obeyed her as her eyes locked with his.

"William, it is your turn. Please, show me how to please you," she begged, running her hand along his length through his clothes.

His breathe caught in his throat. "Lizzy, you need not..."

Before he could say anything more she put her finger to his lips as she sat up. "No, William I want to do this. I need to do this. I need to see you. You wish me to be a good student, do you not?" she said as she opened the front of his breeches, reached in to pull his length into her warm hand.

Darcy gasped at the first sensation of her touch. "Oh, God, Elizabeth!"

"Hmm, you do not look like my horse at all." She moved her hand up and around his tip. As she touched him, a little fluid escaped. She ran her hand around him and whispered, "It is as smooth as velvet and as hard as iron. William, you must show me what to do."

He placed his hand over hers, and moved both of their hands up and down his length, starting at the base and slightly twisting to the right as he reached the top. When he thought she had the rhythm and the pressure he liked, he allowed himself to sink back into pure pleasure. *Oh, Good God, I have never felt such pleasure. Never! Lizzy is exquisite! Indescribable!* That was the last truly rational thought he had, as his hips rose and fell to match the movement of her hand.

Elizabeth remembered her lesson from two days prior, and began to verbally encourage him as she continued the rhythm and movement he had shown her. "Let go, William, let go, let go. This is only for you, only for you, let go, let go."

That tipped the scales, as his movement became frenetic. He erupted into her hands.

When he returned to rationality, he reached into his pocket for his handkerchief and wiped her hands, kissing them. "Thank you, my love, thank you," and with that he pulled her to him.

Once he finished cleaning off her hands, he sought to see if she was uneasy—thankful to see no fear, he shared, "Oh, my love, this fluid on your hands—when we are joined as man and wife—will be the seed that will, God willing, give us a child in the future. Are you well, my love?"

"Yes, William. I love you."

After a few minutes, they gathered themselves together enough to right their clothing, and prepared to leave their glen. They walked hand in hand for a while, in comfortable silence. Occasionally, they would stop to gaze at each other and smile, or perhaps for a short kiss.

After some time, Lizzy broke the silence, "William, have you heard from Georgiana? Is she not due to arrive late tomorrow? How is she?"

"She is well, and I believe she is looking forward to having a new sister, Lizzy. She seems very animated, and excited that she is to come for the wedding. I believe without even meeting her, you have brightened her spirits. I know she is not yet over what happened at Ramsgate, but I hope she is on the path to finding her way past the painful memories. I know you will be able to help her. The Darcys have been in want of a bit of liveliness, I believe."

"You do not seem to want for liveliness, William," Lizzy said as she lightly laughed, raising her eyebrow in his direction.

"Well my love, I do not believe I have ever felt as open, or comfortable with anyone as I do with you. Oh, I have always been close to my cousin Richard, and we have shared a lot over the years. But he is older than I, and has always had a tendency to tease me over the slightest weakness. I have to be guarded in what I say to him."

"Well, you appear to like my teasing? Am I wrong?"

"You are not wrong, Lizzy. Your teasing is delightful. Richard's has a tendency to be embarrassing and calculating. Then there is my friendship with Charles, but I often feel like his elder brother. He needs me to assist and guide him, so it is very rare for me to turn to him with my own concerns or needs."

"You feel you can be open with me, William? I hope you can always share your concerns and needs. It may not be what I learned from my parents, but I would like for us to have the type of union in which we are able to share anything with each other. I know I would like that. I believe we have been able to do so thus far!" Lizzy blushed, slightly embarrassed.

He stopped and turned to her, "Yes, my Luscious Lizzy, I believe that our openness will serve us *quite well.*" He pulled her to him for a long kiss. Both knew they would soon be back at Longbourn and savoured their treasured intimacy.

They talked a bit more about the schedule for the morrow, the arrival of William's family late in the day, and their trip to see the Great House at Stoke.

~~*~*~*

Many people considered Mr. Randolph Hurst to be a lush and a drunkard. But Hurst was actually neither. He was a dissatisfied man. He detested his own life.

He had met Louisa Bingley at a ball in London, and had fallen deeply in love with her over the course of three dances and several conversations that evening. He found that he was a lost man long before he met her detestable sister. Hurst hated, yes hated, his sister-in-law. Unfortunately for him, his wife Louisa, loved her sister and insisted on having her around the majority of the time.

Caroline behaved in every way the older sister, and Louisa allowed her to do so. She did everything she could to control everyone around her, including the Hursts. She was judgmental, catty, and everything wicked in Hurst's estimation.

Over the last several years, Hurst had begun drinking heavily from time to time, to escape the inanity of his own life. Though more often than not, he would simply fake sleep or drunkenness to escape the fruitless, petty, degrading conversations Caroline would engage in with Louisa.

Since arriving in Hertfordshire, it had grown much worse. Hurst recognized, almost immediately, how much Darcy was attracted to the pert Miss Elizabeth Bennet. Well, let us just say that he had *noticed* Darcy's attraction to her; and how Darcy would cope by turning to a window, so that no one would see. But Hurst saw. Hurst could not blame Darcy, as Miss Elizabeth was everything lovely, buxom, and beautiful. Everything that his shrew of a sister-in-law was not!

How Caroline thought she had *ever* had a slight chance with Darcy was beyond Hurst's comprehension. He saw Darcy attempting not to laugh in her presence from time to time. More recently, he saw how Darcy struggled with his anger at her quite catty comments and ludicrous presumptions.

Since Darcy had announced his engagement to Miss Eliza Bennet, Caroline had become increasingly desperate. She had attempted to corner Darcy and tell him of Miss Eliza's unsuitability. She continued to remind Darcy that Miss Eliza had once preferred Mr. Wickham. She tried to *show* Darcy how much more *accomplished* she was than Miss Eliza. Lately, she seemed to be trying to catch Darcy unawares.

Hurst wondered if she was plotting a trap of some type, in order to appear to have been compromised. It would be just like her! Her sole purpose in life for years had been to be Mrs. Fitzwilliam Darcy.

As Hurst came upon the back parlour, Caroline was pacing and muttering to herself and he decided to listen:

... the bright orange one with the orange lace and the plunging neckline. Oh, and my silk orange... Hmmm, yes, that should attract his notice...

As an aside, Hurst doubted that it would attract anyone's notice, except the local gypsies. They might like her orange-coloured clothing enough to take her away with them. Hurst doubted that anyone would find his flat-chested chit of a sister-in-law alluring.

Hurst continued to listen to her mutterings. He was grateful he had heard at least some of what she was considering. He would not let her succeed in her plot. He owed it to Darcy. And he owed it to himself.

Mr. Hurst walked away before Caroline could exit the library. He had a slight smile on his face.

Chapter 12

8 December 1811

Mr. Bennet had just sent Darcy and Elizabeth off on their errand for the day. He had his stable hand prepare his curricle and two best horses for their morning ride, including some warm rugs in case they were needed. The couple had seemed quite happy. Mr. Bennet could not have been more grateful that such a match had been found for his Lizzy. He also knew she would be grateful to have a day away from the demands of her mother and wedding preparations.

Instead of returning to the house, he decided to sit in the garden for a few minutes. Walking toward the garden, he thanked God for the gift of love that his daughter, Elizabeth, and his godson, Darcy, had found together.

As he sat on the bench in the garden, he saw Jane returning from a walk with Mr. Bingley. Jane was his oldest and was, by far, the most serene. He had been expecting Charles Bingley to come for her hand in marriage for over a week now. But he suspected the two had decided not to interrupt the happiness of Darcy and Elizabeth, and were waiting until after the wedding to approach him.

~~*~*~*

Jane Bennet said good-bye to Mr. Bingley and went to her room, contemplating the last two weeks. She had just begun to realize how jealous she was of her sister Elizabeth. Elizabeth always seemed to be able to say exactly what she felt. Some people called her impertinent. But to Jane, Elizabeth was the perfect example of what she wanted to be.

Jane had been the 'good and perfect' daughter for so long that it made her ill. Most recently, Jane had discovered she often had to fight with a dialogue in her head. It was a dialogue of the words she *wished* she could say. Those thoughts were often tumbling through her mind as she spoke.

The night before, when her mother had tried to take the credit for Elizabeth's choices for her trousseau, she had thought and had wanted to say, *Good Lord, mother, do you not know that Elizabeth and I went behind you and changed many of your recommendations! We hate your tendency to over-ornament all of our gowns. We hate lace!* But no! Everyone expected her to be the perfect lady, so she never let anyone know what she was really thinking!

Jane also had been considering what Elizabeth had said of Mr. Darcy's kisses. Jane had determined that perhaps, Mr. Bingley was too much like she was—at least when it came to sharing his feelings. If he did not take the initiative soon to kiss her, she might just take it upon herself. *Yes! Maybe it is time for me to be bold!*

~~*~*~*

After Jane had entered, Mr. Bennet saw Mary walking towards the house with a book in her hand, never looking up as she reached the door. Mr. Bennet chucked as his thoughts turned to his daughter Mary. Mary was by no means unattractive. She just chose not to worry about such things. Mary had lately intrigued Mr. Bennet, as he had noticed she no longer seemed to quote Fordyce. He had also seen her sneaking in and out of his library on more than one occasion. He found himself wondering again, what would become of Mary.

~~*~*~*

Mary Bennet was thought by many to be a boring, over-religious zealot. This was what she wanted them to believe. Mary hid her secret life behind a carefully constructed veil of white lies.

Mary had spent the summer before last in London, with her Aunt and Uncle Gardiner. She was there, pursuing some advancement in her education; taking courses at the local ladies seminary.

But while there, she got to meet many artists that came to her uncle's home. Poets, musicians, and authors all seemed to find the Gardiner's home a meeting place of sorts. It was here that Mary met Lord Byron and his paramour, Lady Caroline.

Lady Caroline Lamb was married to the Second Viscount Melbourne, the Prime Minister. Oh, no one knew that she had a lover. But, Mary eventually discovered that she had been carrying on a secret affair with Lord Byron for some time.

Lady Caroline and Lord Byron used their visits to the Gardiner's as a way of setting up their assignations. While Mary did not initially know any of this, she was intrigued by Lady Caroline, and learned of her interest in writing. Before Mary knew it, she and Lady Caroline had become quite good friends. It was from this friendship that the seeds of her current avocation began.

When Mary did learn of Lady Caroline's secret affair, she found that she could not judge her, as she would before coming to London. Lady Caroline intrigued her, in fact. The two came up with an acceptable *cover* story to remain in contact with each other, and to be able to converse. Mary told a little white lie to her parents.

She told them she had met Lady Caroline while at the Gardiner's. That Lady Caroline was intrigued by Mary's knowledge of Fordyce, as well as other writers of the cloth, and desired to continue their acquaintance through writing. Both Mr. and Mrs. Bennet, hoping that the correspondence might decrease the amount of "sermonizing" Mary imposed upon the family on a regular basis, allowed the ongoing communication.

Lady Caroline had instructed Mary in the form and style of the modern gothic romance novel. She had also helped her by critiquing some of Mary's novice work. Mary was currently writing a romance novel. She hoped to have The Adventures of Mary Anne completed by the end of the year. Lady Caroline had already submitted portions of the novel to a publisher, on her behalf. It had been tentatively accepted for publishing, under the pen name *Lady Mary Anne*.

Mary was still a maid, but she was much more educated in the ways of men and women than most any other unmarried woman would be. Lady Caroline had given her a rare book from India about intimate relations, as well as sharing many gothic romance novels with her. Mary did not describe any actual act of coupling in her stories, as she felt it would be too difficult to do so—never having experienced it herself, but she did tend to let her imagination run free as she wrote.

Her family and friends knew her to be an expert in Fordyce Sermons and, in fact, she was. Her actual behaviour modelled those sermons. But she longed for more. Her thoughts and dreams were of another nature.

On this day she entered her father's library, as she knew he was currently out of the house. Her father had a *locked* drawer in his desk where he kept his *sensitive materials*. Mary had learned she could pick the lock. She had often found her way into her father's library when he left the house. On this day she needed to do some research to find out if there were ways to avoid conception while coupling. Her main character, obvious Mary Anne, had need of such special avoidance techniques. In Mary's novel, her main character was a spy and a vixen.

On some level Mary wondered herself, if there were a way for her to be able to experience pleasure, and not have to experience the consequences. She believed she would be a better writer if she had intimate experience. Yet she had been raised as a gentlewoman, and such things were just not done.

It was not long before Kitty and Lydia ran by Mr. Bennet giggling, on their way to return to the house. Yes, he was glad that he had decided to send them to school! They might be the silliest of girls at this point in their lives. But he found himself wanting them to make as good of a match as Elizabeth had already made, and Jane was soon to make.

~~*~*~*

Other than their brief walk earlier, Lydia and Kitty had been sitting around this morning, discussing their father's revelation that he intended to send them away to school. Lydia had always prided her self on being an exemplary flirt, but she knew now that she had gone too far, and had caused her father's wrath the night of the Netherfield ball.

In the past, where Lydia went, Kitty had usually followed. However, recently Kitty had found that she desired to have a mind of her own. Yet, she simply could not seem to individuate from her most silly sister. On this day, Kitty had begun to think she needed to change her life in order to make a fortunate match, as her sister Lizzy had done.

Kitty had found her copy of Fordyce's sermons and was reading it. She noticed something that she decided to share with her sister Lydia, "Lydia, listen to this:

**'It is a maxim laid down among you, and a very prudent one it is, that love is not to begin on your part, but is entirely to be the consequence of our attachment to you.'"

"Do you think that means we are not supposed to chase after men, but allow them to seek us? You know that Lizzy did not seem to even like Mr. Darcy in the beginning, but is very much in love with him now. He seems so much more agreeable than I would have ever have imagined—so handsome, and so rich. I think he formed an attachment first, do you not? Maybe it would be better, more prudent, to be pursued than to pursue ourselves. What do you think?"

Lydia snorted, "It would not be nearly as much fun, Kitty. Oh, I know that it is *my* behaviour that father is unhappy with, and that because of me we are to go to school. But it might be fun to be in London. I hope we are allowed to go to balls and the theatre. It could be fun indeed."

Kitty returned, "I do not believe that father is sending us to London for fun, Lydia. I believe he is giving us a chance to learn to be ladies, and make as good of a match as Lizzy's. Listen to this:

**'...some agreeable qualities recommend a gentleman to your common good liking and friendship. In the course of his acquaintance, he contracts an attachment to you. When you perceive it, it excites your gratitude; this gratitude rises into a preference, and this preference perhaps at last advances to some degree of attachment, especially if it meets with crosses and difficulties; for these, and a state of suspense, are very great incitements to attachment, and are the food of love in both sexes.'"

"I believe that state of suspense, as well as the crosses and difficulties, have provided the food of love for our sister, Lizzy. Do not you think so?"

"Kitty, do not think me too indiscrete. I can see that Lizzy's courtship has progressed to her advantage. But living as Fordyce speaks seems so boring. Please promise me you are not becoming like Mary. I suppose we are to learn more of behaving as proper young ladies when we go to London. But I, for one, am not looking forward to it," Lydia followed with another snort.

The sisters continued in such a manner for another hour before they decided to go for a walk.

~~*~*~*

Mr. Bennet concluded his musings about his daughters and began to return to the house. Before he began to enter the house, he saw an express rider, and remained outside to receive the express. It was from Matlock, and more particularly, from his friend Edward. As the express rider had been given instructions there was no need to wait for a response, Mr. Bennet re-entered the house and went to his library to read the express.

He began to read the attached article and, in shock, began to laugh:

Flashback, 27-28 November 1811, Mr. Collins' flight from Longbourn

Mr. Collins exited the parlour as Mr. Darcy entered. He was mortified, as well as angry, and decided to go for a long walk to cool his ire. By the time he returned to Longbourn, completely expecting that Mr. and Mrs. Bennet would insist on Elizabeth accepting his suit, he was greeted with news that left him bereft and heart-broken. His chosen bride, his choice for the companion of his future life, his Elizabeth, was engaged to none other than Mr. Darcy.

Mr. Collin's knew that this could not be the truth as his noble patroness, Lady Catherine de Bourgh, had repeatedly gloated that her daughter Anne was engaged to be married to Mr. Darcy. Mr. Collins attempted to intervene with Mr. Darcy, pointing out to him the impropriety and impossibility of such an alliance as he was already betrothed to another.

The two gentlemen had quite an angry confrontation. Mr. Darcy attempted to inform him that he was not, nor ever had been, nor ever would be engaged to his cousin Anne. Mr. Collins immediately sent off an express to his patroness, to alert her to this disturbing development. Yet, by that time Mr. Collins realized he had lost all hope of making a successful match with Miss Elizabeth, and decided to leave Longbourn.

He was angry, he was sad, he was heart-broken, and yet he was also in need of relief for the growing allure he had felt for Miss Elizabeth Bennet. Her bounteous beauty, or more specifically her breasts, had so attracted him that he had been longing for the day he would join with her in wedded bliss. When he realized this was not to be, Mr. Collins made a decision that was against his better sense, against his character, and even against his own moral standard. Mr. Collins decided to take himself to London to find a '*house of ill repute.*'

Oh, yes, Mr. Collins knew it was a moral degradation to even contemplate doing what he was considering. He had done some study in Fordyce's sermons to see if it was an unforgivable sin, and found that it was not. Therefore, he had determined he could find forgiveness for his future actions after the fact.

He had also read a great deal about the topic in local newspapers. It was acceptable by society for men to have these little liaisons. It was probably not acceptable that a man of the cloth do so, but who would know?

Next, he began to contemplate how he could explain his visit to London to his noble patroness. First, he must see about finding a '*disguise*' to wear to such a house, as the clothes of a mere parson would be noted and frowned upon. God forbid, someone should see him entering or leaving! He would be in disgrace.

Mr. Collins told a little white lie to his noble patroness, Lady Catherine de Bourgh. He wrote to her, stating he needed to further his venture into obtaining a companion for his future life, by visiting a distant cousin in London, who was reported to have four lovely daughters. He told her he had found no one suitable in Hertfordshire. (Of course, he forgot he had just sent her an express, in which he told her of his rejection by Miss Elizabeth Bennet, because she was to marry Mr. Darcy.)

Initially, Mr. Collins considered finding the ***rag and bone man to purchase a used set of men's wear. There was no guarantee he would run into him, or that he would have a size that would fit him. So he determined he would need to purchase a new set of clothes. He went to a men's wear shop in Cheapside, to purchase clothes befitting a gentleman.

He told the shopkeeper he was assisting a gentleman who was a member of his parish. The gentleman had been sick for a long time, and had lost enough weight to need a new size of clothing.

He also went to a wig maker to purchase a wig. Mr. Collins decided on red hair, as it was quite different from his current coloring, and there would be less of a chance that anyone would recognize him. He told the wig shop owner he was to be in a play that was being produced in his parish, and was to play Irish gentlemen.

Mr. Collins had woven such a web of convenient white lies; that he found it quite easy to forget he was not telling the truth. The deeper he got into the elaborate deceit he was spinning, the easier it became to lie. After a short time, his lies were so far from being white, that little truth existed in his words.

There was one element in this plan he had not accounted for. He belatedly realized he had no idea where to go in town to find a supposed '*house of ill repute.*' He began perusing the paper for telling news events, and discovered that several bawdy incidents had happened in and around an area of town called Covent Garden. He decided to venture to that side of town in his new set of clothes and wig.

To the gentlemen of London, it was quite well known that there were high class and lower class prostitutes. However, this was not something Mr. Collins was aware of, and he entered the Covent Garden in search of a night of carnal bliss. He happened upon a place simply listed as Madame Unina's. What he did not know was Madame Unina's was a home for the rehabilitation of wayward girls—girls attempting to reform their lives—not a house of prostitution. Unfortunately, Mr. Collins did not know this upon entering the establishment.

So, prepared with cash and ready for a night of pure debauchery, he unwittingly entered a house run by a former Spanish nun. Sitting just inside the establishment were several lovely young women. Several of them were equally as well endowed as Miss Elizabeth, and he was quite eager to taste their lovely mounds. As he had never requested this type of service, he was unsure exactly how to ask. So, he reached down and fondled his manhood, and asked which of them would like to take him on.

"Hello, my lovelies, being an Irish gentleman and new to town, I find myself in need of an extended release. Which one of you would be so inclined to be the companion of my future bliss?"

The girls were shocked as they thought they had gotten away from such men, and began to scream. Madame Unina, the matron of the home, came out to see what caused such a disturbance.

By this time the girls had picked up whatever they could find in the room to use as weapons, and had begun to beat Mr. Collins about the head and shoulders. At that same time, Lady Eleanor was entering the front parlour. She was one of the organizers of a group of respectable citizens in London that had recently formed an organization called ****'*The Guardian Society for the Preservation of Public Morals*'. Members of the society were beginning to arrive for their bi-weekly meeting. One of their recent projects was working toward maintaining a refuge for repentant concubines and courtesans.

Currently, Madame Unina's establishment was one of their main projects. They were having some success, as recently the Lord Mayor of London had agreed to issue a proclamation against streetwalkers, and an increasing number of mistreated and neglected young women were seeking refuge in homes such as this one.

Mr. Collins knew none of this. The screaming had caused several of the men from this group to advance towards him, to assist the women.

Collins was quite shocked that among the group was one of his seminary professors from the Theologian College at Oxford. The seminary was internationally renowned, and attracted students and professors from all over Europe. He began to back out of the room, as the assembled group tried to subdue him with a plan to prosecute him for assault.

What Collins did not know was not only was he backing out of the door, he was backing towards a steep staircase that led to the basement, and that the door was open. Before any could stop him, he tripped and fell down the stairs. He twisted his head as he fell, cracking his neck in the process, whereby he was dead before he hit the basement floor. His wig had flown off in the process. Professor Mischa, a seminary professor from Theologian College, ran down the stairs to assist him. It was discovered that not only was the man dead, but was also Mr. Collins.

~~*~*~*

Mr. Bennet read the highlights from the newspaper article Edward had sent him:

"Reverend Collins was apparently killed in a scuffle between the members of the Guardian Society (an organization founded this year to aid wayward girls and prostitutes in changing their profession), the residents of one of the houses established for restoring these young girls to a moral life, and him. Reverend Collins, according to a source, had mistaken the home for a known brothel.

Madame Unina stated, 'For a man of the cloth to be of such a low character, to seek out prostitutes, is disgraceful. I, of course, regret he died in my establishment, but it was an accident. The Church of Rosings, in Kent, will most likely be much better off without the services of a morally degenerate minister.'

Lady Catherine de Bourgh, who was the patroness for Reverend

Collins, has refused to comment."

~~*~*~*

Mr. Bennet knew it might be inappropriate at such a time, but he could not help it. He laughed so hard he cried.

*There are many Internet sites in which you can learn more about Lady Caroline Lamb. You can also discover more information about her torrid affair with Lord Byron.

**Quotes are directly from Fordyce's sermons

***The rag and bone man would come round all the villages collecting any clothing what people would consider to be rags. Many fine ladies would most likely only wear their dresses a couple of times and then give them say to her Ladies Maid, the Ladies Maid would then either pass them on to a scullery maid or would take them to the Rag and Bone Man who would give her a few pence for them. He would then take what he had managed to get home where his wife would dye them a different colour or sell them at the market in a different town or county. Here a squire's daughter may pick up a silk dress for less than a quarter of the price in London.

****A.D. Harvey , Sex in Georgian England, Phoenix Press (1994), page 100

In 1811 a group of respectable citizens in London formed an organization called 'The Guardian Society for the Preservation of Public Morals'. Probably its most important work was in maintaining a refuge for repentant prostitutes but they persuaded the Lord Mayor of London to issue a proclamation against streetwalkers.

Chapter 13

8 December 1811

It was a beautiful day for a ride in an open curricle, and Darcy and Elizabeth were grateful for the time alone. As the curricle turned on to the open road, after they had passed through Meryton, Darcy reached over and took Elizabeth's hand; kissing it first on the back, then on the palm, and then on her wrist. He inter-laced his fingers with hers, and put their joined hands back on the bench. He looked at her out of the corner of his eyes.

"Are you happy today, my love?" Darcy asked.

"William, I do not know of a time I have ever been happier! It is a lovely day, I am with the only man I will ever love, he loves me to distraction, and I am to be married in three days. Happy does not say enough! I think I can safely say that I am also joyful, cheerful and blissful."

"What about contented, delighted, jovial, exultant, and ecstatic? That is how I feel, Lizzy! I quite agree. Happy does not say enough when I consider how I feel being this close to having you as my bride!" They continued to enjoy their ride in companionable silence for several minutes, until Elizabeth decided to speak again.

"William, father spoke to me yesterday of his connections with your family. Did you not have any idea that he was your godfather when you first arrived here in Meryton? I am still struggling to comprehend that our fathers were best friends."

"I was as shocked as you when I realized your father was '*Tom*'. My father often spoke of his best friend Tom, as well as some of the antics he and my Uncle Edward and had shared with him when they were young. He talked a great deal about their time at Eton and Cambridge. He even spoke to me about some of their adventures on their Grand Tour. I have to admit, remembering some of the things my father told me about Tom—now recognizing them to be about your father—have left me a little embarrassed."

"William, what did he tell you of my father?"

"Well, about their many adventures. They were both bachelors at the time."

"What kind of adventures, William? Do you think their adventures involved ladies?"

"Lizzy, you do not really want to know about the intimate life of your father, now do you? My father never shared specific details with me. He just gave me some warnings from time to time. Particularly, before I departed for my grand tour after Cambridge."

"And did you have many adventures, William? Adventures with ladies?" She turned sideways to look at him, a little unsure of herself, and a little scared of what he might tell her if she were being honest with herself.

Darcy did not respond.

"William, did we not agree to be honest with each other. I do not believe you are uneducated in the ways of love. Can you not tell me?"

"I cannot."

Lizzy said a little nervously, "Cannot or will not, William?"

"Either... both."

"Please, William. Would it not be helpful for your student to know where her Professor was trained?"

"Lizzy, please!"

Elizabeth became very quiet, and removed her hand from his, looking out at the countryside.

Darcy pulled the curricle off the road and into a clearing. They both remained quiet for a while. Darcy was unsure how to proceed; he would do anything rather than hurt her. *Why did I not prepare for her curiosity in regards to my past?*

Finally, Darcy reached out to her and pulled her into his chest. They held on to each other for a few minutes. Finally, Darcy loosened his grip and angled her head up until he could look into her eyes.

"Lizzy, if I had it to do over again, I would have waited."

Lizzy did not say anything and attempted to look away, but when she could not she closed her eyes and stayed silent.

Darcy pulled her to his chest and said, "Lizzy, will you not say something?"

"Of course, you have experience... I should have known you would not want... not wish to tell me about your other ladies..."

Lizzy buried her head again into his chest. A couple minutes later he heard her sob. "Oh God, Lizzy, I would do anything other than hurt you. I have never been in love before you, but I will not lie to you—as I promised I would not—and tell you that I am an innocent. Please let me wait and speak to you of this after we are married. For the time being, know that it has been many years, and not since I went on my Grand Tour."

"But you will tell me?"

"After we are married," he said softly, but firmly.

Then Darcy gently placed his hands on both sides of her face. Gazing into her eyes, he wiped away her tears with his thumbs, kissing each lid as it closed on her fine eyes. Then he moved to her slightly open mouth, and felt himself being pulled into her as he kissed her deeply, assuring her of his love.

They held each other for a few minutes, and then after another quick kiss, William pulled the curricle back onto the road.

Reluctantly, Elizabeth accepted that the topic was over... for the time being, anyway.

After several minutes, Lizzy changed the subject, "My father told me he was at your parents wedding, that he was at Pemberley when you were born, as well as at your christening. William, do you know what happened? Do you know why they lost touch? I confess I am very curious. I know my father well, it does not make sense that he would just lose touch with his godson," Lizzy questioned.

"I am not sure myself. But if I had to guess, I would suspect it has something to do with my Aunt Catherine. I am quite grateful that your father spoke with her when she was here, and not you."

Darcy paused. He did not know whether to tell her what he suspected might have happened. From Darcy's interview with his aunt in London, he knew his aunt had spoken very unkind things to Mr. Bennet.

He looked over at her and she quietly said, "William, whatever you say is alright. I know it is the feelings of your aunt, and not yourself."

"Elizabeth, I do not know what happened. But I do know that my aunt tried to convince my mother and father to set a marriage contract for a union between myself, and my cousin Anne. I would never have married her. It was not my wish nor Anne's, but Aunt Catherine desired it even before she had a child. Consequently, not too long after Anne was born, Aunt Catherine visited Pemberley.

"Something may have happened when I was very young, or maybe even during one of your father's visits to Pemberley. I truly do not know.

"My father always told me that he wanted to be sure I married for love, and I wanted that as well. That is why I have remained single as long as I have." Darcy looked over at Elizabeth. "If I could not marry for love, I would not marry at all. Gratefully, my father always supported my feelings.

"But my mother, I believe, came to believe that if a marriage happened between Anne and myself, it would be good for the family. She mentioned it to me several times before she died.

"I do not know if your father has spoken of this with you or not," he chuckled. "According to what he told me the other day, he and my father had always wished that their houses would be united. They were so close that they wished to become family, and hoped I would marry one of your father's children. Any time my mother and Aunt Catherine would talk about my marrying one of her children, your father and my father would say that one of Tom's children would marry me. It became quite the joke from what your father mentioned the other day."

"So our fathers desired this match, and hoped for it so long ago? Your father would be happy for us, William?" Elizabeth asked.

"Oh, I believe he would be very happy!"

"What about your mother?"

"I am not as sure about my mother. My Aunt Catherine pursued the '*connection*' of the Darcy and de Bourgh families relentlessly. She was determined in her pursuit. My mother was taught to believe you should marry for wealth and connections.

"Lizzy, your father is such a kind man, I respect him very much. He may choose to tell us, or he may not. I do not recommend we press him on the matter. He seems quite happy to have me back in his life. He seems happier still, that I am to be his son-in-law. I can tell you, however, that in my father's last hours, he thought of your father. He asked that if I ever met his friend Tom, to tell him he loved him and that he was sorry."

"Oh, William! I am so sorry you lost your mother and father. But, it is difficult to contemplate that your mother may not have approved of me," Elizabeth had tears running down her cheeks, and as they were out in the middle of open road he pulled the curricle over again and stopped it. He pulled her into his arms and tucked her head into his chest.

"Oh, Elizabeth, do not be sad. I know my father would be happy. I would like to think that if my mother met you, she would love you as much as I do. We both now know you are not without money as so many believed, and not without connections as your father and my uncle have remained friends all this time. You are marrying your father's Godson, who just happens to be a Darcy. So you have connections *and* wealth my dear. Most of all, you have the love of this less than perfect, passionately besotted man," he tipped her chin up to look at him, and wiping her eyes with his fingers, he gave her a chaste kiss this time.

"Is that the only kiss I am to receive now, sir?" she said in her impertinent way.

"That is all you may have on the open road. But we will find the time and place for more before this day is over, I assure you," Darcy said.

"I will count on that, my love," Elizabeth said with a slight smile.

~~*~*~*

When Lord Matlock was announced, Mr. Bennet was surprised as he had only just finished reading his express. Now here he was!

"Edward, you do not know how wonderful it is to see you again!" Tom

Bennet said as he enthusiastically shook Edward Fitzwilliam's hand.

"The feeling is mutual, old friend. I could not help it! I came on horseback, ahead of the rest of the party. I was longing for a little private conversation before the rest of the party descends upon us. Where is your lovely daughter, Tom? Is she with Fitzwilliam?"

Tom led him back to his library and offered him a drink. The gentleman gratefully accepted.

"I sent them on an errand today," Tom answered. "You will remember I purchased the Great House at Stoke several years ago. I took it so Fanny and the girls would not be '*turned out into the hedgerows*', as Fanny puts it, should I depart this earth prior to her. I wanted them to have a place to live, and the place has paid for itself with the income from the tenants. I have recently been contemplating what to do with it, and have considered leasing it. I asked Fitzwilliam to look over the estate for me before he departs on his honeymoon, and give me his opinion. They left in my curricle several hours ago.

"Because Elizabeth knows her mother's taste, and her constant complaints, I encouraged her to go along."

"Tom, do you think it wise to send them off alone?" Edward questioned.

"Well, they rode in the open curricle... They appear quite content and happy together, Edward. It is a love match, which I know would have pleased George."

"I am quite happy for Fitzwilliam. The family has been concerned about him since George's death. He became so serious and consumed with learning how to manage the estate, and caring for Georgiana. He has had little time to think about himself, and even less time to think of marriage. I dare say, from what you have told me of your Elizabeth over the years, they must be very well matched."

"Edward, I think they are perfect for each other. Fitzwilliam needs some liveliness in his life, and my Elizabeth would never have been happy without someone who would appreciate her spirit, her wit, and her intelligence. I know of very few men that could match wits with her. I dare say, I have already seen Darcy best her. They shall never be bored, that is for sure."

"I am very happy for you. To have been re-united with your godson, and have him matched with your daughter, must be a great triumph indeed. How went your interview with my sister? I dare say she was '*most seriously displeased*,'" laughed Edward.

"I enjoyed the opportunity of *one-upping* your ignoble sister at least once in this lifetime, Edward. Will she make trouble for them, do you think?"

"I have already spoken with her on the subject, Tom. I did not demand she come to the wedding, but I have forbidden her to say or do anything that will hurt the family. I still control her estate; she would not be so foolish as to defy me." He looked at his friend of long-standing. "After all these years, Tom, we will now be family."

Mr. Bennet refilled their glasses with port, "What say you then, to Fitzwilliam and Elizabeth?" Tom raised his glass in toast, and Edward joined him.

"Your express arrived just this morning," Tom chuckled. "Did you want me to have some time to think of the news before we spoke of it?"

Edward laughed, "Yes, I wanted to be sure you had time to contemplate the demise of your ridiculous cousin! Can you believe he came to such an end?"

Tom chuckled, "I cannot say I grieve him. Are you aware he made an offer to Lizzy? Fitzwilliam walked into the room as he was attempting to get her to reconsider her resounding '*no*' to his request."

"Good God, Tom; could he have really thought she would consider him?"

"It appears he thought she would. Although, I am sorry to say my wife may have had a hand in the matter. She has long feared being turned out of this house."

"Does Fanny or anyone else in the family know of Collins' demise?"

"There are several pieces of news I must dispense in the next couple days. I am grateful for a little time to discuss them with you. Fanny does not know of my income. I, at times, think I have been quite selfish in concealing it from her, Edward. I wanted to have adequate dowries for all my daughters, and take care of her in my demise. I fear if she knows the truth of my wealth, she will overspend my income.

"At one point, I envisioned she would demand we move to a large estate, decorate it in some garish fashion, and I would no longer know myself. But sometimes I think that in not telling her, I may have left her to her fears, and those fears have driven her nerves into agitation," he confessed.

"Well, she must have less fear in having your second daughter so well-situated. Even if your income was not as it is, I know that Fitzwilliam would aid your family. That alone may remove her fear, Tom."

"I do believe it shall not be long before I have another suitor come to claim my eldest daughter. If William had not been rushed into it, I dare say his best friend Bingley may have beat him to my door. As it is, I would suspect he is waiting until Darcy and Elizabeth are married, in order not to detract from their nuptials."

Edward questioned, "Tom, what do you mean by being rushed into it?"

"Ah, so I did not share that part of the story with you in my letter?" and Mr. Bennet proceeded to tell him about the events of the Netherfield Ball, those that had led to Darcy and Elizabeth's understanding.

"They do not appear to be forced into a marriage you say?" Edward asked.

"No, not at all. They appear very much in love, and happy with the turn of events. Their affection appears to grow each day. I do believe that Fitzwilliam is currently *'courting'* Lizzy in order to assure greater felicity in their marriage. Perhaps I should have done more of that myself..." he said with sadness in his voice.

"Tom, are you all right? Do you still feel regret after all this time?" Edward asked.

"Edward, to be honest, there is not a day that I do not think about her at some point. If I had been more bold, if I had asked to court her first, if..."

Edward cut him off, "Is it not time to let the regret go, Tom? I know you loved her. But that was a long time ago. It is time to let it go. Time to love the family that God has given you. Now you have Fitzwilliam coming into your family. Does that not give you some peace?"

"It does bring me some peace. It binds me back to my friend, George. Fitzwilliam told me he spoke of me in his last hours, Edward. George told him if he ever met me to tell me he loved me and he was sorry!" Tom exclaimed.

"I know the break with George was hard on you," Edward asked.

Tom continued, "It was hard, excruciatingly hard. But it was equally difficult to let go of my best friend. You know over the years, you have replaced him, my dear friend."

"Thank you, Tom. I treasure all the times that you, George, and I had together. I am grateful you have kept in touch with me over all these years. I have not told you 'til now, but George knew that we kept in touch, and was always eager for word of you. You know he loved you like a brother," Edward stated.

"I could not have had truer friends than George and yourself. For that I am quite grateful. I would never have made my fortune without your and Darcy's guidance. I thank you my friend!

"I have one last question for you. I know that Fitzwilliam, and now Lizzy as I have told her some of my relationship with your family, wonder how George and I came to be estranged. What shall I tell them, Edward?" Tom asked with all sincerity.

"Well Tom, Fitzwilliam knows of his aunt's machinations, as he has been subject to them these many years. She has long tried to force him to marry her Anne. He has evaded her over and over, but she has continued to believe he would finally relent. I think the simple answer, and the one you told George, is acceptable. That it appeared your presence was causing conflict in the Darcy household, and you decided it was best to stay away. Tell Fitzwilliam you have always kept track of his life through me. It might be just a half truth, but I think it is enough."

"Thank you, my friend. Wise advise indeed. May I freshen your drink?" And then the conversation changed to more mundane topics until they picked up the chessboard for a game.

~~*~*~*

Darcy and Elizabeth arrived at the entrance to the Great House at Stoke a little over an hour after they had left Longbourn. The drive to the gate appeared to be well maintained. The gate, while not being garish, spoke well for keeping the non-intended off the property. Darcy stopped, opened the gate, and entered. Both were well pleased with the prospect... The park appeared to be well maintained, even though no one was currently living there. A fountain rested in front of the entrance. In the centre was a statue of Adonis, and Elizabeth teased Darcy that it reminded her of him. There was a circle drive in front of the house, and off to the left was a notched roof stable. Darcy drove the curricle down there to unhitch the horses, allowing them to rest in the stable and eat, as there was hay available. With very little effort he located the supplies, left the horses to rest, and returned to escort his fiancée to the front of the house.

Elizabeth suggested that they walk around the house before entering. The house was a light, almost yellow brick with white trim. It was much bigger than a cottage, but had an airiness that reminded her of a romantic cottage tucked away amongst the wood. Trees and flowerbeds surrounded it; the beds seemed a little wild, but full of colourful fall flowers. As they rounded the house to the back, they saw a formal garden. There were well-marked paths, trellises with grape vines, benches scattered around the lawn, and another large fountain with Grecian statues at the four corners and one in the centre. Around the edge of the garden, there appeared to be paths continuing into the surrounding trees.

Elizabeth found it delightful and that she could see herself living in such a place. Though Darcy loved Pemberley, he admitted fancying the smaller, graceful, romantic feel of the Great House at Stoke. Once they had walked back around to the entrance, Darcy took the key that Mr. Bennet had given him and unlocked the door.

Chapter 14

8 December 1811

Though Darcy loved Pemberley, he admitted fancying the smaller, graceful, romantic feel of the Great House at Stoke. Once they had walked back around to the entrance, Darcy took the key that Mr. Bennet had given him and entered.

The entrance way had a marble floor and was wider than they had originally thought. To the left was the drawing room and to the right was a handsome lady's parlour. The rooms were filled with drop cloth covered furniture. With the giggle of a little girl, Elizabeth went around peeking beneath the cloths. "Oh, William, come see!"

Admitting curiosity only to himself, Darcy moved about the room, uncovering several pieces. He was pleased to find settees, and elegant, yet not ostentatious furniture.

They continued to walk through the house. Darcy made a few notes for Mr. Bennet as they went along. The wall covers appeared in good condition. It appeared the partial staff kept by Mr. Bennet was doing a good job, as there was no dust to be found. In fact, they wondered why there were coverings on the furniture, as there did not appear to be dust upon them either.

There was a small dining room (or it could be used as a breakfast room), and there was a larger formal dining room. Darcy and Elizabeth both agreed that their favourite room down stairs was the library. It was there they decided to set up their luncheon. Once they had found that the kitchen actually had running water, Darcy had filled a basin in the downstairs washroom for her to use. They each took a few minutes to refresh themselves.

When Elizabeth returned from freshening up, to her delight, she discovered Darcy had started a fire, and had removed the drop cloths from much of the furniture in the library. At a table with two chairs near the fire, he was setting up their luncheon. There were two armchairs, two sofas, and a large chaise that graced the room. The table might originally have been a game table, but it would do quite nicely for their repast. Elizabeth brought a couple candlesticks she had found and placed them on the table, and with a match from the fireplace, lit them as well as several candles that were placed about the room.

One of the walls of the library consisted almost entirely of windows looking out on the formal gardens they had previously toured.

"This is quite a handsome room, my dear. I believe I could spend many happy hours here. This house may not be much larger than Longbourn, but the ceiling is higher and, in this room at least, the windows allow enough light into the room to make it very welcoming," Darcy said as he approached and pulled her into his arms.

He touched her cheek and then rubbed a finger along the seam between her lips, until she opened them to him and he kissed her deeply. "I have been longing to do that. Come, let us have our luncheon," Darcy said.

"This is the only kiss I am to receive?" Elizabeth queried impertinently.

"No my dear, but more kisses will be served for dessert, if you clean your plate," he smiled and she lightly giggled.

They sat at right angles with only a corner of the table between them. The table was turned as a diamond to the fire. They ate their meal and exchanged small talk. Both were happy to simply be in the other's company. In truth, they were both thinking more about "dessert" than their meal. The fire lightly warmed them, even though the day was warm for late fall. But as the house had not been warmed in some time, they were grateful for the fire to dispel the chill. The sun shining in the windows had also graced the room with a little warmth, and soon they found they were quite comfortable.

Neither ate much preferring to gaze into each other's eyes. And as new lovers often do, they would take a bite off each other's plates, or nibble something from the other's fingers, nibbling the finger a bit as well. They spoke of nothing in particular, but thought of all that was to come in their life as man and wife. Contentment seemed to fill them both. For the time they had in this house, in this room all alone, they were grateful.

Darcy lifted her wine glass for her to drink, and was entranced as he saw the liquid wet her lips. Elizabeth lifted his glass to him and could not help herself from running a finger along his lips as he finished his sip. When they had eaten what they wanted, they packed the leftovers away. Darcy stood and lifted her from her seat and said simply, "Come."

He led her to the chaise. It was made of rich tapestry and was wider than most. Darcy unbuttoned and removed his waistcoat, cravat and his vest as well as her spencer and propped himself into the corner, against the rolled back before pulling Elizabeth against him. He proceeded to remove the pins from her hair, burying his nose into her curls as he kissed the top of her head. He then put his arms around her just below her breasts. She leaned further against him and put her hands on top of his. They sighed in contentment.

"William, is it time for another lesson?" Elizabeth queried.

"Well, my love, as you are longing to become quite the proficient, perhaps we simply need to practice what you have already learned," he said as he kissed along the back of her neck and up until his lips caressed her earlobe. She moaned and turned into his arms, leaning up to nibble his lips. As he had done to her before, she took his lower lip into her mouth and suckled it, doing the same with the top lip before kissing him full on the mouth. And to prove herself the conscientious student, she began a duel with his tongue as her small tongue entered his mouth. He moaned and pulled her firmly against his body.

She turned to face him and pulled up to straddle him as he reached behind her to unbutton the first couple buttons at the back of her dress. As he released the buttons, he kissed along her jaw line, and then along her neck to her pulse point, kissing her deeply until he heard her moans increase. He then moved to her collarbone and continued until he reached the hollow at the base of her neck. His tongue flecked out to circle the small hollow, and her head fell back to allow him better access.

When he knew he had enough buttons opened, he stopped long enough to lower the top of her dress and her chemise. Again with a slight gasp, he whispered in a husky voice, "No stays again today? Anticipating another lesson, my dear? Oh, my Lizzy you are so, so beautiful. I can wait no longer to taste your sweet fruit." He lowered his mouth to trace a path down her neck, kissing around one breast and then the other. He then focused on her left breast as he circled around and around her flesh with his tongue until he lightly tapped the tip of the nipple, then moved to the left breast with the tip of his tongue. Frustrated with his teasing her, she reached up to grasp his head, trying to force him down fully onto her nipple.

Yet, he resisted her and looked up into her eyes. He saw them swimming with dark passion.

"No, No, No, my love. *All good things come to those who wait. Patience my love," and he continued his light tapping on her nipple for a couple more moments, until he changed to short light licks on the tip. Then his teeth just lightly grazed her firm, hard berry as his light ministrations had had their desired effect.

When Lizzy thought she could bear it no longer, he took her nipple fully into his mouth. First, he suckled lightly and circled with his tongue; then releasing it, he bestowed the same attention to its mate. With each pass between the two, he picked up his pace and the firmness of his suckling. When he had her panting, he suckled hard and gripped the tip with his teeth. She moaned and pulled him hard against her as her hips began to rock against him. She was now aware that he was hard and firm below her. She was getting closer and closer to a release, and began to moan, "More, William, I want more."

"What do you want, my Lizzy?"

"I want you to make me your wife, William. I long for it. Please, William! I want to know what that will be like. I do not want to wait. I want to know now. Please, William? Please," she gasped and then looked down into his eyes.

Darcy stopped and pulled her back against his chest and lifted her up to look into his eyes. They both were panting. "No, Lizzy, I cannot. I cannot dishonour you in that way. You deserve a wedding night. In a big beautiful bed after taking a warm fresh bath, and coming together when we are man and wife in the eyes of God."

"William, William, my love, do you not know that you are already my husband in my heart? Please, William, please. I know you love me, and I trust you, you have made it so. You have taught me all I need to know. I am no longer afraid, but I do not want to live with this anticipation of the unknown anymore. I tire of it. I want to be your wife—I am ready to be your wife. We are alone in this beautiful romantic place. I cannot think of a better time for us to join as man and wife. Please, William."

"Oh, Elizabeth, please do not ask this of me. I cannot dishonour your father, my *godfather.* He trusted us in this trip today. I cannot take advantage of you or him in that way. Please understand my love. I cannot," Darcy was finding it more and more difficult to resist her, as his physical response had reached an acute level.

Elizabeth sat up again, straddling him and put her hands to frame his handsome face, and she said directly into his passion filled, ebony pools. "William, my love, I love you. I know you love me. We are to be married in three days. You want me; I feel the evidence of it below me. If you will not volunteer for this, then I fear that I must take advantage of you," and with that she reached down and began to undo his breeches, reaching in to grasp hold of his manhood and lift it out.

She began to stroke his arousal, and Darcy found his body was betraying his will, as he grew harder with each of her strokes. He was putty in her hands, and as she watched his body's reaction, she knew it. Cocking her head slightly to the side, and with her brows raised and her lips grinning she said, "Well what is it to be? Ravish me, or will we go home now?" With that she stopped stroking him and started to lift off of him.

He grabbed her hand as she began to push off and stopped her. "Good God, Lizzy, you are dangerous. Are you sure? Are you absolutely sure, my love. I do not know what I would do if you were to regret this."

She then slid down farther onto his body again, and began to stroke him again, "I will not regret this. But I do encourage you to begin the ravishment now; as I will be angry with you should you refuse me. I am begging you to make me your wife in a most wanton way, and if you were to deny me, then I will be most unhappy."

He put his hand on top of hers and stopped her movements as he said huskily, "Then if we are to proceed with this ravishment, you must cease what you are doing now."

"Why?"

"Oh, my love, my restraint may be strong, but you are pushing me beyond my limit. If you truly want me to make you my wife, then I need to be able to spend inside of you. If you do not stop, I fear I will find my release much too soon."

"Can you only *spend,* as you say, one time a day?" Elizabeth asked.

Darcy lightly chuckled, "Yes, curiosity will kill the cat, but I fear I will be the cat. Oh, my Lizzy, it is possible for me to spend more than once in a day, but it usually takes quite some time for me to recover, and I would much rather enjoy this with you than alone. That is, if you are really determined..."

"William, do not ask me again, I am determined."

He pulled her back and said, "Then you must stand up, for if this ravishment is to commence, we must remove more of our clothes. Shall we?"

She giggled lightly and moved off of his lap, and he smiled as she helped pull him to his feet. Darcy turned Elizabeth around and unbuttoned the remaining buttons on her gown and it fell to the ground along with her chemise.

She reached up to run her hand down his chest from his chin to his waistline and when she reached his waist, her fingers lowered into his waistband to pull out his shirt. As the ties had already been loosened, he raised his arms and allowed her to help him take it off. He removed his breeches as she watched and then sat down as she removed his boots. Elizabeth marvelled at his nakedness. Her eyes raked over his body; from his neck, down his chest, resting on his manhood and then down to his muscular, tight buttocks and thighs. "You truly are like the statue of Adonis, my love."

Darcy picked up the cloth covering that had been on the chaise and folded it, placing it on the chaise before sitting Elizabeth on it. He began to remove her shoes, running his hand lightly up the inside of her leg until he reached the inside of her thigh. Then just for a minute he reached up higher to slightly tease her as his finger entered her small clothes, slightly tapping her bud. He then took her stocking down her leg as he looked up into her eyes, repeating the same motion on her other leg.

"Oh, my love, you are everything that I could have ever imagined in a wife. You are the most beautiful thing I have ever seen in my life. If at any point you want to stop, please know that I will. If I do something that you particularly like you must tell me. Even if you cannot say it in words, you can move my hand, or mouth, or finger to anywhere you want them. Do you understand, my Lizzy?"

"I do, William. But less talking, please. Precede with the lesson, my love."

He chuckled and reached up and removed her small clothes. He gazed at her in adoration. Her naked splendour made him want to worship at her feet. He knew that he must taste her before he made her his own. He had her lean back against the corner of the chaise as he began to kiss her feet, and then her calf and continued up her leg to the inside of her knee. From there he continued, gently opening her legs as he went, kissing along the inside of her thigh.

Elizabeth was gasping, "William, what are you doing? You are not going to kiss me *there* are you?"

He reached up to touch her nub and began to lightly rub her. "Yes, my love, I am going to kiss you *here* and I promise you will like it. I wish to bring you pleasure, extreme pleasure, before bringing you any pain. Please, allow me this. Just lay back and close your eyes if you must. I promise to stop if you do not enjoy it. Is that acceptable to you? You did say that you would trust me?"

"I did, William, but is this part of what must be done? Is this part of making me your wife?"

"It is not something that is required for me to make you my wife. But I believe it will allow me to make you my wife with the absolute minimum amount of pain. Lizzy if you can find your pleasure, if the wetness your body makes is enough to make it easy for me to enter you, it will be much easier this first time. You must relax, my love, just let me give you pleasure."

"I will, William, I will allow you. Oh, William, that feels so good!" she gasped as Darcy's tongue first touched her nub, "Oh, William! Oh, William! Do not stop, do not stop!"

He stopped just enough to say "I have no intention of stopping" and his finger entered her wet folds as he spoke.

Darcy alternated between lightly licking her nub and licking all along the crease of her folds, each pass his tongue going a little deeper. After several passes, her legs began to clench his head, and he moved his hands to lightly keep them open as he moved up to suckle her nub.

Elizabeth lost all conscious thought. All she felt was pleasure. All the focus of her entire body was on the place where William's mouth was touching; the place she had just discovered this week. The place she had been taught could bring her shame, and it had brought her fear. Only now it was bringing her intense pleasure. Darcy lifted her legs up and over his shoulders as he suckled her harder still, and began to rhythmically move one and then two fingers in and out of her honey nest. He could sense her opening up to him, relaxing to his touch and rhythm as he suckled her. He added a third finger, and in between each in and out motion he lightly opened his fingers a bit wider with each pass to prepare her for him.

Then he felt her approach, and heard her increasing moans, "William, oh God William! Do not stop, do not stop! Oh, God!" and with that she sparked and erupted. She screamed at the top of her lungs, "William!" as she rode his mouth, faster and faster.

Darcy lapped at her juices as she was so wet, but he did not allow her to recover. With her one of her legs still over his shoulder, he placed his manhood at her entrance. Teasing her with just a little bit at a time.

He rocked her lightly with each small entrance. He leaned over to suckle her nipple, and he opened her legs just a little more as he entered her just a little farther and a little farther, reaching as far as he could without hurting her. He tapped her nub lightly and then rubbed gently as said, "My Lizzy, this may hurt a little, but I will need to thrust a bit harder in order to break through your maidenhead. This will join us as man and wife, and make you my own. Are you sure? Are you ready, my love?"

He looked up into her warm, emerald pools of love and heard her say, "Oh, Please, William, Please, make me yours."

He lowered his mouth again to suckle her nipple and nibble at her tip. He opened her legs again, and moved in and out a little several times to accustom her to the rhythm. And at the same time she lowered her arm to grasp his bottom as he thrust into her depths.

Elizabeth gasped and he stopped. She said, "William, I am well, it was just a quick sting, but it feels so good to have you deep inside of me. Is this it, are you finished?"

"Oh no, love, the best part is yet to come." And he began to pull back.

"Do not leave me yet, William!" Elizabeth gasped.

"I am not leaving, my heart. We have only just begun," as he pulled out almost to the entrance and then plunged back in again.

"Oh yes, do it again, William!"

And do it again, he did. He pulled out almost to the brink, and entered her fully, again and again; slowly at first, then picking up the pace. Her left leg was just on the outside of his shoulders, allowing her to open more fully. His knees were on the lower part of the chaise and his arms on each side of her head as he built the pace slowly, slowly as his thoughts ran away with him. *Oh, God she is so wet. And the he smell is even better than my wildest dreams, lavender and tanginess. I am inside her, feeling her warm lushness. Plunging into her depths, filling her luscious river of pleasure. I must go slowly, I want her to find her pleasure, to crest with me and it will require all the restraint I have ever learned.*

They whispered words of love and of desire as he plunged again and again into her depths. He moved his body onto her even further to reach her mouth for a deep kiss. His tongue and his manhood keep pace, depth and rhythm with each other.

Elizabeth could no longer feel any pain, just fullness and liquid pleasure. With each entry back into her womanhood, she felt more and more complete. Her hips began to keep time, meeting his hips with each thrust. It was maddening. She held onto his bottom, pulling him into her with each of his strokes, as her tongue circled his. His tongue, moving into her mouth, kept the rhythm of their sex.

Their breathing increased, their moans became more boisterous, their pace faster and faster. Elizabeth kept time with him, meeting his every stroke. He was the master conductor in this orchestra of love and she was the concertmaster, the first violinist, and he was stroking her brilliantly. And then the crescendo of their passage picked up as they headed towards the finale. The timpani were rumbling as their passion ignited. Then, like a cymbal crash, they reached their thunderous conclusion together. Elizabeth was screaming his name on a high note, and Darcy releasing his thunderous applause within her depths.

As Darcy lay upon her in his exhaustion, she rubbed his lower back in a circular rhythm. He lowered her legs and they wrapped around him, her feet resting on the lower part of his buttocks. She liked the feeling of his heaviness, as he lay upon her and inside her.

They lay contented for a few minutes until Darcy moved slightly on his side against the arm of the chaise and pulled her against his chest, her head tucked into his neck. "I love you, my wife. I know there has yet to be a formal ceremony, but you are my wife. We are bound together fully in the eyes of God, my love."

"And I love you, my husband. I am bound to you in the eyes of God. From this day forward, for better or worse."

"Are you well, my Lizzy?" He rubbed her brow and moved her chin up until they were gazing into each other's eyes.

"I am quite well. You may think me very wanton, for I did not remain still and quiet. But I do believe that I will quite enjoy being your wife, William," Lizzy shared as she giggled lightly.

"I would not have you any other way. I know I will enjoy being your husband, my love. But, as much as I would like to stay here with you all day, we have been gone a very long time. Let me use this cloth under us to clean you up as we must to be on our way soon," he frowned as he was worried for her.

Fortunately, Elizabeth anticipated his concern. "William, never regret this day. I will not. This has been everything wonderful. So much more than I had ever, ever imagined it could be. I am very, very happy indeed. I know we must leave. I do not believe I have bled much at all. So please do not worry so. This has been too wonderful for you to fret."

Darcy pulled her to him one last time before they were to ready themselves for their departure. "Oh my beautiful, Luscious Lizzy, my wife," and kissed her deeply and firmly on the mouth.

"William, I thought you said that it took you quite awhile to recover, my love? I believe you have already recovered quite well... And, as you say, I will never become truly accomplished unless I practice..."

And practice they did.

CHAPTER NOTES:

Curiosity killed the cat is from Shakespeare.

*This saying originated with the French, and has been traced back to the early 1500's. In the United States, this idiom was made popular by the poet, Henry Wadsworth Longfellow in his poem, "The Student's Tale" from "Tales of a Wayside Inn" (verbatim wording: "All things come round to him who will but wait.")

It's reminiscent of "Patience is a virtue."

"The ability to wait for something without excessive frustration is a valuable character trait. The proverb has been traced back to 'Piers Ploughman' (1377) by William Langland and is similar to the Latin, Maxima enim..patientia virtus (Patience is the greatest virtue) and the French, Patience est une grant vertu. (Patience is a great value.) Some ten years after Langland, Chaucer wrote in 'The Canterbury Tales' (1386) that 'Patience is a high virtue.' Sometimes followed by the wry rejoinder 'but virtue can hurt you.' First cited in the United States in 1724 in the 'Works of Thomas Chalkley' (1766)..."

Chapter 15

8 December 1811

Darcy and Elizabeth had a wonderful, intimate conversation on their way back to Longbourn. They talked of their upcoming life together. They discussed their hopes and dreams. They spoke openly about the possible consequences for their actions that day, but agreed it was so close to the wedding that no one would ever need know if their interlude had consequences, as their wedding was less than three days hence.

Both agreed that they loved children, and hoped for at least three. Darcy was certain that the first would be a boy, while Elizabeth reminded him that her mother had only given birth to girls. Darcy assured her that the Darcy seed for generations had always given way to firstborn sons. They smiled. They held hands. They stopped several times for a kiss or two. They rejoiced in their love for each other.

When they arrived at Longbourn, they discovered that the Matlock's were due for tea in an hour. Elizabeth retired to her chamber to bathe and change her clothes. She also arranged with her father for Darcy to use his chamber to refresh himself. As Darcy had suggested to her, Elizabeth took a very warm bath to lessen her soreness, although she was not nearly as sore as she had thought she would be. *Must be all the walking I do,* she leaned back in the tub, and thought with a smile.

By the time that Elizabeth entered the main parlour, her family and William were all gathered there. Her mother had a smile on her face. Elizabeth had never seen such an expression from her mother, and wondered what had occurred to cause her mother to look as though she felt—dare say—content?

~~*~*~*

Flashback, Mrs. Bennet's Chambers, earlier that day

Mr. Bennet approached Mrs. Bennet's chambers and knocked.

"Who is it?" Fanny asked.

"It is I, Mrs. Bennet; I had a need to speak with you about a few matters. Might I come in?"

She rose from her bed where she was resting and went to open the door.

"Why of course, Mr. Bennet, please come in," she said, motioning to the two chairs in front of the fireplace. "Please do sit down, and tell me what this is about."

Mr. Bennet pulled the article that Edward had sent him out of his pocket, and handed it to her and said, "Before I speak, I would like for you to read this article. It was in yesterday's London paper, my dear."

Mrs. Bennet perused the article and looked at him in shock, "Dead, Mr. Collins is dead? What a rake, what a scoundrel he was! To be caught in such a situation! But what... oh my word... Thank heavens Mr. Darcy offered for Lizzy when he did, to think she could have been bound to such a man!"

"Elizabeth would never have been bound to Mr. Collins. I would never have allowed it," Mr. Bennet returned.

"Of course you would have considered it! With the entail you would not have wanted us to be thrown into the hedgerows. She would have *had* to marry Mr. Collins!" Mrs. Bennet's voice was beginning to rise. Mr. Bennet took that time to pick up her hand and kiss the back of it.

Mr. Bennet is kissing my hand and being considerate of my feelings! Is it possible that he actually does care about me? I do appreciate him letting me know of Mr. Collins' death.

Fanny smiled at him and coyly responded, "So what distant relative is to inherit Longbourn now, Mr. Bennet? Who is next to throw us out into the hedgerows?"

"Mrs. Bennet, we need to talk of many things..." Mr. and Mrs. Bennet continued to talk for some time.

~~*~*~*

"Elizabeth, you look quite well this afternoon. Did you and Mr. Darcy enjoy your ride together, my dear?" Mrs. Bennet asked.

Elizabeth could not remember the last time her mother had directly addressed her. She answered, as she approached Darcy and sat beside him, "Yes, ma'am, we had a very nice ride today. Thank you."

Darcy added, "Mrs. Bennet, your husband was so kind to loan us the use of his curricle for our ride and picnic. We had quite a lovely day."

Mrs. Bennet observed the couple and flushed a little. She saw in Darcy's eyes a look so pure, so adoring, almost private in nature, and she was grateful that he truly loved her daughter. She also looked at Elizabeth for the first time in a long time, really looked at her, and saw how beautiful she really was. She saw Elizabeth's face was lit up as she gazed at her betrothed. Mrs. Bennet saw all the joy her daughter felt reflected in her countenance.

Mrs. Bennet realized, maybe for the first time, that the reason she had never felt tender feelings for her second daughter was due to her jealousy. The only time she remembered her husband looking at anyone with the same look Darcy shared with Elizabeth, was the day his second daughter was born. Observing the young couple in front of her, obviously in love and anticipating their upcoming marriage, Fanny thought of her own marriage. Before her thoughts would proceed further down that road, Fanny brought her mind back to the present.

"Mr. Darcy, I understand your family is to arrive here shortly for tea. I am sure you will be glad to see them. I understand your sister will be with them. Has it been awhile since you have seen her, sir?" Mrs. Bennet asked.

"I was able to see Georgiana for a brief time on my trip to London. She remained with my Aunt and Uncle, as I was only there for a few days. She will be travelling with them after the wedding to Matlock, as they plan to return there before the holidays. Elizabeth and I hope all of them will be able to join your family in visiting us for Christmas," Darcy explained.

"Elizabeth, that will be a very large party for you to attend to so soon after becoming Mistress of Pemberley. You must be sure to ask me for help, or from your new aunt, should you need it. I know you have assisted your father for some years with matters for the estate, and have assisted me in handling special events here at Longbourn, but Pemberley is so much larger. I am glad your first social event will be with family. Perhaps, it can help hone your hosting skills, before Mr. Darcy has other large parties for you to oversee. You know I am very proud of you, as you have always been so clever and attentive. I am sure you will do fine," Mrs. Bennet stated.

Where is my mother and what have you done with her? Elizabeth thought.

"Thank you, Mama. I appreciate your confidence in me. I will let you know if there is anything you can do to assist me," Elizabeth said, still somewhat in shock of her mother praising her.

"Mrs. Bennet, Elizabeth is perhaps the brightest, liveliest and yes loveliest," Darcy gazed at Elizabeth as he said this, "woman of my acquaintance. I have no doubts about her ability to serve as Mistress of Pemberley. While I have entertained very little since I became master of the estate, perhaps with Elizabeth at Pemberley, she will breathe new life into the estate as she has renewed mine," he said as he turned back to smile at Elizabeth.

"If there were any doubt at all, I am sure that Mrs. Reynolds will be there to assist her in any way. After all, she has been the overseeing the staff there since I was four," Darcy offered.

"Mrs. Reynolds is still there! She was so kind to me when I visited your home, Mr. Darcy. In fact I remember fondly, having a conversation with her about the recent birth of her son. I discovered I was carrying Jane while at Pemberley. Mr. Bennet and I have fond memories of our trip there together."

"Mrs. Bennet, I knew that Mr. Bennet had visited Pemberley, but I did not realize you had been there as well!" They continued to talk of Pemberley until the Fitzwilliam party was announced.

Mr. Hill announced to those in the parlour, "Lord Edward Fitzwilliam, Earl of Matlock, Lady Matlock, Viscount Mark and Lady Harriet Fitzwilliam, Colonel Fitzwilliam and Miss Georgiana Darcy." The Bennets and Darcy rose to greet their guests. After all the introductions were out of the way, every one introduced to Darcy's betrothed as well as the rest of the Bennet family, the large group divided into smaller pairings as tea was served.

Darcy arranged for Georgiana to join him and Elizabeth, so they could get better acquainted, and Colonel Richard Fitzwilliam joined them as well. He was most interested to acquaint himself with the woman that had stolen Darcy's heart. After the initial greetings and agreement to call each other by their first names, Elizabeth said, "Georgiana, I am so happy to meet you! William has said so much about you. He tells me you are a very accomplished musician, and that you love to play the piano and the harp. I hope I will be able to hear you play while you are here for the wedding."

"My brother says that nothing gives him greater pleasure than to hear *you* play and sing," Georgiana said softly, struggling to maintain eye contact with Elizabeth. She continued to look down at her lap every few words.

"I assure you he has exaggerated my talents, no doubt for some mischievous reason of his own," Elizabeth laughed, as she smiled and cocked her head to the side and looked at Darcy.

Darcy smiled and patted her hand just once since they were in company, and said, "No, my dear, what I said was true! I dearly love to hear you sing and play."

"And Darcy never lies! He always tells the complete truth. Is that not true Darcy? Disguise of every sort is your abhorrence. Is that not what you always say?" Colonel Fitzwilliam chuckled.

"Oh, but colonel, I believe I must disappoint you. You see, on the first night of our acquaintance, he has admitted to telling a white lie. You did ask me for forgiveness for that unkind remark did you not, dear sir? Or did you truly find me only tolerable, and not handsome enough to tempt you?" Elizabeth turned to ask Darcy.

Richard and Georgiana looked at Darcy, a little shocked as his cheeks flushed close to bright red, and then they looked to Elizabeth. As she had a mischievous look about her, they lightly laughed. "Darcy you did not say such a thing to the woman you are now to marry, did you? I would imagine it took more than just a simple apology to get past such a remark!" Fitzwilliam questioned.

Darcy, definitely embarrassed that Elizabeth had brought up one of the two white lies that started their trek towards walking down the aisle, decided to tease her back, "Elizabeth, my dear, you would not like for me to recount all of the events of that evening where I apologized to you, now would you?" Darcy said this as **he** cocked his head and raised his eyebrow in her direction.

"Oh, it is to my disadvantage that he knows as much about me as he does. All right, William, you have had your retribution. I concede, sir. I believe William was in very poor spirits the first evening we met, and was trying to get Mr. Bingley to leave him alone and not require him to dance. He told me he had not really looked at me until after he said what he did. Then, he hoped I had not heard what he said. But, I believe he suspected that I had, as he apologized to me before I brought it to his attention. Did you not, William? There, am I forgiven for embarrassing you in front of your family?" Elizabeth fluttered her eyelashes at him as she asked.
Laughing, Darcy said, "You have all the forgiveness you will ever require, and my heart as well, my love," and he kissed the back of her hand.

Georgiana and Richard were both a little shocked, as they had never seen Darcy tease or show affection in such a manner.

Tea was announced and distributed amongst those attending. Mr. Bingley arrived to visit Jane, and was introduced to all that were in attendance. Richard moved to visit with Bingley, and Georgiana tentatively moved to meet Jane.

Darcy invited his aunt and uncle to visit with him and Elizabeth for a while. Lord Matlock shared his sincere best wishes, and his gratitude, that Darcy and Elizabeth's fathers greatest wish was to come true. Aunt Cassandra, as she insisted that Elizabeth begin to call her that even before the wedding, had a lovely conversation about wedding plans and her memories of Darcy as a child.

Mrs. Bennet was the consummate hostess. Elizabeth was amazed. No loud raptures regarding what jewellery and pin money she would have. No disclosures of private information. No discussion on qualities of carriages. No effort whatsoever to embarrass anyone in her family. In fact, Mrs. Bennet was solicitous of everyone in Darcy's family, and very kind in her memories and discussion of her second daughter's wedding. All and all, tea was quite pleasant for all in attendance.

~~*~*~*

A lone figure stood at an upper window, watching the carriages approach from Longbourn. This was her opportunity. Certainly, such auspicious personages would assist her in pointing out the absurdity of the match. She was certain of it.

As the Fitzwilliam and Darcy party were entering the front entrance of Netherfield, Miss Bingley was floating down the staircase in an orange gown that, if it were appropriate for any occasion at all, would only have been appropriate in a formal ballroom.

She approached Lord and Lady Matlock, and with a deep, formal courtesy said, "My Lord, My Lady, I am so grateful for this opportunity to welcome you to our lovely home. Please come into the parlour as I have prepared some tea and dessert. After such an evening in inferior company, I am sure you would like to experience a more superior respite before retiring."

Lord and Lady Matlock looked at each other with a frown. Richard and Georgiana shook their heads in confusion and followed. Bingley looked embarrassed. Darcy's face was angry, so angry that he flushed red. Certainly, if looks could kill Caroline would have been dead, had she any power of discernment of the gentleman in question's demeanour. But alas, said lady was oblivious of her lack of charm appreciated by said gentleman.

The entire party followed Miss Bingley, reluctantly, into the parlour. She had the finest china, and an elaborate assortment of desserts presented on the table. It appeared that the entire staff of Netherfield was there to assist in presenting this formal tea, a tea that none of them desired. They had all enjoyed their evening repast at Longbourn. After tea, they had continued to visit; having enjoyed dinner, as well as tea and dessert, before they had left Longbourn.

Mr. and Mrs. Hurst were already seated. Randolph Hurst looked about as embarrassed as Charles Bingley. He had stayed at Netherfield that evening, attempting to prevent Caroline from doing just what she was acting on now; that being to embarrass Darcy in front of his family. He had shortly realized that Caroline had planned this event to show what an exemplary hostess she was. Hurst knew that nothing she had planned was appropriate for this late in the evening. He wondered what she could possibly believe she was accomplishing by such a spectacle! Yet, he also knew by allowing her to embarrass herself beyond redemption, he might have a chance to aid Darcy in ending Caroline's determination to subvert his wedding plans.

"Oh, Lord and Lady Matlock, please take a seat; as well as you, Viscount and Lady Fitzwilliam. Colonel Fitzwilliam, you and Georgiana should sit over here with Mr. Darcy. Charles, I am sure you would like to visit with Louisa and Randolph. Now, are we not comfortable?" Miss Bingley exclaimed, as she sat next to the settee where she had placed Lord and Lady Matlock.

"James and Lucy, please serve the tea," Miss Bingley instructed. "All of you must be hungry. Please partake of this exemplary dessert our chef has prepared. You know, our chef is from France."

To everyone's surprise, it was Georgiana who spoke first, "Miss Bingley, I do not believe I would be speaking out of line, if I told you that none of us are hungry. We had an excellent meal at Longbourn, and we just completed our dessert prior to departure."

Darcy was astonished by Georgiana's outburst. It would follow propriety for all of them to simply eat again, to make their hostess happy. Yet, secretly, he was pleased she was determined not to give into Caroline's machinations.

Richard said, "Georgiana is quite right. I do not know when I have had a more pleasant meal. Everything was prepared quite well indeed."

"I asked Mrs. Bennet if her cook would provide the recipe to mine for that Sherried Trifle we had for dessert. It was perhaps the best example of the confection I have ever had the pleasure to partake," Lady Fitzwilliam added.

Caroline turned to Lord and Lady Matlock, determined to make her point, "I am sure you are only being polite. I cannot imagine you have ever had to partake of dinner in such company. Surely, you do not agree with your other relatives? I am certain that after the Bennet's have made such a spectacle of themselves, you are wondering how to impress upon Mr. Darcy just what a catastrophic mistake he is making in this match. Perhaps, it is not too late to convince him of this. I will be more than happy to assist you in impressing upon him the importance of changing his mind before it is too late."

A collective gasp was heard around the room, as all in attendance were shocked at Caroline's open rudeness. Caroline, of course, had only said this to Lord and Lady Matlock, but everyone in the room had heard her. The Viscount and his wife, not knowing either the Bennet's or the Bingley's before tonight, felt it was Miss Bingley making the spectacle of herself, not the Bennets. Richard and Georgiana were shocked to hear Miss Bingley's blatant rudeness in her offensive words towards Darcy and his fiancée's family. Darcy rose and strode to the window in an attempt to calm his angry thoughts, before he said something that would damage his relationship with his friend's family. Mr. Bingley and the Hursts were preparing to intervene, however before they could, it was Lady Matlock that spoke.

"Miss Bingley perhaps you, as well as my husband and I, could step into another room. I know I would like to speak with you," she said with a raised brow, that her husband and nephews recognized as mischievous.

Caroline, thinking that she had been victorious, asked to be temporarily excused from her company and escorted Lord and Lady Matlock across the hall to the library. She closed the door; and as soon as she did, the Viscount and Lady Fitzwilliam as well as the colonel found a reason to leave the room, only to walk across the hall to listen to the interaction. Darcy, Georgiana, Mr. Bingley, and the Hursts remained in the parlour.

After Caroline had invited the Fitzwilliams to sit, she sat on a chair across from them. Lady Matlock began, "Miss Bingley, I asked you to follow me out of the room because I did not want to embarrass you in front of my family and yours. What I want to say to you is quite important. I know that I am a guest in your home. I will leave and stay elsewhere, if you like. But I will not, and I repeat will not, have you disparage my nephew's family-to-be. They are the finest of gentle persons, and I am quite grateful to have made their acquaintance this evening."

"However, I cannot say the same thing for you. You have attempted to belittle my nephew's future family, and embarrass him in front of his relations. This I will not have! Do you understand me? I will not have it! I will take my entire family elsewhere if necessary. We are here for Darcy's wedding. We are here to celebrate a union our family has hoped might happen for a very long time."

"But, Lady Matlock, I know you must be quite shocked that Mr. Darcy would connect himself with such an impertinent chit, with no family connections or fortune..."

Lord Matlock interrupted, "Miss Bingley, we will not have it! Do you understand? Miss Elizabeth Bennet is everything that is lovely and proper, which is more than I can say for you! I am quite sorry I have to be so blunt. It is not appropriate for me to say so, but I must. How can you disparage Darcy's fiancée, and think you will stay in his good graces? He is your brother's best friend, is he not? Do you want to be banished from his homes and his company? For I assure you, if you do not change this behaviour now, I will encourage him to do so."

"But Lord Matlock, do you not know that the Bennets have no connections..." Caroline started.

Lord Matlock continued, "Enough, Miss Bingley, I will not hear it. Do you understand? The Bennets have quite good connections, if you believe *me* to be such. Thomas Bennet is one of my best friends in the whole world. I will not have him, or his family disrespected! Now, I would like to return to my family."

"Yes, sir," was all Caroline could say. She was shocked. She had been certain that this plan would work.

The evening soon came to an end and, all retired to their chambers. No one had the words to discuss what had just happened in the parlour.

For Caroline Bingley, sleep did not come easily. She stood looking out her window long into the night. She certainly thought his family would be against this match—they would not possibly believe that Darcy, married to that chit, would be acceptable to the London *ton*. She had planned so carefully only to be thwarted. She was desperate. There had to be a way. There simply had to be away to stop this marriage before it was too late.

Chapter 16

9 December 1811

The following morning, Elizabeth woke before dawn, her thoughts full of William and the day before. She knew she should feel regret or shame; her upbringing insisted that she ought, yet she could not. Nothing about her relationship with her William had been normal, so why should their wedding night not be an engagement afternoon? She was so relieved that nothing of intimacy was as she had feared. Truly, she had never thought to know such pleasure.

Knowing she had an appointment to keep, she rose and began to ready herself for her walk with William. She was eager to see him, and if she were honest with herself, eager to practice her lessons. She was also grateful the hot bath she had the afternoon before, along with her night of rest, had eased the soreness from their intimate activities.

Once dressed, she left the house and walked towards the path. Upon arriving, she saw there were three persons waiting, not just one.

As Darcy approached her, his eyes swept over her body and his thoughts were transported back to yesterday, thinking with lustful fondness of what she had felt like in his arms. But as they were not alone, he lifted her hand and placed a gentle kiss upon her fingers.

"Good morning, my love. Richard and Georgiana have insisted on joining us this morning. They wanted the opportunity to visit with you, and thought they would serve as chaperones."

As they gazed into each other's eyes, they blushed in fond remembrance of the previous afternoon. Breaking the spell, Elizabeth exchanged greetings with Georgiana and Richard, and they began their walk. The initial partnering had Elizabeth and William leading and Richard and Georgiana following a ways behind. It was distance enough to allow them to talk without anyone overhearing.

"I am very sorry not to have this time alone with you, Elizabeth," Darcy began. "I could not find a way to dissuade my sister and cousin."

"Do not think of it, William. We have enjoyed our time alone quite well. We will have a great deal of pleasant solitude in but two days."

Darcy glanced behind him to be sure they were a sufficient distance away from Richard and Georgiana, and whispered, "Lizzy, are you quite well this morning? I should have asked prior to starting out if you felt well enough to walk."

"I am quite well, William. I have very little soreness, almost none at all. Though, I am quite grateful for your kind attention. I know this is not always the case after such an... experience. Thank you for everything."

"You need not thank me. It is I who should be thanking you. I have never felt such joy..."

Elizabeth interrupted him with a slight laugh and whispered, "Oh, William, let us just agree we are both grateful of our day at the Great House at Stoke, and be happy to know there will be a lifetime filled with many more."

"Very well, but I would have you know I am anxious for the day I may hold you again in my arms—two days hence. Now, I do have a couple things I would share with you today," Darcy said.

"Yes, William?"

"Your father gave me a clipping from the London paper. He suggested I tell you of it instead of him," he pulled the clipping out of his pocket. "Would you like to read it?"

Elizabeth took the clipping. She slowed her pace, but continued to walk as she read. "My word, Mr. Collins is dead! And in such a fashion! It is quite shocking, indeed!" She looked up at Darcy, who was trying to hide a smirk.

Once Elizabeth had looked at him, neither of them could help themselves. In their amusement, both stopped on the path and laughed so hard that Richard and Georgiana caught up with them, watching them with curiosity.

"What in the world has transpired to cause my staid cousin to act in this manner, Darcy?" Richard asked.

This caused a renewal of their amusement, and soon, tears were running down their cheeks. Whenever they tried to stop, they would look at each other and begin laughing again.

"Brother, are you well? Please tell us what is so funny. We would really like to know. Elizabeth can you tell me?" Georgiana asked.

Elizabeth handed the article to Georgiana and Richard and they read it. In the meantime, Darcy and Elizabeth managed to get themselves under control.

Richard started chuckling as he finished the article, "You mean, this was my aunt's parson? That *this* was his demise?" Richard started laughing. Georgiana, still not quite understanding, looked to her brother.

"Brother, I do not understand. This man was a parson? He was given the living at Hunsford? Is that it? Elizabeth, did you know him as well?"

Elizabeth calmed her self and said, "Oh, Georgiana, I did know him. He was my cousin. He was to have inherited Longbourn upon my father's passing. He also," she glanced at Darcy, "Made me an offer of marriage, that your brother happened to walk in on. It happened the same day your brother proposed to me. So you see, we have already laughed at the absurdity of this man's presence in our life. I know that it is not proper to laugh at another's demise. But to have died in such a way..." she giggled, in vain she attempted to prevent herself from laughing again.

"Georgiana, do not think us unfeeling. Mr. Collins was such a pious, overbearing man; that to think of him attempting a liaison in such a manner is beyond ridiculous."

"But, Elizabeth..." Georgiana began. "What does this mean for the entailment? Does your father have another relative?"

"You know, I have no idea. I am sure that my father will investigate the matter. Come, Georgiana, walk with me for a bit. Let us get to know each other, as we are to be sisters," Elizabeth said as she linked her arm with Georgiana.

Darcy and Richard fell into step behind them, following at a distance.

"Darcy, I do not think I have ever seen you so happy. Not even as a boy! You were always such a serious lad. I am very happy for you, old man. Very happy, indeed."

"Thank you, Richard, I *am* very happy. Elizabeth is oh, she is so many things, and I cannot even voice them all. She is bright and intelligent. She is generous and devoted to all those she loves. She is beautiful. Her liveliness infiltrates my spirit. It is as though she is a bright light that has found a way to shine into my soul. I feel alive, maybe for the first time. I do not think I knew how desolate and dark my life had become until I knew her."

Richard looked at him. "The *ton* will be quite surprised, I think, that you have connected yourself with a woman of no fortune and no connections."

Darcy glared at him, challenging him with his eyes, "Richard, I will not have you question me! I managed to control myself with Caroline's vitriol last night, but I will not endure yours as well!"

Richard, surprised by the expediency with which he had raised Darcy's ire, quickly moved to amend himself.

"Darcy, I am not questioning you. I am certainly not degrading your choice, or challenging your judgment as that *orange nightmare* did last night. But you must know your decision will be looked upon with curiosity."

Darcy calmed a bit, "Richard, she is not without connections. Her father was best friend to my father, and your father as well, I believe. Mr. Bennet is my second godfather. As you see, her family is well connected with mine, and yours as well. As far as her fortune, she has dowry enough to satisfy the inquiring minds of yourself and the *ton*. As it is, I am not at liberty to speak of it, but Mr. Bennet has been quite prudent in his financial dealings. He has had my father and yours as a guide, among others."

"So he *is* the Tom my father spoke of? *He* is also the T.B. that now owns Wickham's debts here in Meryton, I take it?"

"Yes, he is, Richard. But if you wish to know more, I ask you to speak with your father. The rest of the story is not mine to tell."

They walked on for a bit before Richard ventured, "Darcy, old man... ah... I... by the way your Elizabeth looks at you with such adoration... she looks quite plucked, cousin. Should I have waited to send you that book until later, old man?"

"Richard, I will not have you speak such..." Darcy turned and gave him a cold, piercing gaze.

"Oh, do not worry that anyone else will notice. But as a man of the world, I recognize the signs. There is an intimacy between the two of you that transmits it, I dare say."

"Richard, I insist that you say no more!" Darcy replied angrily.

"But you do not deny it, either, cousin. She is all that is lovely!" He said as he waggled his eyebrows at Darcy.

Darcy grabbed Richard's collar and drug him behind a tree, and out of the sight of the ladies. He pushed him up against a tree as his glare was as sharp as the cold steel of his rapier's blade. "I will not have this!"

Richard was startled but unwisely said, "Close to the words my mother spoke to Miss Bingley last evening. All right, I will not speak of it. But you walk differently as well, cousin..."

Darcy hands closed around Richard's throat as he pressed him against the tree. "Richard, if you were not my cousin, I would call you out."

Richard whispered through his cousin's painful grasp, "Point taken, Darcy, I am sorry. Let us rejoin the ladies, shall we?"

~~*~*~*

"Elizabeth, did you have many proposals before my brother?" Georgiana asked tentatively.

"No, only one other than Mr. Collins and your brother. It was when I was but sixteen, an older gentleman that had danced with me at an Assembly asked me if I would marry him. I had always determined I would marry only for love. I did not love him. I also knew I was too young."

"I was too young as well," Georgiana said quietly.

"Pardon?"

"I was too young as well. I had a marriage proposal as well. I am quite grateful events transpired as they did. I would not like to be married now," Georgiana whispered.

Elizabeth knew of what she was referring, but chose not to press her. She was only beginning to know Georgiana, and she wanted her new sister to trust her. She knew if she was to remain open and honest, she might convince the young girl it was safe to trust her. With time, she hoped Georgiana would feel comfortable enough to tell her of her experience with Mr. Wickham.

For the remainder of the walk, the ladies talked pleasantly, with Darcy occasionally joining in. Richard was silent as he had lost his voice.

~~*~*~*

Bingley summoned Caroline to his study. When she arrived, he closed the door behind her, escorting her to a chair.

"Caroline, whatever possessed you to behave in such a manner in company last evening? You have offended every member of the Fitzwilliam family, as well as the Darcys. I will not have it! If you are unable to maintain proper behaviour, then you will leave my home," Bingley said firmly.

"Charles, certainly you do not mean that. I was every bit the accomplished hostess last evening. Providing my guests with superior desserts, accompanied by the appropriate number of servants to serve them in a proper manner. I do not understand what you could mean."

"Caroline, you cannot possibly be ignorant of the rudeness you exhibited before our guests last evening. Your offer to Lord and Lady Matlock of providing aid to prevent Darcy's marriage was heard by every person in the room! I assure you, you could not have offended Darcy more if you said it directly to him! You will be very lucky if he ever speaks to you again, much less if he is willing to ever have you in his home," Charles spoke angrily.

Caroline paled a bit and said, "Of course, my Darcy... oh, I mean Mr. Darcy must have misunderstood my meaning. I was simply suggesting to Lord and Lady Matlock that I might aid with the plans for Mr. Darcy's wedding. It would not do for anything to be less than proper and appropriate as possible. We would not want their family to find anything wanting in the preparations."

Bingley's voice rose, "Caroline, do not take me for a fool! You are lying. I heard everything you said! Colonel Fitzwilliam heard your entire conversation with his parents, I dare say. He indicated as much to me just a little while ago. You are treading on quite thin ice, Caroline! You may or may not heed this warning, but I assure you I am quite sincere in it."

"I have already asked Louisa to act as hostess for dinner this evening. You may remain and attend the event only if you answer with simple *yes* and *no* answers. I will not tolerate any snide remarks to anyone in attendance. If I hear you have said anything disparaging about any member of the Bennet family, you will find yourself on the road in my carriage tonight. If you are unable to temper your behaviour, then I will give you the bulk of your remaining inheritance now, subtracting all the overages you have had on your monthly allowance each month since father died. Oh yes, I have kept track of such, and believe me you are well into the bulk of your 20,000 pounds. I believe you only have around 14,000 left. That is all you will see if you do not heed my warning. Do we understand each other? I dislike being this firm with you, Caroline, but have left me with little choice," Bingley finished with calmness.

Caroline nodded to Bingley in acknowledgement of his words. But defiantly, she did not believe him, nor was she ready to give up her last chance to claim Mr. Darcy for her own.

Caroline returned to her room. *Oh, how I hate Eliza Bennet. She is the cause of all of my difficulties. I simply must think of something, something to prevent this wedding. Otherwise, Eliza will be the death of me, and all of my dreams.*

~~*~*~*

Mary Bennet had brought a small note pad with her that evening to the engagement dinner at Netherfield. She had it tucked into the middle of her copy of Fordyce's Sermons. She was determined to observe conversations for material she needed in regards to an upcoming scene in her book.

Her sister, Elizabeth, simply glowed. Mary had never known of a time when she had seen Lizzy so happy. She was particularly radiant whenever she was in the presence of her fiancée. Mary had watched them carefully. She was unsure if she had ever seen true, pure love until she had observed her sister and Mr. Darcy. The looks that radiated from their eyes! Their bright and pleasant smiles they shared only with each other! The little excuses they came up with to touch one another in some small way! How their heads inclined just a little closer to the other when they spoke. She wrote down these observances then moved closer to hear their conversation, close enough to be able to take a few notes.

"William, have I told you lately that I love you? You know, when I think of it, it was just one of those chance encounters that we ever found each other. But I am quite grateful, beloved that we met for now I only dream of you," Elizabeth said.

"I was always determined to marry only for the deepest love, and if it were not for your love and acceptance, I might have been alone all the days of my life. I am serious, in only one night things have changed to bring about my heart's desire. I thought I would be single until the end of time until I chose you to be the companion of my future life. You make me want to be a better man," Darcy said, looking into her deep emerald eyes with such sincere love.

"I long to be by your side always. But, I am sure that the obligations of love and duty will, from time to time, cause me to have to travel away from you. It is my hope that when I am gone there will be no more tears from you while I am away. But I will always be loving you from afar, and hopefully God's grace will lead me home to you," Darcy continued.

"Well, my love, I know I will find this is a marriage worth the earning for God has given me the role of a lifetime in making me your wife. I hope that come what may, I will have the determination to accept such wonderful sources of happiness as have been given to me by loving you," Elizabeth said with a look of heart-felt joy on her face.

Mary thought this to be an odd conversation. She was not quite sure why. To hear them whispering sweet nothings to each other was quite entertaining. However, she decided to move to another seat to hear others speak.

Mary moved over to where Colonel Fitzwilliam and Miss Darcy were speaking with Jane and Mr. Bingley.

"Miss Bennet, you must be so happy for your sister. I know I have never seen my brother happier. I think they are perfect for each other," Georgiana said to Jane.

"I do not ever remember my sister being happier. I know she is grateful she is to have you as a sister," Jane said.

"I have always wanted a sister. And to think, now I will have five!" Georgiana exclaimed.

"Miss Mary, how are you this evening? Are you excited about the upcoming wedding?" Colonel Fitzwilliam asked.

"Oh, Colonel, I am quite excited for my sister, indeed. I am grateful I am to have such a handsome brother, oh, and new cousins as well," she smiled at him and cocked her head with a raised brow, in an attempt to imitate Elizabeth's most alluring look.

The Colonel laughed, "Well, it appears I am to have many new cousins. What are you writing, if I may be so bold to ask?"

Mary was not sure exactly how to answer him, but it was obvious he had noticed her writing so she said, "I have recently been working on writing a story, and I find I quite enjoy observing the art of conversation. Each individual in this room has a different manner of speaking, and different manners of facial expressions. I find it quite an educational experience."

"The study of human character can be quite a challenge. Why, as a younger son and a military man, I have long learned to take advantage of understanding what someone is saying with their facial and body language, sometimes even before they open their mouths. For instance, look over to where Miss Bingley is sitting," he slightly motioned in her direction. "It is obvious by the set of her chin, by her narrowed eyes, even by the stiffness in which she sits so upright and rigid that she is unhappy. She does not wish to be here this evening. Can you see that?"

"Why yes, Colonel! I can see that! But I dare say that is how Miss Bingley usually behaves amongst our company. I believe she feels my family is quite beneath her. I do not understand that, however, as her father was in trade. My father is a gentleman, so in reality she is beneath us in rank. Do you think she believes others can not see the disdain she carries on her person?" Mary responded.

"Quite astute, Miss Mary. Quite astute. Now, what see you as you observe my parents speaking with yours?" Richard asked.

"Your father and my father seem quite diverted. Their eyes are crinkling at bit at the corners, and their expressions are open and engaging. They both appear to be attempting not to laugh, actually. There is just enough tension in their faces, even though they are both slightly smiling and their eyes are moving about to observe the room. Yes, I believe that they have found some joke amongst us, and are attempting to make sport of it without bringing it to anyone's attention," stated Mary. "What about our mothers' sir? What do you see in them?"

"I can tell my mother is feeling quite mischievous. I have seen that look on her face when she is contemplating how to deal with some type of spectacle, or when attempting not to laugh. Your mother looks a little nervous, but also in awe. Her eyes are wide open, and she is very attentive to the conversation. But knowing mother, she is not planning her mischief with your mother, but rather with someone else in the room," the colonel said.

Dinner was announced. And a very fine and expertly planned dinner was served. Conversation was light, and as the last course was cleared, Lord Matlock stood and raised his glass, encouraging all to join him. "I would like to take this opportunity to make a toast on behalf of my favourite nephew and godson, Fitzwilliam Darcy. Fitzwilliam, on behalf of all three of your godparents—Lady Matlock, Mr. Bennet, as well as myself—we would like to tell you how proud of you we are. You have grown to be a well-respected and honoured member of the community. Your management of Pemberley and your guardianship of Georgiana is an inspiration to many. Your family members love you. You are respected by the *ton*, and you have made an exceptional match with your Miss Bennet. Miss Bennet, on behalf of myself and my family, we are honoured to welcome you into ours. Your wit and wisdom, your intelligence and liveliness, and your care and kindness are exemplary. We could not be more pleased to call you niece. So, to Fitzwilliam and Elizabeth, may your marriage be blessed with happiness!"

"To Fitzwilliam and Elizabeth!"

All joined with the exception of Miss Bingley, who was still trying to understand what she heard...*godfather... Mr. Bennet... it could not be...*

The gentlemen did not separate from the ladies that evening. They were all enjoying being in company with each other. The evening progressed amicably. There was a little music as Caroline, Louisa, Mary and Elizabeth took turns at the pianoforte; with Elizabeth eventually convincing Georgiana to join her in a duet. As the evening was about to come to a close, the party was interrupted by a knock at the door and an unusual little man entered the parlour door unannounced.

"Greetings all. I understood from a recent express there is a dearth of clerics in the area. Particularly, with the demise of Mr. Collins in such a horrific way, there have been many who have wished to avoid this part of the country. As some feel that something in the Meryton area must have affected him to cause him to act in such an unscrupulous way. To die at the hands of former prostitutes no less! I know you will be most heartily glad that I have arrived to perform the necessary role of parson for the upcoming wedding ceremonies. All I ask is a place to stay until after the wedding. I am monstrously glad to be able to assist you in this matter. Show me to my room, good man," the gentleman said to the footman as he left the room, assuming they would allow him to stay for the night.

If jaws dropping had a sound, there would have been a massive chorus sounding at the moment. "Who, or rather what in the world was that?" Richard questioned, giving voice to what they all were wondering.

Chapter 17

10 December 1811

Darcy and Elizabeth had agreed, rather reluctantly, that they would not see each other again until they met at the church. There were many last minute details that needed to be taken into consideration before the wedding.

Elizabeth had, however, decided to sleep in a bit later than normal on this last full day of her life as a single woman. But thoughts of her husband were her first waking thoughts as they were foremost on her mind. *I never thought that I would discover a love like I have for William!* Her thoughts were full of nothing but her husband to be.

Oh, I can think of nothing but William's touch. There is so much more I wish to learn. I wonder if it is done... if it is something he would like... for me to taste him.

Elizabeth found that her hands just had to move. She was imagining Darcy's hands touching her. She could not help but tease her nipples, squeezing them, until they were hard buds. She could remember Darcy doing the same. And then licking and nibbling them...

~~*~*~*

As Darcy first awoke, his first thoughts were of Lizzy, and how happy he was they were to be married the next day! *Just think in but two days I will awake with Lizzy in my arms!* At least that was what he desired, and he believed she did as well.

Darcy regretted his agreement not to see Elizabeth on this day. All he could think of were her eyes, her scent, her taste, and her breasts... He could not stop from stroking himself, imagining her beneath him.

Ah, so beautiful, so exquisite. So, so wet, and all for me... so adventurous, and the taste of her, like rare nectar. I wonder if she will be willing to taste me... to feel those luscious ruby lips surrounding my manhood. Oh, and to have her in my arms again... to plunge myself into her depths again and again. To make her mine every day anew. . .

~~*~*~*

Elizabeth had moved her hand down to touch herself. *Oh, to feel him inside of me... deep inside of me... hard, firm and hot... to feel his kiss, deep and wet... his tongue rhythmically plunging into my mouth, matching time with his member...*

~~*~*~*

Even though neither knew it, they came to their pleasure at the same moment, as three miles separated them. Rising and climbing to higher and higher planes. Both tipped over the horizon at the same time. Both called the other's name.

"My William!!"

"My Luscious Lizzy!!"

Both were thinking of how they would be waking in each other's arms in two days time!!

~~*~*~*

Elizabeth finished her breakfast and sat in the front parlour to do a bit of mending, thinking over all she needed to do during the day. She had already packed her trunks. They were new trunks her fiancé had sent her, as he had ordered them while in London. She had planned enough clothing for her honeymoon, though Darcy refused to tell her where they were going. All he had said was they would not be gone very long as they were expecting family for Christmas. The bulk of her things would be sent to Pemberley. Darcy had arranged for someone to pick up that trunk later in the day.

Her wedding gown had arrived. It had already been fitted, as well as the few things she would take with her on her honeymoon. Her aunt Gardiner and her new aunt-to-be had both, separately, given her some lovely silk gowns and lingerie. Elizabeth blushed as she thought of Darcy's seeing them on her.

She had agreed to spend some time with Jane a little later in the day, and her mother had asked to speak with her this morning. Elizabeth knew she would not get away without this '*talk*' with her mother. Her mother must feel it was her responsibility to tell her of her duties. But Elizabeth no longer needed her guidance, and could only guess that her advice would be unhelpful.

She giggled when she remembered Darcy pretending to be her mother, telling her what he suspected her mother would want to say. Elizabeth had been trying to think of a way to avoid the interview all together. *I wonder if there will be a time I can think of being with William in an intimate manner and not blush.*

With that thought, her mother came into the room.

"Elizabeth, I would like to speak with you now."

"Yes, Mama, I will be there shortly."

A couple minutes later, Elizabeth knocked and entered her mother's room. Her mother asked her to sit.

"Elizabeth, you might have guessed why I have asked you to my chambers. I need to speak with you of your duties. Your duties as a wife to Mr. Darcy," Mrs. Bennet said.

"Mama, you need not..." Elizabeth started.

Mrs. Bennet interrupted her, "No, Lizzy I must tell you these things. It is my duty as your mother. Now, I know you must have questions about what will happen tomorrow evening."

"No, Mama, I really have no concerns or question at all. I am not worried. I trust William."

"Elizabeth, you do not know of what you are speaking. A husband does not care for such things. It is not his job. You will be expected to remain still..." Mrs. Bennet began.

Elizabeth interrupted her, "Mama! I know what I need or want to know. You need not trouble yourself! William has told me he is committed to me, and desires our marital bed to be as joyful for me as it is for him. I trust him."

"Elizabeth, have you truly had such an intimate conversation with you fiancé? It is not proper! What was Mr. Darcy thinking to speak with you of such things?"

"Mama, I had concerns and I decided to speak to him. Our relationship started in such a way that we have decided there will be no secrets between us. He has asked me to speak to him about any concerns or questions I might have, on any topic."

"Elizabeth, it is just not done. Oh, what he must think of you?"

"He loves me, Mama. William has assured me that allowing me to feel pleasure is his duty. He has assured me that it is."

"But Elizabeth, it is not proper for you to find your pleasure. That is not what society demands of a proper wife," Mrs. Bennet said.

"Well, William insists propriety need not have a place in our bed chamber," Elizabeth said.

"He has spoken to you of such? That is most singular, shocking, in fact!" Mrs. Bennet looked her in the eyes.

Elizabeth blushed slightly but said nothing.

"Well I see, well, fair thee well," Mrs. Bennet said.

Is it possible that Lizzy and Mr. Darcy have already... oh, well, she has always been so independent... Mrs. Bennet paused for a few minutes, and then finally decided to let it go.

"I will leave you to yourself in this matter then, Lizzy. I wish you well, but if you should ever have any questions you will speak with me, will you not?"

Elizabeth answered her, "Yes, I will, Mama."

"There is one more thing of which I would speak to you, Elizabeth. You know that I knew your William's mother," Mrs. Bennet paused here for a moment. *I wonder if I should encourage her not to let anyone think she is inferior...*

Mrs. Bennet continued, "Anne Darcy was a strikingly beautiful woman. She was the perfect picture of proper society. I found myself feeling quite, I should say, inferior when I first met her. I want you to know you are everything intelligent and lovely, Elizabeth. You have all the skills you need to be Mistress of Pemberley. Never, ever let Mr. Darcy, or anyone in his family, make you feel like you are second-class.

"Know your strength, intelligence and wisdom will aid you, my dear. I am here if you have questions or need encouragement. I know Longbourn is not nearly as large as Pemberley. But I have managed this estate as its Mistress for many years. I may not have said it often, Lizzy, but I love you and I am proud of you."

Elizabeth rose and walked across to her mother's chair and touched her on the arm, "Thank you, Mama, thank you for your confidence in me. It means a great deal."

~~*~*~*

A little while after Elizabeth left her mother, she found herself out in the gardens, walking with Jane. Jane seemed a little subdued, and Elizabeth was introspective. But they began to talk.

"Sister dear, it is quite difficult to believe that in less than twenty-four hours you shall no longer be a Bennet, but shall be Mrs. Darcy, Mistress of Pemberley. Are you not frightened? Is it not overwhelming to you?" Jane asked her.

"Jane, I have no fear. I could not have said that even ten days ago, but I have spent much time in William's presence; I simply cannot wait to be his wife. No, I do not feel fear, simply anticipation. The last two weeks have simply flown by, and now it is as if I am in some type of in-between place. No longer Miss Elizabeth and not quite Mrs. Darcy. But in my heart I am already William's wife."

"Elizabeth, I know mother was to speak with you today. Are you not concerned about the wedding night? Do your duties as Mr. Darcy's wife not concern you? You just seem so calm. Are you, I mean do you not have any fear at all of what is to come?"

Elizabeth blushed bright red and turned away, but Jane saw her. In Jane's new determination to speak her mind and be bold she questioned her sister, "Elizabeth, what is it? I know you are trying to hide something from me. I know you that well. What is it? You know me too well to think you can hide it from me. I also know you well enough to be able to tell if you are lying to me. So you might as was well tell me. I am your older sister, and I demand to know what would cause you to blush so."

"Jane, I simply cannot speak of it."

"Elizabeth, what are you hiding from me?" Jane asked and managed to get her sister to turn around towards her. Elizabeth would not look at her in the eyes.

"Why cannot you look at me, Elizabeth? Do you have something to tell me? I am listening. I will not back down."

"You may be quite shocked if I speak of it, Jane. Shocked indeed," Elizabeth said. But she looked up at her sister, and smiled a big smile as she cocked her head slightly to the side.

"Alright, I am not concerned about my wedding night because it is no longer an issue. So there! Are you glad that you pressed me to tell you what you did not want to know?"

"Oh, Lizzy, do you mean that you... that you and Mr. Darcy... that you have already... you cannot mean... Lizzy is that what you mean?" Jane stumbled on her words.

"Oh, yes, Jane! That is exactly what I mean. This must, has, to be a secret between you and I. No one else need ever know. Are we in agreement?"

"But when... how... where?" Jane gasped.

"Father sent us on an errand in the curricle the other day. That is all I will say about when and where. But how, oh Jane, it is simply amazing. William is everything wonderful."

Suddenly Jane changed from astonishment to curiosity, "Oh Lizzy, tell me what is it like? Is it horrible and unpleasant, as Mother has alluded to? You do not seem to think that it was."

"All I will say Jane is nothing you have heard need be true. When it comes to your time to be married, I would not recommend you follow my path. But if you have any questions, any doubts and fears, you should speak of them with your fiancée or your husband when they occur. If you need to know anything else, you may speak with me. I would encourage you to forget everything mother might say to you. Perhaps, it might not be so long until you need this advice, sister dear? Are you and Mr. Bingley close to making your own announcement?"

"Oh, Lizzy, I am so glad to speak of it to you. He has asked me to marry him and I have accepted. But he is waiting to speak to our Father until after your wedding. He wants nothing to overshadow yours and Mr. Darcy's wedding. He said he wanted his best friend to have his special day without getting in the way. Oh, but Lizzy, he is everything that a man ought to be. I love him so. You say I should speak to him of any concerns or fears I have?"

"Yes, I would recommend that."

"And what if I want him to kiss me?"

"He has not yet kissed you?"

"No, and I find I tire of his adherence to propriety. I want to feel his arms around me. I have been thinking about kissing him. Are you shocked?"

"Well, Jane, I would encourage you to let him know you want his kisses. He may not want to offend you and take a chance on having you reject his advances. If you want him to kiss you, you might move closer to him, put a hand on his face and look at his lips."

"Thank you, Lizzy. Know that I will miss you and write to you often."

~~*~*~*

"Bingley, I want to tell you just how grateful I am to you for all but forcing me to come to Netherfield. When I think of all I might have missed if I had not come..." William trailed off.

"Darcy my friend, you need not thank me, you know. I do believe before too long we will be brothers..." Charles said.

"So, have you asked the lovely Miss Bennet to marry you? At last!" Darcy exclaimed.

"You beat me to punch, old man! I was preparing to ask Jane within a day or two of the ball here at Netherfield. You were faster than me. I did not think you had it in you. But I dare say, I have never seen you more content. I am very happy for you, Darcy. Very happy indeed!"

"Bingley, you have not answered my question, now have you?"

"I have asked Jane to marry me and she has agreed, Darcy. She truly is an angel. We have both decided to wait to ask for her father's consent until the day after your wedding. I believe she was going to tell Miss Elizabeth today. So you see, we will indeed be brothers."

"Well, I dare say I could not have chosen a better brother for myself. I will be quite honoured to have you in my family, Bingley. Initially, I was unsure if Jane felt for you what you felt for her. But, I think she is much like I am, or rather was before Elizabeth. I know she has strong feelings for you, as Elizabeth has assured me that she does. She is reserved at times, and maybe a little shy. But with you as her husband, I know you will do very well together."

Charles moved to pour some brandy for both of them and handed a glass to Darcy, "Here's to the lovely Bennet sisters!"

Darcy raised his glass and joined him in the toast.

~~*~*~*

Caroline Bingley was preparing herself for the evening's events. She had dressed carefully in a very special, quite alluring (if she did not say so herself) orange gown and robe, along with her orange slippers. She had loosely braided her hair with an orange ribbon woven into the strands. Everything was set.

Earlier in the day, Caroline had slipped into the housekeeper's chambers, found, and stolen the key to Mr. Darcy's room. She knew that he had begun to lock his door each evening, and the only way her plan would work was if she could slip into his room undetected.

The house had been quiet for nearly an hour when Caroline quietly opened the door to her bedchamber, and looked down the hall to see if anyone was about. Seeing no one, she quietly walked down the corridor towards Mr. Darcy's room. She slipped the key from a ribbon she had worn around her wrist and placed it into the lock, taking care to be very quiet as she turned the key. She peered around the corner of the door, discovered the room was dark with only embers from an earlier fire. Silently, she tiptoed into the room, and closed the door behind her.

Caroline approached the bed. Since the sleeping figure was facing away from her on the other side of the bed, with caution, she pulled back the covers and slipped in beside him. She moved a little closer to the warm figure, and spooned behind him. She waited until her hand and arm were warmed by the covers, and then placed her arm over his side and pulled herself closer.

He closed his hand over hers and raised it to his mouth to kiss it, pulling her even closer until her breasts, nay; her entire body was pressed against him. She sensed he was beginning to wake as his breathing began to increase in rhythm. He turned around, pulling her hard against his chest, moved her head up to meet his, and kissed her hard and firm on the mouth. Caroline had never been kissed, and her excitement was more than she could have imagined. His tongue ran along the seam between her lips, forcing them open as he invaded her mouth. He lowered his hands to her buttocks, pulling her against his hard manhood, undulating his erection against her. She became more and more excited as her heart rate rose and her breathing quickened. She had never imagined such rapture, such ecstasy. Suddenly, without knowing what was happening to her, she reached her pinnacle of pleasure and screamed; a piercing, brutal scream, "Mr. Darcy!"

All along the hall, doors were open and guests began to peek out of their doors, looking out into the hall.

Further down the hall, the last room on the left, a lone figure woke out of a deep sleep. *Did someone call my name?* Tired, the figure rose from the bed, put on a robe, and began to open the door and walk down the hallway.

Back at the door to the bedchamber, Bingley was first to arrive and opened the door as the key was still in the lock. Caroline moved her head towards the door, and looked up in triumph as her brother entered the room. Behind Bingley joined the figures of his valet, and Lord Matlock. Her smile grew brighter as she saw one of Mr. Darcy's family members in the doorway.

"Caroline, my God, what have you done?" her brother cried.

Caroline prepared to answer him in victory when over the corner of her brother's shoulder appeared Mr. Darcy, asking, "What is all the racket about, Bingley?"

Caroline turned to look at her bed companion and the shock was too great. She fainted.

Chapter 18

11 December 1811, 12:01 AM

"What on God's earth possessed her, Darcy?" Lord Matlock questioned his nephew. He and Darcy were sitting in Bingley's study, sharing a glass of port.

"I do not know, Uncle. But I believe, unfortunately, she thought herself to be in my chamber," Darcy returned.

"What do you mean?" questioned Lord Matlock.

"Uncle, up until the night before last, that was the bedchamber I was using," Darcy returned with irritation and concern.

"Good God, Darcy! Do you mean to say she was attempting to compromise you? She thought herself in bed with you? My word! To what further lengths will that woman go? I cannot believe it! Well, actually I can after the interview your aunt and I had with her the other night!"

Darcy stood and began to pace. "She has been unwavering in her pursuit of me for years, Uncle. But until my engagement to Elizabeth, her attempts have been decidedly less calculating. Since my engagement, she has been like a lioness on the prowl. She has searched for a way to separate me from the herd so she could pounce. I have been keenly aware of it, and have had a heightened sense of alert."

"Darcy, I do not think I really need to ask you this; but did you ever consider her? Did you ever give her notice? Did you do anything that might cause her to believe she had a chance to win your favour?"

"No, absolutely not! She is the sister of my best friend, and I have attempted to be civil to with her, but that is all. I have not been insensible to of her machinations. I have let Charles know I had absolutely no interest in her, and he has told her. Yet, I think she must have believed she would eventually wear me down, and I would accept her. She has had no reason to believe I would court her, other than her own vanity," Darcy said as he stopped pacing to have a sip of port.

"Well, I thought you had better sense than that. But I also thought that she might have changed since your engagement. Perhaps her bitterness has made her more desperate?"

"I suppose so. To be honest, I have paid her no mind as I have been pleasantly engaged with my soon-to-be wife," he smiled and looked away as he said it.

"Ah, yes, I am sure you have been preoccupied. You must have a friend in this household protecting you if your bedchamber was changed," Uncle Matlock said, stretching his arms over his head and locking his hands behind his head.

"I am not sure if someone knew of a plot, or they were simply protecting me from the possibility of one. All I know is that my valet said Mrs. Hurst suggested that I move to one of the larger married apartments; as the next time I am here, I will be here with Elizabeth. He said the Hursts thought I would like the larger apartment. I admit I did not think too much of it at the time. I will have to ask the Hursts if they suspected anything. I cannot tell you, though, how grateful I am that it occurred. There was a key in the lock, Uncle! She had gone so far as to obtain it to unlock the door. I shudder when I think what could have happened if circumstances had been different," at this Darcy winced slightly, as he rubbed his brow and then his hair distractedly.

"Darcy, how trustworthy are the servants here at Netherfield? Do you suspect any gossip of this evening's events will make it to Longbourn before the morning?"

"Oh, good God, I must send an urgent message Mr. Bennet right away, and ask him to have Elizabeth meet me at first light. I know she will be busy preparing for the wedding, but I cannot allow anything to spoil our wedding day. If she should hear anything of this, by the time the gossips have their way with the news, she might hear that I *was* in that bedchamber. Perhaps I should ride down there myself now," he rose, preparing to leave the room.

"Darcy, sit down. A message will do quite well. I will have my valet hand deliver it to Tom myself. In fact, I will send him a message as well, and inform him of your need to see Elizabeth in the morning. Speaking of which, it is now your wedding day, old boy! I think it is time for you to return to your bedchamber. You have escaped Miss Bingley, hopefully for the last time. Let Bingley do his duty as a brother to sort it out. You deserve some rest so you will be your best on your wedding night, aye?" Uncle Edward chuckled and finished his port.

"Yes, I suppose you are right. Charles will inform me of what happened in the ..." but as Darcy began to prepare to leave the chamber, Charles Bingley and Randolph Hurst entered the study. The four discussed the event in detail before returning to their bedchambers.

~~*~*~*

Mr. Bennet was awoken around one in the morning by Mr. Hill. Two messages had been delivered to him. One was from Edward Fitzwilliam, summarizing the events of the evening, as well as the innocence of his godson in the matter. The second was a note from Darcy, asking him to wake his second daughter shortly before dawn; asking that she meet him on their *path*, as the note said, so he could tell her of the events. Darcy was quite adamant that he did not want Elizabeth to hear about the matter through gossip, and doubt his innocence; or be concerned that the events of the previous evening would affect their nuptials.

The next morning Mr. Bennet tapped lightly on Elizabeth's door, and hearing nothing, opened it. She was sleeping so peacefully, he hated to disturb her rest, but knew that she would want to speak with her fiancé. He entered the room and tapped her on the shoulder. Elizabeth groggily opened her eyes and looked at him, giving him her attention. "Elizabeth, my dear, I have received a note that your fiancé would like to see you for a few minutes on your *path* just after dawn. I thought you might like a chance to slip out before the house awakes."

"Thank you, Papa." She looked at him slightly alarmed. "But is it not bad luck to see the bride before the wedding, is there something amiss?"

"No, no, my dear, I do not believe there is anything amiss. As far as seeing the bride before the wedding, I am sure that is why he wished to see you so early. He knows you will not be dressed yet for the wedding. Oh, and you need not worry yourself. He assured me in his note that he had no intention of abandoning you at the altar this morning," Mr. Bennet teased.

"Oh, father, do not tease me so! I shall get up and get ready. I would not want to disappoint William on our wedding day, thank you."

"There is not a thing in the world you could do to disappoint him. I could not have found a more perfect match had I designed the man myself. He is simply besotted with you, my Lizzy," Mr. Bennet said with a chuckle and left the room.

Elizabeth prepared herself hurriedly to meet William, and walked to the footbridge to await her fiancé. It was her wedding day. Every time she thought of it, she smiled brightly. She saw him coming from a distance.

Darcy was so urgent to see Elizabeth that he spent little time in preparation. He had on his shirt, but wore it open with no cravat. His shirt was casually tucked into his breeches and he was wearing his long coat. As he looked down at himself, and realized he had the appearance of one who had just rolled out of bed. *Hmmm, and to think Tomorrow, I will not have to leave my bed to see my wife. I cannot wait to hold her naked body in my arms again. Ah, there she is! She is so beautiful, yet as haphazardly dressed as myself; just fresh out of bed, indeed... so lovely.* He noted she appeared to have dressed as quickly as himself, and basked in the lovely picture she created, progressing towards him.

As Elizabeth approached him, she gasped at the sight of him so casually dressed. She saw him stop, and with the warmth of his smile, all her worries dissipated. She ran to him and jumped into his arms. He twirled her around as they laughed until their lips met. They both pulled back to look at each other. "Happy Wedding Day, my love," Darcy said as he kissed her again. He tried to control his ardour, as the reason for this early assignation was to inform her of the events of the previous evening, not to delight in her flesh. There would be plenty of time for that later in the day.

"Yes, William, Happy Wedding Day. But, sir, is it not bad luck for the groom to see the bride before the wedding?" Elizabeth smiled as she asked.

"It is quite early. And we are not yet dressed for the wedding. So I have not truly *seen* you, is that not right, my Lizzy?" Darcy reasoned as he kissed her lips lightly. "Let us sit on that log over there; I need to tell you about some happenings last evening."

Elizabeth frowned and looked at him with a twinge of worry on her face, "I hope nothing is wrong, William?"

"Nothing is wrong, my love, at least nothing that will effect our wedding. But I wanted to tell you of the events of last night. I could not bear to think of you hearing it from anyone else. It is of a nature that, if presented to you in a particular manner, might have brought you pain."

"Oh, William, please tell me of what you speak. I am now quite concerned."

Darcy began to tell her what he had heard, and what he had observed the previous evening. He told her of hearing his name being screamed, and finding himself in front of a room where Charles and his uncle were standing. He told her of seeing Caroline in bed in the arms of a gentleman, and her shock at seeing him at the door.

When he had finished, he took her hands into his and continued, "My love, Charles and Mr. Hurst spoke with Miss Bingley at length last evening. I am told that Mrs. Hurst questioned her in private. It appears that Miss Bingley was quite desperate to try and compromise me in a way that would disrupt our wedding."

"Miss Bingley had a friend near Hartsfield, a Lady Weston. Lady Weston had written her of an incident in which her friend, a Miss Emma Woodhouse, was accosted by a parson in the area. The parson had assumed, quite wrongly, that Miss Woodhouse was expecting his addresses. He asked her to marry him, and before she could respond, grabbed her improperly. Miss Woodhouse is well, after all that transpired; and happens, coincidentally, to be engaged to a long time family, Mr. Knightley. But I knew none of this until late last night."

"Miss Bingley invented a plot to invite Mr. Elton to Netherfield. She thought with the lack of clerics in the area, having him offer his services to perform our marriage ceremony was quite a ploy. But as you and I know, your father had already arranged for a parson to perform the ceremony today, so services of Mr. Elton were never needed," he brought her hand to his mouth and kissed her fingers, then her wrist and then her palm.

"Mr. Elton was the man that showed up at Netherfield while your family was dining there the night before last," Darcy explained as an aside.

"Miss Bingley, it appears, stole the key to what was gratefully my former bedchamber."

"Oh William! How did you escape? That is to say, she did not... it did not... you are unharmed... nothing happened?" Elizabeth stuttered.

"Elizabeth, I am very well. I assure you, but I will get to that. That is why I needed to tell you this story. I would not have you doubt me, or our felicity. Or my loyalty and devotion to you," Darcy said as he pulled her to him and kissed her on the mouth – a hard, deep kiss expressing the depth of his feelings. When they had pulled apart and calmed themselves, he continued with his story.

"Mrs. Hurst said she had promised him... I fear you will not like this part, my love." He paused and stroked the back of her cheek, and kissed her nose lightly.

"She promised him that if he would help her, she would help him find his way into a compromising position with you. I understand she led him to believe you would welcome his attentions. We both know that it is not true." Darcy placed a finger under her chin, beckoning her to look at him. "My love I can see how troubling this is to you. But it did not happen. You have nothing to worry about. I do believe that woman, if she can even be called such, belongs in Bedlam. Let me continue," Darcy said as he kissed her quickly.

"Hurst said that he heard her muttering to herself about having to find a way to stop the wedding. He has been on alert since our engagement was announced, as have I. He did not know what she was planning, but decided to protect me by changing my bedchamber. As I have been distracted, I thought little of it when my valet reported I had been moved," Darcy smiled, and looked deeply into her eyes.

"Hurst told me he had observed Miss Bingley attempting to open my door one night. He noted that the closer the wedding approached, the more desperate she was becoming. I thank God for his attention!" Darcy exclaimed.

Elizabeth sighed and placed her arms around him, "Yes, thank God. We owe him quite a debt of gratitude, William." They held each other for a few moments.

"I agree we owe Mr. Hurst a great deal, and have arranged to send him a case of fine port from Pemberley. But I should finish my tale."

"Miss Bingley used the stolen key to open the door to the room she thought was mine. The room apparently was quite dark, and she really did not see who was within the covers of the bed. She got into the bed and... oh... Elizabeth... proceeded to seduce the man in the bed sleeping there... who... was *thank heaven...* not me."

"Who was in the bed, William? Who is now attached to her, as I expect that Mr. Bingley will insist that they marry? It was not Richard was it? Lord, he does not deserve that!"

"No, no, it was not Richard. Surprisingly Richard, the soldier, slept through the entire event! No, it was Mr. Elton!" exclaimed Darcy as he chuckled a bit at the irony.

"Mr. Elton, Lord, so Miss Bingley is to marry a parson?"

"Yes, indeed, my love. Miss Bingley is to be Mrs. Elton! Charles has insisted that they marry quickly. It will take place as soon as a special license is obtained from London. Hurst has offered to depart after our wedding and travel to London for it. I suspect they will be married within the week. It will be a very small ceremony."

"I imagine that Miss Bingley is not happy about that!"

"Charles told her he would not spend any extra funds on a wedding for her. Her inheritance, what is left of it after all the advancements that Bingley has been giving her, will serve as her dowry and will be given to her husband. Bingley has cut her off. She must live on her husband's income."

"Miss Bingley... a parson's wife!" Elizabeth began to laugh, which caused Darcy to laugh as well. Needless to say, as had happened in the past, their laughter infected the other, and it took them some time to calm themselves. Darcy wiped her tears of laughter as well as his own as they quieted.

"Whatever parish he serves will need to prepare itself for orange vestments and robes at their services," Elizabeth said with a smile.

"I wonder if they make orange wedding gowns," Darcy speculated.

"And orange veils," Elizabeth supplied.

"And instead of coins, at the end of the service, they should throw oranges," Darcy laughed a deep big laugh, and they were off again. Laughing until they cried.

When they calmed themselves, Darcy drew Elizabeth onto his lap and kissed her long and tenderly, and then rested his forehead against hers.

"Miss Bennet, for that is the last time I shall call you that, I must return you to Longbourn; as we both must prepare for our wedding," Darcy smiled widely and gave her a light kiss.

"I love you, so much, William, I long to be your wife," Elizabeth replied.

"In the sight of God you are already my wife, Lizzy. Today will only legalize what we already know to be true. But I love you as well. I long to be able to formally call you Mrs. Darcy!" He removed a box from inside his coat and handed it to her, "Open this gift when you return to Longbourn, and wear them if you desire. They were my mother's." He tucked her arm into his. "Come, let me walk you back," and with that, they slowly walked to the house.

Preparations at Longbourn and at Netherfield were accomplished, in between nerves and frenetic activity. There were a few panicked moments at Longbourn, belonging to Mrs. Bennet, when she discovered her second daughter had escaped for a walk on the morning of her wedding. At Netherfield, Georgiana and Richard found much entertainment in watching the staid and proper Mr. Darcy become flustered and nervous the closer it came time to depart to the church.

But all preparations came to fruition, and Fitzwilliam Darcy stood at the front of the chapel with his dearest friend, Charles Bingley. He could not ever, in his entire life, remember a time in which he had felt more joyous anticipation. Elizabeth was to be bound to him, and he to her, for all the days of their lives. Lightness infused his soul. He need never again be caught by the darkness of isolation, desolation, and loneliness that had trapped him for so long.

His soul had already joined with Lizzy's. They were one flesh. They had already agreed it to be so, but now the eyes of the church and their families, they would be legally bound to each other.

The music began and Miss Jane Bennet walked down the aisle. Darcy was not paying attention at the time, but if anyone had looked in Charles' eyes at that exact moment, they would have thought Charles was the groom.

Darcy's breath caught when Elizabeth appeared in the doorway with her father. Light filtered in from the windows, giving her a heavenly glow. She was a vision in pale lavender. Her head was covered in very special lace, imported from France, that his aunt had brought for her. It had graced the heads of all of the Fitzwilliam brides for three generations. Darcy's mother had worn it when she married his father. Around her neck, she wore the pearls Lady Anne had worn on her wedding day. They had been inside the package Darcy had given to her that morning. She was a vision – all that was lovely, an ethereal creature, a goddess in light. Darcy was transfixed.

It is not the work of this fiction to recite the words repeated in all ceremonies. But they were exchanged. A ring was given. Prayers were said. Tears were shed. Vows were made before God and man.

Mr. Bertram spoke of the love he had witnessed in the couple. "It is rare as a pastor that I am able to witness a true love match. But in Fitzwilliam and Elizabeth, I see the love they have for each other, and it is the kind of love that I read of in I Corinthians 13:

*'Charity suffereth long, [and] is kind; charity envieth not; charity vaunteth not itself, is not puffed up. Doth not behave itself unseemly, seeketh not her own, is not easily provoked, thinketh no evil; Rejoiceth not in iniquity, but rejoiceth in the truth; Beareth all things, believeth all things, hopeth all things, endureth all things. Charity never faileth.

After a final prayer, Mr. Bertram proclaimed, "May I now present, Mr. and Mrs. Fitzwilliam Darcy."

~~*~*~*

Later in the carriage, Darcy pulled his bride onto his lap and kissed her long and deep.

"William, will you not tell me where we are going?" Elizabeth cocked her head, raising her brow as she gave him her most alluring smile.

"No, Mrs. Darcy, it is a secret. And we know that all good things come to those who wait..." Darcy advised, kissing her again.

*Text is from the King James Version of the Holy Bible. The New International Version interprets the original test as:

Love is patient, love is kind. It does not envy, it does not boast, it is not proud. It is not rude, it is not self-seeking, it is not easily angered, it keeps no record of wrongs. Love does not delight in evil but rejoices with the truth. It always protects, always trusts, always hopes, always perseveres. Love never fails."

Chapter 19

Mr. and Mrs. Fitzwilliam Darcy were celebrating their newly spoken vows in a way lovers often do. Well, as best as one can in a carriage without consummation.

"Oh William, I love you, my husband. Will you not tell me where we are going?" Elizabeth said as she climbed into Darcy's lap and began to nibble on his earlobe.

Darcy pulled her close to him, one arm around her waist, while the other hand was busy slipping beneath her low neckline and along her lush bounteous breast towards its goal – her increasingly hard nipple. One of his favourite fascinations with his wife was watching her bud ripen beneath her dress... he was enjoying it presently.

"No, my love. Did I not already tell you good things would come for those who wait, my impatient bride?" They whispered words of love to each other as they kissed, and Darcy revelled in exploring her breasts.

Elizabeth, being the competent student, reached down to the front of his breeches and began to stroke his hardening member, as she said, "William, can I see to your relief, my love?"

William found that Lizzy's attention to his manhood caused him to consider taking her in the carriage, and not to proceed in such a manner he stilled her hand. "Oh God, Lizzy, what you do to me! Love, you must stop. I want and need you more than I could ever imagine. But I have plans to experience you in a luxurious, large and warm bed; not in a rocking carriage in which there is too much chance of discovery." William said this as he reluctantly picked up her hand to arrest its progress, and brought it to his lips to kiss each individual finger and suckle on her thumb.

"Come, my love, let us rest for the remainder of our journey. As you know with all the events of last evening, I have slept little. I have plans for you this evening that require my attention, so let us spend some time in repose until we arrive."

"Oh, of course, William," and she moved off of his lap to lean her back against him. Shortly they were both asleep, he with his arms around her and her head resting against his neck.

A little more than an hour later the carriage stopped and the footman came to knock on the carriage door. "Mr. Darcy, sir, we have arrived."

Elizabeth and William both woke from a sound sleep, and looked at each other and smiled. As they righted their clothing, Elizabeth said, "Are you going to tell me where we are, William?"

"I believe you will know the moment we alight from this conveyance."

Darcy put his finger to her lips, "No more questions, Lizzy. Let us leave the carriage and all will be revealed."

Darcy opened the door, and the footman assisted them in stepping out. Elizabeth took a moment to get her bearings. There were large torches lit in front of a house that looked familiar, "Stoke, we are at the Great House, oh William, how did you do this?" She looked around, and it was like the house had come alive in three days. There were lights in all the windows and there were two servants standing at the front door. The grounds had been manicured. The hedges were clipped to exquisite detail.

Elizabeth looked up at William and smiled at him.

"I take it you are happy?"

"Oh William, I am, I am speechless! But it has only been three days, how, how did you accomplish all of this?"

"Your father suggested we use it for our honeymoon. Many of our staff from the townhouse in London are here, and have been opening the estate," he said as he escorted her towards the door.

"I wanted the place we shared our wedding night to be very special. And this place, where we joined as one, seemed a wonderful choice. Are you happy?"

"I could not be happier, William!" Elizabeth exclaimed. They walked to the door, where the doorman and William's butler awaited them.

The Darcys walked into the entryway and were greeted by Mrs. Newsome, Darcy's chief housekeeper from London. "Mr. Darcy, sir, Mrs. Darcy, ma'am. I believe all is ready."

"Thank you, Mrs. Newsome. May I present my bride, Mrs. Darcy, Elizabeth this is Mrs. Newsome. She has been our housekeeper at Darcy House in London for many years, since I was a child. She has been supervising the readying of Stoke for our wedding night," Darcy said as he introduced them.

"Mrs. Newsome, I am overwhelmed at all the work that has been done here in such a short period of time!"

Elizabeth was taking in the view. The house was essentially the same, but it had come alive. There were fresh flowers almost everywhere she looked. All the covers were gone from the tastefully appointed furniture that seemed to suit the entryway, and the parlour she could see to her left. Everything appeared to be so clean it glowed.

"Mrs. Darcy, I am quite honoured to meet you, and happy for you and Mr. Darcy. We are happy to serve you, Mistress. Mr. Darcy, I have bath water ready whenever you desire. Dinner can be ready within a half hour.

We can serve you in the dining room, or bring it up to a lovely sitting room in-between the Master and Mistress' rooms upstairs. Do you have a preference, or would you rather ring us when you decide?"

"Mrs. Darcy, do you have a preference?" William asked her.

"Mr. Darcy, if the sitting area is as lovely as Mrs. Newsome says, it would be nice to eat informally upstairs, and then have our baths after dinner. Would that be all right with you?"

"Quite fine, my love," Darcy said and they went upstairs.

The newly married Darcys had a lovely meal in their sitting room. Neither was very hungry as they were both thinking of the night to come. They chatted and laughed and fed each other, and kissed in between nibbles.

When she had finished eating, Elizabeth excused herself to ready herself for bed. The Mistress' chambers had been prepared to exquisite detail as requested by Mr. Darcy. There were roses and lavender flowers arranged in vases throughout the room. The bedchamber was quite large, over twice the size of Elizabeth's chamber at Longbourn. The walls were covered in a yellow linen embossed wallpaper, with light tapestry drapes of light and medium yellow, cream and lavender covering the windows, pulled back with golden tassels.

The four-poster bed was the largest Elizabeth had seen, and it was covered in an expensive yellow and lavender patterned silk coverlet and pillows. A settee was at the foot of the bed. Two large armchairs and a chaise were arranged near the fireplace, which currently had a large warm fire in the hearth, and there was a small table between the chairs. There was a large fluffy rug in front of the fireplace. Bedside tables were on each side of the bed. Elizabeth felt it matched her own tastes quite well.

She went through to her dressing and bathing room. The water was warm, and a maid assisted her in disrobing, and put her favourite lavender oil into the water. There were candles throughout both rooms. The atmosphere was comfortable and very romantic.

When she had completed her bath, her maid assisted her in putting on a gown her Aunt Gardiner had given her for her wedding. It was the colour of Champagne and made her skin glow. The neckline was quite daring in front and back, and it had very thin straps. She had a matching robe that she put on and tied it in front. "That is all Sarah," She said.

"Mistress, do you not wish for me to assist you with your hair? " Sarah said.

"No, Sarah I will be fine, thank you, you may retire. I will not need you again tonight. I will ring for you in the morning when I require you. Thank you," Elizabeth said as she found a lovely new brush and comb set on her vanity table. The handles were made of jade and they were emerald encrusted. The card read, *This set reminded me of your exquisite emerald-coloured eyes. I love you Mrs. Darcy, Your William.*

"Mrs. Darcy, if you do not mind me saying, you look quite beautiful. I am sure Mr. Darcy will be quite pleased," Sarah said as she smiled. "Good night, Mistress."

Sarah had taken Elizabeth's hair down, but Elizabeth preferred to brush it herself as it calmed her. She did not see Darcy enter the room, but sensed him shortly before he came up behind her. As he lifted the brush from her hand he said, "Allow me, Mrs. Darcy."

In truth, Darcy had longed for the freedom to do this. He loved her lush, brown hair. It had auburn lights in it, and was full and wavy, always smelling of lavender.

As Darcy brushed her hair, Elizabeth leaned her head to one side and then the other to give him easier access. She was unsurprised when he placed kisses along one side of her neck, and then the other, in between strokes of the brush. When he finished, he turned her towards him on the stool to admire his handiwork, and gazed at his lovely bride. His fingers ran into her hair near her cheekbones as he kneeled, and through her locks to the end. He brought his hands back up to her cheeks, and put his hands into her hair, but held them there, pulling her slightly closer to him and gazing deeply into her eyes.

His thumbs rubbed the corners of her mouth and she smiled, her lips slightly opened in anticipation before he moved closer and kissed her long and deep. Her legs naturally opened for him as he continued to kneel at her feet, pulling into her body as the apex of her sex was on the edge of the stool. His hands dropped to her waist and down to her bottom, pulling her into his body as his tongue began to duel with hers.

He pulled back to look at her tenderly, "Mrs. Darcy, are you ready for bed, my love?" Darcy asked as he rose, but neither William nor Lizzy calculated their longing for each other. As he lifted her to her feet, she moved automatically into his arms, and their kisses became more urgent. Stumbling, they found themselves flush with the wall, and William pressed hard against her torso as his tongue continued its tango with her own.

Elizabeth could do little but moan. Her thoughts had already ceased, and her hands were not idle as they moved to his buttocks. She pulled him into her apex, as they were both quickly reaching a feverous state. Darcy stopped long enough to remove the robe that had opened and to move the straps off her shoulder until the gown pooled at her feel. Her lush naked flesh was pressed against him and she managed to remove his robe and help slip his nightshirt over his head.

Now naked flesh to flesh, her hands resumed their journey. Elizabeth moved them over Darcy's flat nipples and leaned in to tweak them with her tongue lightly as Darcy felt his manhood slip back and forth along her warm folds.

He stilled her and moved to capture her warm, firm nipple in his mouth; suckling hard and releasing, until she was moaning louder every time he suckled.

He picked her up in his arms and moved her towards the bed. "Oh, my wife, I fear I cannot wait any longer," Darcy groaned. He placed her on the edge of the bed. Her apex he tested with his fingers and found her dripping with wetness, such was her arousal. Standing, he replaced his fingers with his manhood, entering her easily the first time, unsure whether she had any pain remaining from their previous encounter. He moved slowly and cautiously.

"Oh, God, William! Please, please my love, I need you. Do not hold back, I will not break," Elizabeth begged.

That was it. William lost conscious thought. She wanted him as much as he wanted her. He plunged hard and deep into her wetness. In and out, he pressed. He lifted her legs to wrap around his body. His movements were kinetic, faster and faster. Elizabeth meet his pace, moving forward each time he plunged into her. There was nothing but the two of them, and their bodies uniting.

Like a stallion, Darcy was a magnificent beast. Taking her, possessing her, plunging into her again and again; building, swelling harder than he ever remembered. He was a champion, and he was racing toward the finish line. He had to win! He had to cross the finish line along with her. He felt her pleasure began to crest, and although neither thought it possible, their pace increased to chaotic frenzy.

Elizabeth crossed the finish line just two seconds ahead of him. She screamed his name in her ecstasy, and he finished with her, erupting into her depths and screaming her name..."L-l-l-l-i-i-i-z-z-z-z-z-y-y-y-y." He collapsed upon her in exhaustion, then falling to his knees on the floor.

When he had slightly recovered, he lifted her to the head of the bed and joined her there; pulling the covers over them and cuddling her close to his side, they fell into a deep, satisfied sleep.

~~*~*~*

Longbourn, later that night

Tom Bennet stood looking out of the window at Longbourn. His favourite daughter, his Lizzy, his jewel, was married to his godson. He smiled as he thought of the joy he saw in their eyes as they looked upon each other. They truly loved each other, of that he was sure.

What irony that his child was now married to the son of the only woman he had ever loved. His Anne. He still carried the pain with him to this day. Edward had asked him to try and let it go. Encouraged him to accept William, a part of Anne, to help heal this pain and find peace.

Could he do it? Tom was not sure. But he was beginning to realize that he had never even allowed himself to try. Fear of abandoning the love he had felt for her and falling into a useless void, was what had kept him from letting go of the pain.

Anne had been gone over ten years now. Tom had a wife and five children, one married to Anne's only son. Could he allow himself to rejoice? Could he just celebrate having her son in his family?

Tom knew that it was time to try. He needed to do it for his family.

Chapter 20

Several hours later, Elizabeth Darcy woke to the marvellous feeling of flesh upon flesh. Her new husband of just hours was spooning her naked body from behind, his hand resting in sleep upon her breast. She could hear and feel his soft breath, as well as the rise and fall of his chest against her back. She noted that her breath matched his. How curious! Did it happen as they slept? Were they now so connected as one flesh that they even breathed in sync? It made her warm all over.

Elizabeth realized there was something else pressing into her lower body. She smiled, as even in William's sleep, he wanted her. She could arouse him in his dreams. She contemplated their conjugal bliss of several hours previous, the ferocious nature of their coupling. In addition to the feel of his arousal pressed into her, she longed again for his touch. Her body was responding by creating liquid pleasure, preparing itself for William.

Elizabeth was ever the eager student and wished again to practice. Her hips began to undulate, pressing back against Darcy and his erection. The movement of her warm flesh brought Darcy slightly back from the edge of sleep. He said nothing, but began to caress her breast with his hand. His hips began to move back and forth, pressing into her loins. He moved his hand down and lifted her leg up and back over his hip and leg, opening her folds for him, wide open, allowing easy entry from the rear. He pressed forward and moved to place his manhood into her envelope of pleasure, beginning in **tempo largo.*

He advanced until he was fully within her depths. He kissed her neck, then alternated nibbling her earlobe and circled his tongue around her outer ear. Each time he plumbed her depths, he squeezed the ripe bud of her nipple when he reached her apex, and as he pulled back he released her.

Elizabeth luxuriated in his arms as her body came alive yet again. She could do little as he was behind her. But her hips kept tempo with William, moving back and forth in time with his advancement into her hot, wet folds.

They took their time, a rhythm as old as mankind, yet the pace was a sleepy **adagio*; slow, easy and graceful. As their excitement began to build, he moved his hand to the center of her pleasure; rubbing **andante, andante*, flowing and graceful. He nipped at her earlobe and then suckled it hard into his lush mouth as his manhood swelled within her, and his pace began to amplify **allegro*, lively and brisk, pressing harder into her depths with each plunge. She kept to his rhythm, his **glissando*, moving at yet a faster rate, **vivace*. He then began to punctuate his movements by holding when he reached her depths, and then a quick retreat and return, **rubato*.

The mood and spirit of their composition of love was **con amore, con spirito, con fuoco, con moto and oh, so dolce*. The vocalizations of their passion rose to such heights that their moans and gasps were **fortissimo*, accentuated by **sforzando* strokes, and as Darcy's plunges into her depths reached **prestissimo* tempo, they reached their ultimate **crescendo* and triumphed in the last bars of their musical union.

A little while later as they luxuriated in each other's arms, Elizabeth said, "William, how did you come to love me? When did you know?"

Her husband thought carefully before making his answer. "Lizzy, it came on so gradually. I was halfway there before I even knew I had begun. But I knew beyond a shadow of a doubt that I loved you the night of the ball at Netherfield. And you, how did you come to love me?"

"I saw you before Mr. Bingley even moved into Netherfield. You were riding across a field on your stallion at top speed, and you were smiling and laughing, racing Mr. Bingley. I was struck by that first glimpse of you. Yet, I did not know for sure that I loved you until I heard those words of love in your marriage proposal."

William gazed upon her, sinking deeply into her fine eyes and kissed her long and deep. As the kiss ended, Elizabeth tucked her head into his neck and turned to kiss him on the chest, as she made a decision to ask a question she was concerned might anger him.

"William, I have another question for you. You may be angry with me for asking again, but you did promise you would tell me when we were married. It is obvious to me that you have some... I will say expertise in the ways of physical love. Have you been with many women?"

Darcy moved until he could look into her in the eyes, trying to judge the mood from whence the question originated. What he saw was stress and playfulness. "Lizzy, what are you feeling? Why do you ask me this now?"

Elizabeth reached up to touch his cheek. "William... I can never imagine feeling like I have this night with any other person... and I guess... oh, I do not know how to say this... I am jealous that you have been with other women. Concerned I might not bring you as much pleasure as they did. That they might have been more experienced in the ways of love and have brought you more delight." She looked away from his eyes as she said this, and moved to her opposite side away from him.

"Elizabeth... Lizzy... please do not turn away from me. Please look at me!" Elizabeth turned back and shyly looked at him.

"I have never, do you hear me, never felt such pleasure as I have felt with you. Please know this. I had a physical union before, but I have *never* made love. I have by no means been united with someone body, mind and soul. I have never experienced love and ecstasy before. I have the skills that come with having had a physical release with another person; this is true. If I had known, if I had had any idea that one day I would live to regret that; if I had known that it might bring my new bride any pain at all, I would not have done it.

"I have only been with two women in the past. I feel ashamed to tell you this, but they were courtesans, women who were paid for their services. My father took me when I was but fifteen to a courtesan for, as he told me then, education into the ways of love and the ways of restraint. I was with this lady for one weekend. The only other time I was on my Grand Tour, which was seven years ago, Lizzy. I have been with no one, no one but you since that time. I promised you that we would always be honest with each other, and now you know all. I am so, so sorry if it brings you pain."

"Truly, William, you have never been with a woman you loved? You have never made love to another besides me?"

"No, my love, never. Only you. Now, I find that I must have you again, unless you tire of me."

"Never will I tire of you William," Lizzy said as she pulled him to her and their passion flared again.

~~*~*~*

Elizabeth woke the next time from the most exquisite dream she could ever remember experiencing. She was in the midst of experiencing the heights of pleasure when she awoke. She did not immediately see William, but she was experiencing the pleasure she was having in her dreams. She looked down, and Darcy was busy delighting her pleasure center. "Oh God, William. Oh God, I... ah... believe... this is the most delicious way to be awoken."

Darcy suckled on her hard nub as two of his fingers explored her folds, moving in and out as he suckled hard and then soft. Elizabeth put her hands into the curls of hair on his head and pulled him harder to her. Her breathing was already at such a state, and her arousal so heightened that it took very little time for her to climb to her heights of pleasure. Yet, William did not stop. He continued to suckle and plumb her wet tunnel, now with three fingers, and she crested over and over until she was exhausted. He finally moved back up to the top of the bed to hold her against his chest. Darcy allowed her to recovery as he softly held her close.

After her breath returned to normal, Elizabeth said, "William, should we not alight from this bed at some point today? Will not the staff wonder if we are ill if we do not leave this chamber?"

"The staff knows that this is our honeymoon, my love. I doubt they expect us to leave this chamber."

"Well, we will need to eat at some point," Lizzy cocked her head at him and grinned.

"What of poetry; is not poetry the food of love? I can quote you some Shakespeare," Darcy chuckled back at her.

"Poetry does not fill the stomach, William."

Darcy laughed.

"William... can a woman taste a man like you have tasted me?" Lizzy looked at him, a bit embarrassed, from below her eyelashes.

"It is not proper, Lizzy," William answered and pulled her back against his chest, breathing deeply.

"But William, did you not tell me that propriety would have no place in our bedchamber? You did say that, did you not? Is it done? Can it be done? Would you like it?" Elizabeth innocently asked him.

"Oh, Good God, Lizzy. You are exquisite. My adventurous, curious cat," but he did not answer her.

Elizabeth pulled up to look at him and moved to kiss his chest and nipped at his nipples. She began to kiss down his chest, as she got closer and closer to his manhood. Darcy exalted in his fortune to have married such a passionate wife. He would never tire of her. He would always delight in her luscious flesh.

Elizabeth continued to make her way down his body. Taking her time to suckle on parts of his flesh as she made her way to his Zenith. When she reached his now hardened length, she peered up at him, questioning with her look. "It can be done, but you need not..." he said. But she was too quick for him, her tongue reached out to circle his tip. Round and round her tongue lapped at him, tasting a little fluid that had escaped from its center.

She moved to the base and began her own slow *glissando, up and down his length, circling the tip with her tongue each time she reached the top, and then licked down his length again. Darcy had lost conscious thought. His hips undulated and he was moaning as if in pain, but he had never imagined such pleasure.

Elizabeth tentatively put her mouth completely around the tip, and lowered her mouth as far as she could and began to suckle his hard, firm length. She began to move her mouth up and down, suckling as she moved, and with a sudden inspiration, moved her hand below her mouth so his entire length was covered. She tried to pace her movements in a similar tempo to those they had employed as they mated earlier. Darcy's pace was increasing as he rhythmically mated with her mouth. Faster and faster were his movements, and Lizzy did her best to keep with his timing. She began licking his length, as she suckled until he exploded in to her mouth.

Elizabeth was a little startled, but she was exhilarated that she had conquered him—that he had surrendered entirely to her ministrations. That she was the victor of the conquest! She moved up to lay back upon his chest, content that she had seen to his pleasure.

~~*~*~*

Charles Bingley had been quite busy over the last two days. He had set in motion a plan for his sister's wedding. She had compromised herself, and there was nothing to do but to insist on the marriage. She had been angry about the financial aspects of the match. But other than that, he had been quite surprised when she said that she would *'delight in the pleasurable ministrations of her soon to be husband.'* He shuddered when he remembered seeing them in each other's arms. He wanted to gag when she started to talk about her celebration of Mr. Elton's flesh. *Oh, Well,* thought Charles, *at least she will not be completely unhappy with Mr. Elton.*

Then there was the wedding of his best friend, Darcy. Bingley was quite happy for Darcy. He had found a woman that could intellectually stimulate him as well as compliment his romantic sensibilities. Charles knew he could never be happy with the second Bennet sister, as she was too smart for him. But of his lovely Jane, he longed for the day they would marry as well.

Despite his anxious wishes, he knew it was in his better judgment that he and Jane have a longer period of engagement. It would be best for both families. Elizabeth and Darcy's wedding had been a hurried affair, and now Caroline and Mr. Elton's would be even faster. In order to maintain propriety, and in order for his family to maintain its position amongst the *ton*, they had tentatively decided on a March wedding, granted that Mr. Bennet gave his consent. Bingley thought back on his latest walk to Oakham Mount with his beloved Jane.

~~*~*~*

Charles and Jane walked in companionable silence. As soon as they were out of site of Longbourn, Jane moved her hand from around his arm, down to hold his hand. Charles blushed as she intertwined her fingers with his. He found he could not look at her.

"Charles, do you not wish for me to hold your hand? We *are* engaged, sir. Do you think your future bride improper for wanting to feel the touch of your hand?"

They continued to walk, slowing their pace. Charles continued to look at the ground.

Jane stopped and dropped his hand. Crossing her arms in front of her, she glared at him as she said, "You *do* think I am being improper do you not? I cannot understand it, Charles! You are almost stogy in your rigid control of propriety. I find that I have had quite enough of it." Jane's face showed her frustration.

Bingley glanced up at her. "Jane, I, ah... are you disappointed in me? I am just trying to do what is just and honorable by you, particularly until your father grants us his consent."

Jane reached up to touch his cheek, and smiled into his eyes, "Well, Charles I find that unless I can convince you to drop the pretense of this controlled propriety, I may withdraw *my* consent to marry you. What say you to that?"

As she moved closer to him, Charles blanched as he looked at her, "Jane, dearest Jane, what is it you want from me? I do not understand!"

"Sir, it is quite obvious that you do not understand. Though, I cannot believe you are so ignorant— perhaps you are," she said as such moved even closer to him, placing her hands on his shoulders and looking up toward his mouth.

In almost a whisper, Charles asked, "What is it you want from me, my Jane?"

"I want you to shut up and kiss me, you fool!"

Kiss her he did, long and deep. And with that, lessons on making Jane happy officially began.

~~*~*~*

Bingley arrived at Longbourn, and Hill knocked on Mr. Bennet's library door to announce him.

"Ah, Mr. Bingley, I wondered how long it would be until you came to ask for my eldest's hand, do come in." They discussed the arrangements for Charles and Jane's wedding for some time.

The interview had gone better than Bingley had thought it would. He was amazed at the dowry Jane had! Why her dowry was larger than Caroline's! He was quite glad he had ignored his sister's insistence that he could not marry a woman of no connections and no money. As she was now sister to Darcy. and had quite a fortune, neither was a problem.

~~*~*~*

Later that night, Mrs. Bennet was in her chambers thinking of the good fortune of her two elder daughters. *To have Elizabeth already married to one of the most well-known and wealthiest personages in the country. And now to have dear Jane set to marry Mr. Bingley*, Fanny began to feel some freedom for the first time in a very long time. Finances would no longer require her to move in with her sister or brother should her husband pass before her. She need not worry any more, for her oldest daughters' marriages would throw the younger girls into the paths of fine, and perhaps other wealthy men.

What Fanny Bennet did wonder was how she had managed to marry a man who did not love her. Oh, he had desired her when they had first married. In fact they had anticipated their vows. Thankfully it was just two weeks before her wedding, as Jane had been born two weeks early, or at least that is what they had told their family. But she did not believe he had ever loved her. Tom had never looked at her the way Mr. Darcy looked at Elizabeth. He had never fawned over her as Mr. Bingley did Jane. He had provided for her. He had protected her and provided her with children to love. But, no, he had never loved her as she loved him.

*Musical term definitions
LARGO-slow and dignified; stately
ADAGIO-slow; in an easy graceful manner
ANDANTE-moderately slow, but flowing
ALLEGRO-brisk; quick lively
VIVACE-brisk; spirited
PRESTO-quick

PRESTISSIMO-at a very rapid pace
GLISSANDO-a rapid series of ascending or descending notes on the musical scale; rapid sliding up or down the musical scale
RUBATO-extending a note or phrase, compensated by shortening another one nearby
CON AMORE-with love
CON FUOCO-with fiery manner
CON SPIRITO-with spirit
CON MOTO-with movement
DOLCE-sweet
FORTISSIMO-very strong and loud
SFORZANDO-strained and sharply accented
CRESCENDO-musical notation indicating that the composition is to become louder

Chapter 21

13 December 1811

All too soon, the Darcys' brief honeymoon came to an end, and the couple prepared to depart for Pemberley. They had a little over a week to travel to Derbyshire, settle into their new life together, and prepare for the Christmas holiday. Their families were to arrive by the twenty-second of December.

Darcy had sent several expresses to Pemberley regarding preparation of the Mistress' chambers, and readying the house for the arrival of his new wife. He sent an express from Stoke informing his staff of the guests that would be arriving shortly for the holiday, and asked that they drape the house in greenery to decorate for the holiday events.

The Darcys left Stoke on the morning of their third day as man and wife. Their intimacy and their comfort with each other had changed them both in a very short time, as there were few instances where one of them was not seeking a touch from the other. They knew their actual honeymoon phase would last for a long while. Elizabeth, who had doubted a woman could find any pleasure in the act of joining with her husband, had experienced the heights of ecstasy. And Darcy, who had thought that he had some sense of what this time would be like with his new bride, had found that even the farthest reaches of his imagination had been completely exceeded.

All the way to Derbyshire, Darcy's thoughts drifted toward the fantasy of Lizzy in his bed at Pemberley at long last. *Good God, I have wanted her there for what seems like forever. Just the thought of sealing our marriage vows... with her at Pemberley... experiencing that long desired intimate experience between us is almost more than I can bear to anticipate.* They would talk of other things, but his thoughts constantly returned to that ultimate fantasy. His ardour seldom cooled completely, as his eagerness never abated.

They spent two nights on the road, and on the third day, Darcy and Elizabeth chatted eagerly in anticipation of arriving at Pemberley.

"William, I am so excited about seeing my new home. But I must confess I feel a little intimated about being Mistress of such a grand place."

Darcy reached over and took her hand, kissing the palm, before entwining his fingers with hers. "Lizzy, I thought you told me that your courage rises with every attempt to intimate you," he said as he lightly laughed.

"It is not fair that you throw my words back at me at such times, William," Lizzy said with a grin.

"My love, you need not have any concerns. Your intelligence and wit, as well as your kindness are all you need to learn the responsibilities of being Mistress of Pemberley. It took me quite some time to learn all I needed to be Master; and there are still aspects that I leave to my steward, stable manager or other senior member of the household. That is why we have such a competent staff."

Darcy pulled her toward him until her back was resting against his chest, "Mrs. Reynolds has been managing the household for some time. Georgiana has attempted to serve in the capacity of Mistress, but has had no real desire to do so. You need not take over any responsibility earlier than you desire. We have a wonderful staff that are very good at their jobs."

"Thank you, dearest, that does help to know that you will have patience with me learning my new role."

"Oh, Lizzy, if you choose never to take on the responsibilities for overseeing the household it would truly matter not to me. I much prefer you to spend the majority of your time attending to your duty as my wife. In fact your duty as my wife, in *my* bed at Pemberley, is almost all I can think of at the present." He said this as he turned her toward him to kiss her deeply, whispering something very suggestive into her ear about his intentions for her as soon as they arrived home.

Lizzy giggled and looked up at him, "Are we close to Pemberley, William?"

"You, my love, are trying to change the subject; but we are, in fact, quite close. I believe we are on the outskirts of Lambton. Is that not where your Aunt Gardiner grew up? I enjoyed talking with her about her memories of the town. She had memories of my parents as she had met them. She also used to come to the Harvest Festival that my parents gave each year for the neighbourhood. I like your aunt and uncle quite well. I am glad they are coming along with your family for Christmas."

"Well, I like your aunt and uncle as well, William. Aunt Amelia was so kind to me. My mother had a veil made to go with my dress. But your, I mean our aunt explained about the *'Fitzwilliam lace'* and all the Fitzwilliam brides' heads it has adorned. I was so honoured that she insisted I wear it. I know I am a Darcy now, but she insisted I was a Fitzwilliam as well. I like her and Uncle Edward a great deal. Uncle and Father are so close. It is all too hard to believe at times, is it not, that our families have been connected all these years and we were unwitting of it?"

"I am quite glad I was your father's godson. As much as I like him, it would be quite unfortunate if I had been his son," he said as he kissed her neck, his ardour increasing as they were now so close to Pemberley.

Elizabeth laughed and said as she nibbled on his earlobe, "I am quite glad as well."

They pulled apart a little, and looked at each other and laughed. Darcy noticed where they were, and informed Elizabeth they were approaching the boundaries of Pemberley.

Elizabeth found she had a little flutter of nerves in her stomach, but she was also quite excited. Darcy said, "I will have the driver stop when the house first comes into view, love. I want you to see my favourite prospect."

A few minutes later, Darcy tapped on the roof of the carriage and the driver came to a stop as Pemberley House came into view. "Well Lizzy, what do you think of your new home?" Darcy asked as they looked out the window toward the house.

"Oh William, I do not think I have ever seen a place that fits so beautifully into the landscape! It is a thing of beauty," and she turned to look at him. "I cannot believe I am to live in such a place. I find I am still quite in awe; it will take a little time to become accustomed with my new station in life."

Darcy pulled her to him and kissed her long and deep. Pulling back, he looked longingly into her eyes. "You will have a lifetime, my love, if you desire it. I fear that if we continue our delay, my desires will get away from me even before we arrive. As it is, I need to calm myself before we face the staff. But we will not tarry! I am ready to have you in my chambers now," and with that he tapped on the roof and the carriage again began to move.

As they approached the front door, it appeared all those they employed had come outside to greet the newlyweds. Try as he might, Darcy had never determined how they always seemed to know when he was approaching. He disembarked from the carriage, turned to lift her down, and approached them. "Mrs. Darcy, this is Mr. and Mrs. Reynolds. Mrs. Reynolds has been the head housekeeper at Pemberley since I was four years old. Mr. Reynolds is the head butler here. They are like family to me, and will help you in any way you might have need." Curtsies and bows were made as appropriate.

Then Darcy greeted the entire assemblage, "I want to thank all of you for your warm welcome to my new bride, and myself. As Mrs. Darcy is now Mistress of Pemberley she should be afforded all the respect you have for me. I know you will all do your best to welcome her with open arms," he turned to Elizabeth and nodded.

Elizabeth curtsied and said, "I look forward to getting to know you as I serve as your Mistress," she stopped and gave them all a warm smile. They all applauded.

Darcy then said, "Well, I believe that Mrs. Darcy and I are quite tired from our trip. If you will all excuse us," he said as he turned to Mrs. Reynolds. "Mrs. Reynolds, will you see that someone brings hot water to our chambers at around six o'clock. We will come down to dinner at seven," and with that he picked up his new bride in his arms, and carried her into the house, grinning as he did so.

The work force of Pemberley, in unison, dropped their jaws in shock. Not only had they very rarely seen him smile, they would never have imagined their very sombre Master to act in such a frivolous manner. *Yes, Mrs. Darcy was going to bring Pemberley back to life. Yes, indeed!* They all thought!

Mrs. Reynolds looked to her husband and said, "Well, I believe we may see children within these halls before too long!" They both laughed.

Elizabeth protested, slightly, as William was carrying her through the entryway. "William, what will they think of me to be carried off in such a manner?" but she giggled a little as she said it.

Darcy began to climb the stairs with her in his arms. "They will think that the Master is besotted with his new bride."

"William, do you not want to give me a tour of my new home?" Elizabeth asked as he finished climbing the stairs.

"There is only one room I want to give you a tour of presently, Mrs. Darcy," Darcy said as he stopped, and kissed her hard but quickly in the hall.

Elizabeth laughed, "So you are taking me to the library?"

He rounded the corner toward the family apartments as he said, "I am most certainly *not* taking you to the library, love. I have fantasized about having my new bride in *my bedchamber* for way too long. I find that it is imperative that the tour of your new home begin in the Master's chambers."

Darcy stopped in front of his door, opened it with one hand, entered his chambers and put her on the floor, quickly locked the door, pressed her up against the wall, and kissed her hungrily.

Elizabeth was just as stimulated. She grabbed eagerly at his bottom as he pressed into her womanhood. The neckline of her gown was quite low today and he easily lowered one side of her gown to reach her breast. With his other hand, he began slowly gathering up her skirts. They were both too aroused to disrobe.

Her hands moved around to unbutton his breeches. She reached in and pulled his manhood into her eager hands, stroking his length until he stopped her with his hand. "Oh God, Lizzy, please stop! I must be inside of you now." He moved up her skirts and hooked one of her legs over his arm.

The look of hunger in his eyes was more intense than she had ever seen it before. He paused just long enough to lock with her eyes and then move to her mouth, which was slightly open in anticipation of his passion. Darcy pressed forward. His tongue and his manhood entered her at the same instant, the deep thrusting of his tongue wrestling in an intense struggle with her own. Elizabeth pressed against him, as he plunged into her depths.

She felt like he was impaling her into the wall. His mouth began to whisper sensual, intensely sexual words into her ear. "Oh, God Lizzy, you are so warm and so wet. To feel myself buried in your depths, I may never again return to the surface." He moved his hands down to her bottom and pulled her toward him. "Oh, how I have longed to escape into you. Do you like to feel me deep within you? What do you want, Elizabeth?"

"Oh God, William, do not stop, please do not stop!"

"Tell me. Tell me what you want," he trailed the back of his fingers down her chest, slightly teasing her ripe nipple with his fingertips. And he pressed once into her and back out, stopping again.

"Please, Will, Please I need you. I need you in me now!"

"Does wanting me make you feel wanton, Mrs. Darcy?" and he plunged forward forcefully and withdrew slowly, stopping yet again.

"If you want... if you want me to be wanton, I am wanton, Will. Please just fill me again. Please, please," and she pressed herself against him, but he resisted.

"No, no, you have not sufficiently shown me that you truly want me," he said as he again drove deep into her, stopping inside her this time.

"Do you like that, Lizzy? Do you like feeling me deep inside you? Do you want me hard and fast, wife? Beg me, beg me to take you!" Darcy commanded.

"Oh God, Will, take me. Plunge into me, deep within me," tears were escaping from the corners of her eyes as she begged him to fulfill her.

Darcy began to move swifter and harder, as he lifted her up all the way off the floor, wrapping her legs around his waist and pressed her flush against the wall and his manhood pressed again and again into her lush recesses as he kissed her intensely. Their bodies moving in time with each other, he kept his rhythm as they reached their pleasure together.

Darcy collapsed against her just a moment. Somehow they gathered themselves together enough to finish disrobing and he carried her to his bed and pulled her under the covers with him. He was stunned. He had never imagined doing anything that wild with his bride, his Lizzy. He was not sure what to think of himself, much less what Elizabeth might have thought of him, to have taken her in such a way. His thoughts were a jumble, but he reflected for a moment on what she might be feeling and knew that he simply must say something to her. He pulled her head up to look him in the eyes, his eyes questioning her. She blushed and hid her head.

"Oh Lizzy, I am sorry, my love. I had no idea I could become such a beast. Please say something to me," he quietly begged her.

Elizabeth did not look at him, but she whispered into his chest. "Oh, William, are you ashamed of me? To think I have acted the part of such a wanton wench. I... I... simply had no idea I could ever say such things. I have acted no better than a common harlot."

"Oh God, Elizabeth, I am so sorry that I have done something to make you doubt yourself. You are all I could ever want in a wife, in a mistress, and a lover. You are everything I could ever want and more. You have nothing, nothing to be ashamed of. It is I who pushed you to act in such a way. I behaved like a common rake. I should have known better. Are you all right? Please, please tell me," he tried again to get her to look at him.

She whispered into his chest again, "I am more than all right, that is the problem, I fear." She tentatively lifted up her head to look at him. "You are not ashamed of me, William? You are not upset with your wench of a wife," the corners of her mouth just slightly curled upwards, as she was hopeful that he had been pleased and not ashamed.

"If you are a wench then I am a rake. We are quite a pair, Mrs. Darcy," he said as he smiled. "You are not upset with me for taking you in such a way, Lizzy?"

Elizabeth spoke quietly but sincerely, "I would not always want it to be so, William, but I have to admit that I found it quite thrilling. Is this something that you learned from the courtesan, William?"

"Good God, no, Lizzy. *You* are the only one that inspires such fantasizes in me, my love," Darcy said as he rubbed her lips, realizing that they were red and swollen from his fierce kisses.

"You have had fantasies of me?"

Darcy chuckled, "We just fulfilled one of them, I believe. But it was never that intense in my fantasy. You are so much more than my most fanciful whimsy!"

"Will you tell me more of your fantasies, William?" she asked with some curiosity.

"No, my curious cat, but I promise to show you them from time to time. Will that be all right with you? I would not want to dishonour you in any way. But there are some fantasies I would hope to have come true with time."

"Can you tell me any in particular, William?"

"I will only tell you that if I ever call you Miss Bennet, you will know that I intend to fulfill one. Would that be agreeable to you?"

"You had fantasies of me before we were married?" Elizabeth innocently questioned.

"Lizzy, I believe I began having fantasies of you even before you came to Netherfield to stay with your sister. But from that first night on, you visited me in daydreams, taking me into flights of imagination I had never experienced before."

Elizabeth reached up and kissed him lightly. "And this, today, was a fantasy you had of us?" She raised her eyebrow and cocked her head to the side, smiling at him.

"Oh, yes, indeed, along with this," Darcy said. He rolled her over underneath him, as he proceeded to fulfill yet another fantasy, welcoming her to his bed.

~~*~*~*

Tom Bennet sat in his library, absently flipping through the latest paper. He had gotten a short message from his son-in-law when Darcy and Elizabeth left Stoke to return to Pemberley, and was thinking that they were due to arrive at Pemberley that very day.

Tom had some very nice memories of Pemberley, but his *last* memory was not a pleasant one. He had eavesdropped on a conversation between Anne Darcy and her sister Lady Catherine de Bourgh. The conversation had pierced and broken his heart. He thought back to that day, long ago.

~~*~*~*

1790

Tom Bennet was in the library at Pemberley several days prior to Easter. He was looking at some of the rare books, in the back corner when he heard two female voices enter.

"Anne, you simply must do something about George's insistence in maintaining a friendship with that man and his chit of a wife", Catherine said.

"Catty, you know I do not have a say in George's affairs. He keeps them to himself. I have no say in whom he has as a friend and whom he does not. We have known Tom Bennet for many, many years. I met him myself when he spent the summer holidays at Matlock. I can say nothing to George. You know that," Anne responded.

Catherine said, "Anne, you must see, surely you must see that their connections are so far below you. They can do nothing but harm you. For Tom Bennet to continue to openly serve as godfather to Fitzwilliam is bound to lower the opinion of the *ton.* To have a man of no connections and little wealth connected to this family is unsupportable. I will not have it."

Anne spoke, "Catty, this is not up to you. Honestly, it is not up to me either. George chose Tom as Fitzwilliam's godfather. I cannot go against his wishes. He has been a most devoted godfather, as well. In fact, he has been more a part of his godson's life than even Edward has been."

"That is precisely my point, Anne. He may have been a better choice until he chose that woman born into trade. Why she is the silliest chit I have ever known! Surely you see how Mr. Bennet's connection to that woman has made it imperative for you to cut your connection with him and his kind. It will do you all irreparable harm. Do you not see that? George is a fool not to see it himself," Catherine said.

Anne responded, "Well, I will say Tom's choice of wife has definitely lowered him in my esteem. I cannot see what would have caused him to choose that woman! In that you are right. There must have been something about her arts and allurements that captured him. I always thought him to have better taste. You know, at one time I thought he was going to ask if he could court me? Instead to settle on that... that... ridiculous woman, well I do not understand it."

From back in the corner, hidden from view, Tom felt like Anne had stabbed him with a knife. Pain began deep in his soul.

"Well, you see what I am saying then. Maybe if you, Anne, told

Tom he is harming Fitzwilliam by associating with your family, he would chose to cut off the association himself. You say that he once saw something in you, but I imagine even then he realized he was so below you, that he could never reach beyond his realm to consider a match with someone from such noble connections as you, dear sister!" Catherine exclaimed.

"Well, I know George will never choose to let go of his best friend, so better that I not even contemplate such a thing. Do you really think the Darcys associating with the Bennets will harm Fitzwilliam, Catty? Do you really think that?" Anne asked with concern.

"It will, and it most likely already has. He is a gentleman. That is for sure, but what of the wife? She has no ability to censure her thoughts and behaviour. Her manners are absolutely shocking. Pemberley should not be associated with such a woman," Catherine said with force.

Anne thought and said, "Yes, Catty, I have to agree with you. Tom was a fool to marry her. I will never understand it. But I do not know what can be done. I cannot ask him to leave us be. But I cannot allow him to harm my family with his low connections."

In the back corner of the room, Tom Bennet's began to cry heart-wrenching, silent tears. Anne, *his Anne* wanted him gone, was ashamed of him. She wanted to find a way to rid him from her life, saw him as a fool. He wanted to die.

~~*~*~*

Tom Bennet sat at his desk and cried. He cried bitter tears, sobs of a life lost, of a day gone by. He remembered the pain with which he made the decision to leave Pemberley forever. To let his best friend, his only love, and his godson live in peace; away from the influence of himself and his wife.

Oh, God, what pain he had endured all these years! To love them enough to let them go! To know in the depths of his soul that the only woman he had ever loved had wanted him away! She had wanted to rid him from her life; was ashamed of him all because of his choice of a wife. He made the decision for the Darcys. But he also made the decision for himself because it was too painful, too raw, too soul-wrenching to ever have sight of Anne Darcy again.

He had written to George, and told him it was better for Fitzwilliam that he had to cut off contact. In all honesty, it had also been for himself.

Something began to dawn on Tom Bennet. It began to come into the light of day, surfacing from within the pain. He had blamed Fanny all these years for losing his best friend, godson, and true love. He had never forgiven her. It had driven a wedge between them that had never lifted. He knew he was wrong to place the blame on Fanny. He was now able to see Anne Darcy for what she was, and how she chose to judge him.

When they came to Pemberley that Easter season, he had light and hope. He had his young Jane, and his wife had found out she was pregnant with his Lizzy while at Pemberley that season.

But a piece of Tom Bennet's soul had died that day. He sobbed heart-wrenching, regretful tears. Tears that had never come again since that day. He cried for George, for the best friend that he had walked away from. He cried for Anne, an unrequited love, a love never returned, a love of a long-departed soul. He cried for himself, for the man that had died at Pemberley, and the friend he had left behind so long ago. He cried for the lost years with his godson. Yet, it was thoughts of Fitzwilliam that began to lift him out of the depths of his sorrow. He thought of the years of happiness lost with his wife. He had foolishly closed himself off to her because she was not Anne. It was time to set things right. Fanny had already changed in the short time since he had let her know they had no financial problems.

Why had he *ever* kept that information from her? It was time to make a new start. Perhaps, returning to Pemberley for the holidays would allow him the opportunity to face the demons of the past. It was time to let go.

Chapter 22

It had been several days since the Darcys arrived at Pemberley, and Elizabeth was attempting to learn her new duties as Mistress. She sat in her newly refurbished study. William had commissioned Lady Anne's former study to be done in Elizabeth's favourite colours. She knew she could redo it in anyway she wished, but she loved it just the way William had planned it for her.

Mrs. Reynolds had given her the grand tour of the house. She loved the library, and had particularly enjoyed viewing the galleries. The music room, she could tell, would be a favourite. But she was actually embarrassed when Mrs. Reynolds had asked her how she had liked her new chambers. She had spent very little time in them, only passing through only on her way to her dressing chamber, either before she retired each night or as she dressed each morning.

William had told her he had work to do today. He needed to catch up on matters of business that had been neglected during their courtship and honeymoon. But in truth, Elizabeth knew they would not have gotten very far in their tour had he been her guide. They would have been *distracted* in one room or another. She smiled at their increasing intimacy.

She and Mrs. Reynolds had talked about menus for the large family gathering due to arrive in a few days for Christmas. Elizabeth utilized her expertise, having previously noted what each member of Darcy's family preferred. They discussed a plan for which chambers would hold which guests, as well as decorations. It was decided that the staff would decorate the majority of the rooms with greenery. They would find a Christmas tree, as Elizabeth had read about the new tradition many were using for holiday decorations, and they would use Lady Anne's decorations to decorate the tree after the family arrived.

Looking through her correspondence, Lizzy found a letter from Jane and quickly opened it:

~~*~*~*

Longbourn, 15 December 1811

Dearest Lizzy:

Can anyone be as happy as I? It will not be long before I hear dearly beloved myself, dear sister. I need assistance with coming back to earth!

You must have come to the conclusion by now that Papa has given my dear Charles his blessing on our union. If there is a better man, I do not know whom! Oh, I know you most likely believe your William exceeds him in essentials. But, then we both have our preferences, do we not dear sister!

You may believe we have kept to perfect chastity, but I will not lie to you, dear sister. Once I convinced Charles to engage in a few stolen kisses, I found my expectations of what we bear in a marriage as women is not what I had once feared. I find I cannot wait till I am wed! Oh, I do believe our determination to wait until we are wed will stay in place. But it was bliss to experience the ecstasy of our first kiss. You may be shocked at me, if you dare!

We have planned our wedding for April. I will not complain. But with the fate and free will of Caroline and Mr. Elton's recent scandalous marriage, as well as the loose lips of Meryton's gossips, Charles feels the only way for us to reclaim some of his family's reputation is to wait a proper period time before we wed.

I should tell you of Caroline's wedding. Of all the indignities I had expected to experience, it was not as bad as I had originally considered it would be. Of course, her deception and plan to ruin your hopes came to naught but her own consequences. Perhaps it is never too late for love in her case. She seems quite happy with her lot in life. I have worked to keep an endeavour at civility between us, particularly during the brief period before her wedding. After all, she might not be the sister I always wanted; but nevertheless, she is to be my sister.

She wore an orange wedding gown, as we suspected she would, and had managed to obtain a beautiful piece of French lace she had dyed to match her dress—yes, it was orange as well.

Only Caroline insisted that her betrothed matched her in sense and sensibility, as he wore an orange vest under his hunter green formal waistcoat. Not every gentleman would care enough for his bride's opinion to wear such a thing, but he appears happy she is to be the companion of his future life.

Well my mother is calling me to attend her guests. I remain your beloved sister,

Jane

~~*~*~*

Lizzy continued to review her correspondence. Mary wrote that she had completed her book and had sent it to Lady Jane, who would carry it to the publisher. Kitty and Lydia wrote of their anticipation of the start of school after the holidays. Her mother and father appeared to be pretty much the same.

Putting her correspondence aside, Elizabeth decided she had accomplished all she must for the day, and walked to the library to peruse the shelves for something to read.

As she was looking over the stacks, she heard steps behind her and a deep voice behind her saying, "Miss Bennet it appears that your ankle has healed."

Hmmm, Elizabeth smiled, *so we are role-playing*. She turned around to face William. "Ah Mr. Darcy, sir, I am quite sorry. You see, I must admit to being dishonest with you, sir. I was trying to escape, to get away from you. I am afraid that I misunderstood your character. I am quite sorry, Mr. Darcy. Do you think you might forgive me?"

"No indeed madam, I do not believe I can forgive you so easily, Miss Bennet." Darcy approached her as she was backed up against the stacks. "It was most cruel of you to lie to me in such a blatant and imprudent manner. I do not think I will be able to forgive you so easily, Miss Bennet."

"I beg you for your forgiveness, Mr. Darcy. I am very, very sorry. Is there anything that I can do to show you the sincerity of my desire to make amends, sir?"

"I am unsure at this time, Miss Bennet. But at this point I find you have been most naughty. I fear there may be a need for some form of punishment," Darcy said as Elizabeth saw his piercing ebony pools stare deeply into her eyes. If she had not known they were role-playing, she would have been quite sure he was severely angry with her.

"Mr. Darcy, sir, I humbly beg for your forgiveness. Truly, I regret my impertinent and dishonest manner of escape. I am also sure that I do merit chastisement." Elizabeth looked up into his eyes, as he pressed her against the bookshelf.

"Yes, Miss Bennet. I do believe you deserve punishment, indeed. And you will receive it." Darcy paused, ran the back of his hand down her cheek, and stopped at her mouth to run a finger along her lips. Elizabeth reached out to bite his finger.

"Miss Bennet, this will simply *not* do. It is most improper for you to attempt to bite me when you are supposed to be begging forgiveness. I find there is nothing else to do but to begin your instruction," and with that, Darcy put her over his shoulder and moved with her to the couch near the fireplace. He sat down and put her over his lap face down.

"Miss Bennet, you do believe that you deserve my censure and punishment, do you not?" Darcy said as he caressed her round buttocks through her skirt.

Elizabeth was wiggling and attempting to escape. "Mr. Darcy, this is highly improper, unhand me, sir."

Darcy began to lift up her skirts until they were all above her waist, and he returned to caressing her bottom, "I fear, Miss Bennet you are long past the point of escaping your spanking. You will be disciplined, and most severely, I fear," he said began to caress her naked bottom.

"Mr. Darcy, you cannot mean to... you do not intend to..." Elizabeth squirmed in his lap.

He leaned down and whispered in her ear, "Oh, but I most assuredly do intend to," and as he said that he lifted his hand, and swatted her bare cheek.

"You have been quite impertinent with me, Miss Bennet," and he swatted her opposite cheek.

"You have lied to me more than once," and he smacked her on one cheek and then the other, just hard enough to sting a little, but not enough to hurt her.

"Mr. Darcy, please, please, I am sorry! Please, please forgive me!" Elizabeth squirmed yet again, and Darcy's manhood sprang to life beneath her.

"Then there have been all those times when you impudently teased me in front of company," and he lightly smacked both cheeks yet again, and then rubbed them. Darcy was becoming quite aroused.

"And of course, there were all those times when you deemed to show me your erect nipples through your gown," and he swatted and rubbed each cheek yet again.

Elizabeth continued to wiggle against him increasing the strength of his erection. Her breath was becoming faster, and her arousal at his spanking excited and surprised her. "Mr. Darcy, might I do something else to make this up to you. I can feel your manhood pressing against me. Cannot I see to your relief?"

"That truly deserves a spanking, for that is an extremely naughty offer, Miss Bennet," and he spanked her once more on each cheek and then rubbed her bottom. One cheek and then the other, getting closer and closer to her womanhood with each pass, until he inserted one of his fingers into her folds as he rubbed her buttocks.

"So, Miss Bennet, you think you will work off your penance by assisting me in finding my pleasure? Well we will see if you are able to bring me release, and then I will decide whether to grant you my forgiveness," he moved her onto her knees with her body facing over the back of the couch. He moved to his knees, and began to caress her folds with his tongue and fingers from behind. When he was sure she was every bit as aroused as he, he rose to his feet.

Elizabeth was a bit startled by this position, but quite aroused. She continued to be amazed by William's creativity, and his spontaneity. Such variety! Never would she have imagined he could find such a variety of ways in which to take her, and with that her thoughts left her, as he impaled her from behind with his length.

She leaned forward over the couch, pressed her backside more into his body as he plunged forward over and over into her. Darcy's hands were on each side of her hips and after just a few strokes he brought one hand around to caress her hard nub as the other spanked her cheek. As he moved, Darcy's moans were louder than she had ever heard before, and this position allowed him greater depth and more range of motion. She felt him slide in and out again and again as he caressed her. Finally, the tightness broke free to bring her own release with Darcy following quickly behind her. He collapsed forward onto her, but not wanting to harm her, pulled her back to sit on top of him on the chair behind them. Still inside her as he began to soften, he lightly caressed her breasts through her gown and said, "I find that you have truly gained my forgiveness."

Then his voice softened to that of her husband, "But have I gained yours, my love? My Luscious Lizzy, I love you so."

Elizabeth pulled her head back to rest under his neck and reached up to kiss his chin. "I am quite well, William. I think you could have been quite an actor on Drury Lane should you have chosen it, my love."

"I have not yet shocked you beyond your ability to accept my lovemaking, have I?"

"Well, I never imagined that you would take me in the same manner that my horse mates. But we have already discovered that you are not at all like my horse," Elizabeth giggled.

"If I ever go too far will you stop me, my love? I would never wish to harm you. You know that do you not?" Darcy asked her quite seriously.

"I do know that, William. But I find I must ask you a question?" she said as she played with the messy curls of his hair.

"I am listening, my Lizzy," Darcy said.

"You told me several days ago that you had numerous fantasies about me before we married, and you warned me you might decide to role play one of them. That should you ever call me Miss Bennet I would know you were playing out a fantasy. But, William, did you truly think of this when we were in the library at Netherfield? I fear I am quite shocked you would have wished to do something like what we have just done, then. Did you want to spank me then, William?" Elizabeth questioned.

"Oh, Good God, Lizzy. How do I explain this to you?" He said as he pulled her to rest against his shoulder. "I could not have possibly imagined all of this in the library in those short minutes we were there. Although, I did think that I should punish you for your white lie. But no, such were not my thoughts at the time. Later however, when I returned to my chambers, I will admit I thought of what might have happened if that scene had played out differently. I will admit to you, as I told you I would never lie to you, that I have imagined quite a number of variations on what we just did over the past few weeks." He lifted her head to look into his eyes, and to see if she was shocked.

"Lord, William, I should be quite shocked to hear you admit such. But you are so creative, of course, you have thought through some of the fantasies we have staged. That actually makes sense to me. I could not imagine that you just impulsively came up with this recent scene we have enacted," she said as she giggled and kissed him lightly.

"Well, I do perhaps ad lib a little bit, depending on your reactions and what you say," he kissed her nose.

Lizzy looked down at his chest a bit embarrassed to admit to what she wanted to say. "Well, I admit to having a couple fantasies of my own."

"Truly? Before we were married? Or since then?" William was curious indeed. "Will you tell me about these fantasies, my Lizzy, so I can help make them come true?"

"No, my love! But when you least expect it, I will show you," Elizabeth said and kissed him lightly. Then she turned to face him and kissed him deeply. "I love you, William."

~~*~*~*

Over the next couple days, the Darcys enjoyed their solitude as they attended to business matters and preparations for the holiday. Elizabeth had sent an express to the Gardiners with a request to obtain something special for William for the holiday. William had already obtained Elizabeth's gifts while in London. They were content with each other, and continued to enjoy their growing adventurous intimacy.

The twenty-second of December soon arrived, and their family began to arrive at Pemberley. Lord and Lady Matlock came with Georgiana and Richard. The Bennet party included two carriages. One included Mrs. Bennet, along with Mary, Kitty and Lydia. The other carriage included Mr. Bennet, along with Jane and Bingley. The Gardiners were due the next day, as they had decided to spend a night with Mrs. Gardiner's family in Lambton.

The new Mr. and Mrs. Darcy were at the front entrance awaiting each of the carriages as they arrived. Her sister Lydia was the most inappropriate, but at least she was enthusiastic.

"Lord, Lizzy, I mean *Mrs. Darcy;* oh, how nice that sounds! What a mansion you have managed to get for yourself. You are so rich now, I imagine you will forget about your poor relations," she said as she giggled quite loudly. "So have you managed to plan a ball for us, so we can dance with all of Mr. Darcy's rich friends?" she asked as she hugged her sister.

Elizabeth glanced at William to see how he handled her sister's embarrassing behaviour. He responded, "Why, Miss Lydia, I know you are not yet *out*. But we will make sure to allow some time for you to dance over the holiday, should you chose it."

Lizzy greeted all of her relations with joy. As she reached her father he said, "Well, Lizzy, how do you like Pemberley? Are you enjoying your new home? I declare that now that you have left Longbourn, it is difficult for me to have five minutes of sensible conversation each day."

"Oh, Papa, I find I like Pemberley very well indeed. But I am happy to see my family."

Mrs. Reynolds had a team of servants at the ready, to assist each guest with their trunks and get them to their assigned chambers. She had the precision of a drill sergeant, but the pose and kindness of a hostess at a fine Modesto. All the guests were to settle in and rest before dinner.

If any had noticed, Mrs. Bennet had not spoken a word other than, "Good to see you, my dear, Mr. Darcy," as she greeted them. She was as silent as perhaps she had ever been.

~~*~*~*

Fanny Bennet remembered the last time she had arrived at Pemberley. She had been shocked by the size and the elegance of the estate. Tom had told her of his time there with the Darcys, and of his long friendship with George Darcy. But she had not realized the enormity of what George's friendship had brought to her husband.

She had not imagined that Tom was a friend of such a man. So fine an estate! And he had such a lovely wife. Why she was a Lady, the daughter of the Earl of Matlock.

Fanny had not held in her exclamations on that first visit. When she heard her youngest's appallingly inappropriate exclamations upon arriving today, Fanny was mortified to remember that her words were not any more prudent on that first visit.

It was not that Fanny had not been raised to act as a lady. She was the daughter of a tradesman, but her father had been very successful. He saw to it that his family had the best he could afford in the way of education and clothing. She had truly wanted for nothing at the time.

Through his friends, her father had managed to get her invitations to many of the finest balls in all of England. She had enjoyed an unofficial season in London, though because she came from trade, she had not the connections to be presented at court. Though most had not known that.

In fact, Tom Bennet had not known when first he met her. She remembered the first time she saw him. He was quite handsome, and he had the warmest smile and the most expressive eyes she had ever seen. He had asked her to dance, and the first time their hands had touched; well, it was as if she had fallen in love at first sight.

Fanny Gardiner had not always been a silly creature. She believed he had seen in her a lively, intelligent companion. They had shared their love of books and music, and enjoyed observing the folly of others.

But today, as she sat in a chamber at Pemberley—thinking of their history and the effect that this place, this house, this family had had on her family— tears began to fall from her eyes. He had never loved her. She knew that. She had not wanted to accept it, but she knew it to be true.

She remembered that fateful day they had arrived here at Pemberley. She had seen his eyes when they took in the presence of Lady Anne. Maybe Tom did not know she had seen it, but she had. She had known he was in love with Lady Anne, a deep unrequited love that left him bereft of the ability to love another.

Fanny had tried to act the part of a lady while at Pemberley. But she had been so desperate to gain Tom's attention, she had acted the part of a silly schoolgirl. Instead of capturing his attention, she believed she had finally lost it forever when they were in this house.

Fanny's tears changed from silent to deep sobs. She remembered that day well. She had seen Tom go into the library, and had decided to wait just long enough for him to settle in with a good book before joining him. She had hoped for a private intimate moment with her husband there.

Before she could enter, she saw Lady Anne and Lady Catherine enter the library. Lord, how she wished she could have remained ignorant of what she had heard. She had moved quietly to the door that had been slightly ajar, and had listened to a conversation that had broken her spirit, perhaps forever.

She remembered that conversation. How Lady Anne and Lady Catherine had criticized her. They discussed how below them she was. How she had lowered Tom in their eyes, and how the association with the Bennets would forever damage Tom's godson if something were not done.

She knew her husband was in the room, hidden behind a bookshelf most likely. Hearing what she heard, she knew how it would affect him. She learned that Anne, too, thought him once in love with her and had thought he might ask to court her.

A pain as sharp and piercing as a knife slashed into her heart. She was ashamed. She was heartbroken. Part of her died that day. She had slipped from the door, and returned to her chambers and cried for her loss. Cried for the love that she would never have, that Anne would have instead. Cried for the pain she had caused to her husband, by connecting himself to her.

A tear fell onto her hand, today, she cried for all those things yet again. She felt more alone than perhaps she had ever felt in her entire life, here at Pemberley. She had contemplated that coming here might be difficult. But never imagined that this soul-wrenching pain would collapse upon her spirit so completely.

She also cried when she considered the silly, hardened creature she had become. In order to protect herself from her husband, and not feel the pain of knowing he did not love her, she had created the *'silly, nervous, fluttering, Mrs. Bennet'* her family now thought her to be. But that was not Fanny at all. Fanny was a woman who deeply loved a man that did not love her.

Chapter 23

Tom Bennet rose with the dawn and looked out the window of his chamber at Pemberley. God, he was back here! He never imagined what it would be like to return. How unbelievable it was to realize that his daughter, his Lizzy, had replaced Anne as Mistress of this place. When he remembered the pain he had felt for so long, it seemed like vindication that Lizzy was Mistress of Pemberley. Tom Bennet and his low connections, not good enough for Anne, had been a part of creating the new Mistress. He smiled as he thought of it.

The early morning light filtered into the chamber, and he turned around to look at the room. He believed it was the same chamber he had occupied all those years ago. His daughter would not have known it, so it must have been Mrs. Reynolds who remembered.

Tom saw a book lying on the small desk near the window. He had not noticed it the night before. Looking at it closer it was a copy of Much Ado about Nothing. It was extraordinary as he looked at it, as it looked like a copy he had many years ago, a first edition.

He absently picked up the book and noticed a note placed into the front flap, which read,

We found this in the Mistress' chambers when we were preparing it for your daughter, Mr. Bennet. It appears that this book belongs to you. Perhaps, Lady Anne borrowed it from her husband many years ago, and forgot it was in her dresser. We thought you would like to have it back.

It was his book. He sat down and stared at it. *Why did Anne have this book in her chambers?* He had given it to her the spring before she met George. Tom had completely forgotten he had given it to her. He opened the front cover and there was his name on his bookplate.

Flushed and somewhat apprehensive, he felt his heart began to race. Anne had kept his book, kept it all these years, and kept it in her chambers. *Good God!*.

Tom began to absently flip through the book, studying it at length. He noticed there was another blank bookplate in the back of the book. He had not put it there, as he would have remembered. As he felt along it, he noticed that it felt thicker than the one on the front, and his curiosity could not be contained, He pried up the edges of the bookplate until a piece of paper feel out into his hand. It said simply, **T. B.**

Could this letter be from Anne? Tom looked around the room to see if anyone were watching him. Realizing how silly that was, his hands began to shake. What would have happened if it had been his daughter who had found his book, with a letter to him, in the dresser of her husband's mother?

Thomas began to rub his hands through his hair nervously. Then he picked up the paper again. Could he open it? What did it say? Would it destroy his life forever? Would it reconcile him with his past?

Dare he open it? Maybe it would be better just to burn it. *Yes, perhaps it is better not to feel the pain of whatever this might say.* He did not need any more pain. He just wanted to live out the end of his life.

But at the same time, Tom Bennet knew he was not really living his life anymore. He had been dead for so long that perhaps there was something in this letter, or whatever it was, that would allow him to move on.

The conflict was there. But could he destroy something that might have to do with him and his life? He knew he could not leave this as an unknown. He would always regret it.

So, he said a prayer, and with all the courage he could muster he opened the folded paper and began to read:

~~*~*~*

Tom,

I write this letter to you, knowing I will most likely never post it. But hoping that in writing it, I will find peace.

What do I say? I picked up this book, your book, from the library the day you left Pemberley—never to return. I had placed it there, as I did not want George to wonder at my having it. But when I heard that you had left Pemberley without saying goodbye, I knew something was horribly wrong. I found myself picking up this book. The name is ironic, as I know the reason you left was *NOT* much ado about nothing. I know it in my heart now.

As much as I fear it, I believe you must have heard a conversation I had that day with Catherine.

Tom, you must know that I have allowed myself to be guided by my family, particularly Catherine, for the majority of my life. At some point, I just stopped arguing with her. I found it easier to just agree with her.

If you heard our conversation, you *MUST* know—I need you to know— that I did not mean to agree with her. It was a white lie designed to stop her meddling. You have been the best godfather Fitzwilliam could have ever known. He loves you. He cherishes your fun, warm spirit.

You are George's best friend and have stood by him through thick and thin, through the death of his parents, as well as my own. You were here for him through the last trimester of my difficult pregnancy. I know he feared for my life, yet you were a great comfort to him.

You are his brother, Tom. You truly are. He loves you that much. He has not been the same since you left. Even worse, since you sent him a letter he has refused to let me read.

Catherine was wrong, Tom. You must know that. You must know I do not believe you could ever be a bad influence on Fitzwilliam.

You must also know that I know of your feelings. You have attempted to mask them, and you did it quite well. But I have known since that spring at Matlock of your regard for me. I want you to know I thought I was beginning to fall in love with you that Summer. That memory has been encased in this book for me. My family insisted I marry for wealth and connections. I chose to follow their directions and turned you away. I did not give you encouragement, and I let you believe I did not regard you.

There are times I wonder what it would have been like if we had been together, Tom. But you would never have been happy in my family. They would have changed you. They would have forced you into the *ton* and into the society of which you hate. Your joyful spirit, your wit, and even your intelligence would have faded away until it died. I would not have been good for you. You chose a wife with liveliness and humour. Yes, she is at times a little too lively, but I truly like her. You need to allow yourself to be happy with her, Tom.

Let go of the past. Know that your best friend, George, misses you. And, if I should happen to be able to make myself send this letter, or if you should ever happen to come upon it, know that I miss you as well. It is certain that Fitzwilliam misses his godfather.

Who knows, maybe yours and George's wish will come true someday, and one of your daughters will marry Fitzwilliam. It is possible.

Please forgive me, Tom. For hurting you, and for not having the courage to let you know how wrong I truly was.

Yours, etc.,
A.D.

~~*~*~*

Tom was in shock. He read the letter a second time, and then a third. He tried to take everything in, and understand all that was written in this letter. He fought back the tears that began to well up in his eyes.

Anne never meant for him to read this. He did not know when she wrote it. If it was in the weeks after he left Pemberley, or even months or years later.

She had cared for him. She was not ashamed of him. She wanted him to move on. Could he allow himself to do that? He knew not.

He spent the remainder of the day in deep thought. Wandering about the garden paths, remembering happier times here at Pemberley, and beginning to contemplate what his life could be if he allowed himself to move on.

~~*~*~*

The house party met later for a grand dinner. Fitzwilliam sat on one side of the formal dinner table, Elizabeth on the other. Both gazed across the table at the other and smiled. It was the first time they would not be able to hold hands as they ate.

The Gardiners had joined them earlier in the day, so the party was now complete. Mr. Bingley and Jane sat to one side of Lizzy, and on the other were her aunt and uncle. Lizzy addressed Mr. Bingley, "Mr. Bingley, how is your family. Are the Hurst's celebrating the holiday in town?"

Bingley said, "Randolph and Louisa are actually celebrating a second honeymoon of sorts. They travelled to Bath for the holidays, and are enjoying some time alone."

Elizabeth thought to herself that they were probably glad to be away from

Caroline, but knew she could not voice such a thing. "And Mrs. Elton?"

Jane's head moved up to listen, as she had not mentioned Mr. Bingley's sister and her recent wedding directly. "Mr. and Mrs. Elton returned to Highbury after their wedding. My sister writes that she is quite the toast of the town. She has met a lady with whom she would like to make a special acquaintance. Miss Emma Woodhouse is engaged to a gentleman that knows Darcy, a Mr. Knightley."

"Why, yes, Mr. Bingley. Mr. Darcy mentioned he had known Mr. Knightley quite well. In fact we are currently planning to attend the wedding. So, Mrs. Elton sounds as if she is happy in her new situation?" Elizabeth questioned.

Bingley spoke in a whisper, "Mrs. Darcy, you need not be so polite. I know you are familiar with what my sister attempted to do to disrupt your wedding. You need not make small talk about my family to be polite. I am appalled, still, at her lack of decorum. I hope she is happy in her new life. But needless to say, she has drawn her own lot."

"Well, I hope the Eltons have a lovely holiday, none the less. And I thank you for your kindness. So, you and Jane must tell me more of the plans for your wedding," and thus began a discussion of the wedding to come.

On the opposite end of the table, Darcy sat between Mr. and Mrs. Bennet and his aunt and uncle Fitzwilliam. Darcy, Tom and Edward led the conversation. Mrs. Bennet ventured to speak with Lady Amelia. "Lady Amelia, I believe you have spent the last days at Matlock. Am I correct in that, madam?"

"Why yes, Mrs. Bennet, we have spent some quiet time at our estate for a much needed respite before the holidays. But you must call me Amelia. We are family, you know. Edward and Tom are such good friends, it would not seem proper for us to not to be friends as well."

"Why I would be honoured, Amelia. And you must call me Fanny."

"I will do just that, Fanny. I have heard you are beginning preparations for the wedding of your oldest daughter. How exciting it must be to be in the midst of wedding planning. I remember assisting in small ways when Mark married. But as the mother of the groom, I did not get much say in the wedding arrangements. I wish I had daughters!" Amelia exclaimed.

"Well, I wish I had a son, Amelia, as I have had five daughters," she said as she looked to Darcy. "But with as fine of a son-in-law as Mr. Darcy, I now have a son in which to show my pride. I have so much of which to be grateful. And, of course, my daughter Jane is soon to marry Mr. Bingley. I am quite blessed."

Tom overheard the conversation his wife and Edward's were having, and was pleased for her decorum. Had he missed it? It seemed quite a long time since she had complained of her nerves. Did it only take removing her worry about her fate to affect this change? Maybe he should have told her long ago about his wealth. Had he ever been fair to his wife? Tom became introspective as he continued to reflect on the changes he noticed in Fanny.

In the middle of the table, the new siblings talked with each other.

Mary was speaking with Georgiana. "Miss Darcy, do you like to read? Have you read any good books lately?" They began to talk of books, and feel into a conversation about novels the two of them had both read. Kitty and Lydia were separated. Lydia was sitting next to her mother and father, and was quiet. Kitty sat between Mrs. Gardiner and her sister Mary.

Towards the end of the evening, Darcy announced, "My wife, the most beautiful and accomplished Mistress of Pemberley, Mrs. Darcy, suggested to me that we begin a new tradition. She has recently read of the decorating of pine trees as a custom that began in Germany. Some families here in England are beginning to adopt the practice. So we have a tree to be decorated in the parlour. After we have separated briefly, let us all meet there and decorate the tree as we enjoy some traditional music from our family musicians.

The rest of the evening, the families celebrated a coming together as a joint family. They decorated the tree. They sang Christmas hymns. They lit the Yule log, and rejoiced in a quiet spirit of holiday harmony. Elizabeth sang a special carol she had recently discovered from Italy.

DORMI, DORMI, O BEL BAMBIN (Traditional Italian)
Dormi, dormi, dormi, o bel bambino
Re divin, Re divin.
Fa la nanna, o fantolino,
Re divin, Re divin.
Fa la nanna, o fantolino.
Refrain:
Fa la la la, Fa la la la la, Fa la la la,
Fa la , Fa la, Fa la, Fa la.

Perchè piangi, o mio tesoro?
Dolce amor, dolce amor!
Fa la nanna, o caro figlio,
Tanto bel, tanto bel,
Fa la nanna, o caro figlio.
Refrain

[English Translation
SLEEP, O SLEEP, MY LOVELY

Sleep, o sleep, my lovely Child,
King divine, King divine.
Close your eyes and sleep my child, King divine, King divine.
Refrain:
Fa la la la, Fa la la la la, Fa la la la,
Fa la, Fa la, Fa la, Fa la.

O my treasure why are you weeping!
My Sweet love, sweet love,
Close your eyes my Son, my dear one.
So beautiful, so beautiful,
Close your eyes, my Son, my dear one.
Refrain]

Lizzy and William gazed at each other across the room, from time to time during the evening. They had spent a long day in company, and were longing for some quiet moments together. Lizzy, for her part, was quite tired from her responsibilities as hostess, and she longed to be with her husband. Darcy was anxious to join her, quietly hoping his uncle and her father would both wish to retire early, so he could join her in their chambers.

It had been such a busy day, that they both got their wish.

~~*~*~*

Darcy was reclining on the bed awaiting his wife, when she entered their chambers. She wore a red gown. Where she had gotten such a gown, he had no idea. But he was quite indebted to its creator, for it inspired a variety of innovative thoughts in his head.

Lizzy had other ideas in mind for this evening. This was to be the night she gave William his Christmas gift, hence her manner of dressing. She sauntered towards the bed and whispered, seductively, "O mio tresor, mio amor." (Translation: Oh, my treasure, my love.)

With these five words, William was immediately erect. His wife appeared to have planned something. He would lay back and enjoy.

"*Non so piu cosa son, cosa faccio (Translation: I no longer know what I am, what I am doing)," she approached the bed, a seductress in red. She arrived at the edge and reached out her hand to drag her fingers down William's face, stopping at his mouth to lightly run a finger along the crease.

William opened his mouth and tried to trap her finger between his teeth, but she was too quick for him. "Non, non, William," she said as she waved her finger at him, gazing into his startlingly dark eyes, pools of ebony. "Tonight is my night. My fantasy. La mia fantasia. I am an opera star you met after a production in a theatre on Drury Lane, Mr. Darcy."

"Oh, Contessa Bennetta, siete quanto più c'è di bello, mia cara," Darcy said as he joined her in her Italian fantasy. (Translation: Countess Bennet, you are all that is lovely, my dear.)

Elizabeth crawled up on the bed straddling him, William had already stripped down to his breeches. She brushed his chest with her nails, lightly and teasingly.

"*Solo ai nomi d'amor, di diletto, mi si turba, mis'altera il petto," Elizabeth said as she leaned down to kiss him hard on the mouth, her hands teasing his flat nipples into hardness. (Translation: Just the words "love" and "pleasure" disturb me, throw me into turmoil.)

She moved back to a sitting position still straddling him, just below his waist and teasingly slipped one side and then the other of her gown off of her shoulders until it pooled where the gown met his body, "*E a parlare mi sforza d'amore, un desio ch'io non posso spiegar." (Translation: And I am driven to speak about love, by a longing I can't explain.)

She rubbed her hands on her own breasts, moving his hands away when he tried to do it for her. "No, sig. Darcy! Sono stasera in carica!" (Translation: No, Mr. Darcy! I am in charge tonight!)

She moved down until she was slightly below his manhood, opened his breeches, and pulled his manhood into her hand and began to rub him, "*Parlo d'amor vegliando, parlo d'amor sognando." She pulled up her gown just enough to be able to move her moist opening, posing over him, teasing him as she rubbed her folds over his tip. (Translation: Waking, I talk about love; dreaming, I talk about love.)

"*Voi che sapete, che cosa e amor; Sento un affetto pien di desir," she impaled herself with his hardness as she sunk onto him, as Darcy groaned in rapturous response. (Translation: You, who know what love is like, I feel a tenderness, full of longing.)

Lizzy began to move on top of him, establishing a rhythm, riding her stallion. Beginning at a slow walk, "*L'alma avvampar, palpito e tremo." (Translation: My soul in flames. I shiver and tremble.)

Darcy found he could no longer lie passively; he put his hands on her hips to assist with her rhythm, and pumped his loins up and down meeting her in her increasing rhythm. Her stallion increased his gait to a trot, "*Dall'altro canto faremo l'amore." (Translation: On the other hand, I'll make love.)

Their pace increased quickly into a gallop, Darcy adding to her operatic overture, "O, il mio amore, il mio amore, come adore voi!" (Translation: O, my love, my love, how I adore you!")

Then words became decidedly unnecessary. Darcy was moving at a fast and rapid pace from below, and Lizzy was riding him from above. They thought of nothing but the other. Their voices of love became groans and moans of their increasing pleasure. Faster and faster they galloped. Closer and closer to the end of their journey, until Lizzy screamed, "Wwwwwwiiillllliiiaaammmm!" Closely following her Darcy reached his pleasure as well, as he pumped and pumped into her, gasping her name.

Outside in the hallway, a lone figure stood still, listening to the sounds of love. She had walked down the hall to the gallery and back, contemplating how to become the wife she would want to be. Never had she contemplated hearing what she now heard. She heard the groans and moans of her daughter and Mr. Darcy, as they found their pleasure together, screaming the others' name.

Mrs. Bennet returned to her chambers flushed and warm. *Oh, Lord,* how she wished for what her daughter had in her marriage!

*The majority of the Italian words in this scene are from The Marriage of Figaro and Don Giovanni, both by Wolfgang Amadeus Mozart, words can be found in the lyrics of the following arias from that Opera: Non piu andrai, Act II, Le Nozze de Figaro; Voi che sapete, Act II, Le Nozze de Figaro; Finch'han dal vino ("Champagne Aria; Don Giovanni, Act I)

Chapter 24

Fanny had arisen early, thinking of the evident felicity of her daughter Elizabeth's marriage. Mr. Darcy was obviously besotted with his wife. It was quite apparent he did not think badly of Lizzy because of her wanton (Fanny realized she had no other word to describe what she had heard the night before) behaviour with him in his bedroom. Elizabeth appeared to be greatly in love with her husband. It was quite obvious, by what she had heard, that Elizabeth was happy with Mr. Darcy's attentions—literally rejoicing loudly in her pleasure.

Mrs. Bennet was quite curious. She had never known that type of physical pleasure, had never considered women could feel such... joy... ecstasy. She began to contemplate whether she could find a way to speak to her second daughter about it. Dare she?

Fanny knew her long-established pattern of turning away her husband had become expected. Was her decision to turn him away partly to blame for the palpable distance between them? Was there a way to scale the wall she had so carefully built? Did she even want to attempt it?

After all, they were at Pemberley. It was here she learned what she had always suspected, that her husband loved another woman. It was here that their pain and their distance with each other grew to severe proportions. Fanny had not completely denied Tom her bed until a number of years later.

Fanny had discovered she was pregnant with her second daughter during that fateful trip to Pemberley. Her resentment of her daughter settled in even before her birth. Mr. Bennet had seemed to delight in the idea of another child, while avoiding his wife as much as possible. Fanny knew he had chosen to blame her for his self-imposed banishment from Pemberley and the Darcys. So, she blamed Tom for the child she carried, and grew to hate it. The pain of that time settled onto her second daughter even before her birth. If Elizabeth had been a boy, she would have been able to have victory over the pain. Yet, she was not.

Mrs. Bennet tried again thrice more to bear her husband a male child. She suffered his attentions in order to bear him a son... yet it did not happen. When she was with-child the fifth time, she had told him it would be the last time she would try. After Lydia was born, she simply denied her husband her bed. It had been a very long time.

After breakfast, Mrs. Bennet found herself in the Pemberley library. She had spent very little time reading books over the last twenty years. Her customs and habits had begun to reflect her white lie of a life. As she pretended to be silly and nervous, her activities began to reflect her role. The more she pretended, the more nervous and juvenile she became.

Why did I ever grow to be the childish, foolish, shallow creature I have become? she thought as she began to look over the shelves. Fanny had at one time enjoyed reading many things. She had enjoyed poetry, and biographies, and had always enjoyed novels. Today she was looking for anything that would tell her of romance, of the romantic affection she desired. *Perhaps a novel*? she thought.

She doubted, should the Darcy library have any literature that was more *instructive in nature*; that it would be out in plain view. But she chose to look anyway.

As she was studying the shelves, occasionally pulling a book out to read the title and peruse its pages, Elizabeth entered the library.

"Good morning, Mama. You seem to be looking for something. Might I assist you?" Elizabeth had actually been observing her for several minutes, trying to determine what she was doing here. For all of Elizabeth's memories, she could never remember her mother looking through books in *any* library.

"Oh, Lizzy, I have never seen a library like this. It is quite exceptional!" Mrs. Bennet said to her daughter as she ran her finger along a shelf of books.

"Well, I have to say I was not aware you had spent that much time in libraries," Elizabeth said with a grin.

Mrs. Bennet laughed, "Well, you would be right if you considered the majority of your lifetime. But before your father and I married, I studied a great deal – about a large number of topics. I have always enjoyed reading poetry, and Aesop's Fables were my favourite at one time. I actually enjoyed reading Milton among other things."

Elizabeth rose her eyebrow, "Truly, mother? I had no idea. Why ever did you stop reading?" Elizabeth said as she walked toward her.

"Well, it is a long story, Lizzy," Mrs. Bennet said as she turned back to the shelf. She was little self-conscious, and unsure whether she could or should have such a conversation with her daughter.

"Well, I am at leisure at present, and would truly like to hear your story if you are willing to tell it. I can order us some tea. Would you like to sit and talk? I truly cannot remember the last time we did such. We talked a little before the wedding. I would like to get to know you, particularly as I am now a married woman and mistress of this estate. Would you like that?"

Elizabeth asked.

"Why yes, Elizabeth, I believe I would like that very well indeed," said Mrs. Bennet, with tears in her eyes, as Elizabeth rang for tea.

They settled into the luxurious armchairs near the fireplace, and soon the tea service was delivered. Elizabeth poured and they settled in to share with each other.

"Mama, I know so little of your early life with Father. Were you very much in love? I heard that you met at a ball in London, but little other than that."

"Oh, Lizzy, my family was determined I would marry well. They assisted me in improving myself by extensive reading. I did meet Mr. Bennet at a ball. I saw him across the room, and I believe I fell in love with him at first sight. He smiled in my direction, came over to me and asked me to dance." Mrs. Bennet paused to take a sip of tea, and Elizabeth offered her a biscuit.

"Your father, he was so handsome. I, of course, said yes and we danced that set and then the last. I was so excited to be singled out by such a fine man. He was there with his best friend that night, you know, your husband's father he was. George Darcy was a nice-looking gentleman; but your Darcy is so much more handsome, my dear, even to my aging eyes," she lightly laughed. "Why, I see much of his mother in him. She was quite beautiful..." she looked down a little sad. Elizabeth wondered what that could mean.

"Was Mrs. Darcy there as well? Were they already married at that time?" Elizabeth asked.

"Oh, she was there..." Mrs. Bennet whispered. "Lizzy, I was not of the *ton*. I was only a tradesman's daughter. I had no connections or wealth, and was below Mrs. Darcy's notice, I fear. I do not speak ill of her. It was what she was taught. But, she and I never truly spoke. We only tolerated each other. I always felt inferior when I was around her. Your father and George Darcy were such good friends. I do not believe they took note of the fact we did not ever become friendly.

"Lizzy, my daughter, you cannot imagine the joy I have at you being mistress of this estate. I am so proud of you. You are the consummate hostess. You have done quite well in attending to the needs of all your guests. I have no fear for you even exceeding the past Mistress of Pemberley, in your value to this estate and your husband," Mrs. Bennet stopped to sip her tea.

"Lady Anne was a fine mistress, but I believe you will surpass her in every way. You generously share your warmth with everyone around you, and she would not have done that. I have never told you how much I admire you, your wit and your intelligence. I was never as wise or clever as you. I regret that I have not been the mother I should have been to you. Will you forgive your foolish mother, Elizabeth? For I truly love you, I do!" Mrs. Bennet exclaimed.

Elizabeth seemed somewhat startled by her words, but in response Lizzy reached out for her hand. Squeezing it she said, "Oh, Mama, thank you for such kind words. I also know I have not given you the time or the chance to know me. I fear I have always been my father's daughter, and did not give you the consequence you deserved as my mother. So, what say you to us starting over as mother and daughter?"

"I would quite like that," Mrs. Bennet said. They drank their tea and they nibbled on biscuits and talked of Pemberley, of events in their family, small talk. Mrs. Bennet also spoke of books she had read in the past. She was attempting to work up to a conversation she wanted to have with Elizabeth. It was an improper conversation for a mother to have with her daughter, but nonetheless, she needed to ask Elizabeth a few questions.

"Lizzy, you appear to be quite happy with your husband. You seem to love him a great deal, and he appears utterly besotted with you."

"Oh, yes, Mama. I do love William. I never imagined I could be so happy, so content."

"I know the last time we talked you said you had no concerns, no questions or fears of your... ah... marital intimacy. Has that proven to be true?" Fanny was quite nervous about moving into this conversation and how detailed, how much she should ask her daughter, but she moved tentatively forward in her conversation.

"Oh," it appeared that Elizabeth blushed deeply as she rose from her chair and walked toward the window. "I am quite content, Mama," she said, yet she could not bring herself to look at her mother.

"Are you simply content, or is it everything you imagined? I remember being a little startled when we last talked. It sounded as though you and Mr. Darcy had been quite open in discussing the matter. I just wondered if it was all you had hoped it to be, my dear," Fanny said with sincerity and hope her daughter would be willing to speak with her.

Elizabeth picked at the edge of her sleeve and turned to look towards her, yet still struggling to look into her eyes, "Oh, mother, marital love is glorious," Elizabeth chanced a quick glance at her mother. "William is truly the best man I have ever known. But he is also loving and passionate. I have not spoken to anyone of this at all, Mama. But I imagine you know of what I speak," she walked back to her chair, still unable to look at her mother in the eyes.

"I know the topic, my daughter. But I fear that I... I... do not know that much... It has not been my experience. I know I should not say that to you as your mother. But, I was taught... I was taught to simply lie still, be silent and you know, let it be over quick. I... ah... I... ah... oh Lizzy, I do not want you to be embarrassed, but I know that has not been your experience for I was walking by your chambers last night..." Fanny could not go on.

"Oh, heavens, Mama! You could hear us? Oh, Lord, do you think everyone..." Elizabeth said as she buried her head into her hands.

"No, dear, I was walking the hall as I could not sleep. I must have happened by at, ah... near the end, I suspect," Fanny blushed more than she believed she ever had, and looked at her lap. "I am so embarrassed, Lizzy. I should not have been listening. I should have walked on. But I find that, I, wish that I... I want to know more. Oh, I do not know how to say it. I am mortified," Mrs. Bennet stuttered.

"*You*, are mortified? Oh, Lord, I cannot let William know. He would..."

Mrs. Bennet cut her off again, "Oh, Lizzy, no you cannot tell him such a thing. And you know a little white lie never hurt anything!"

Elizabeth started to laugh, "Ah, white lies, well they have always had significance in my relationship with William in one way or another," she said as she chanced a glance back at her mother.

Then she said, "No, I will not tell him you heard, certainly not! But... ah... Mama... are you telling me that you... that you have not felt... do not know... ah... pleasure? Is that what you are trying to say?" Elizabeth said, as she again looked around the room, unable to look directly into her mother's eyes.

"Lizzy, I was here today searching your library for a book... for an instruction manual, maybe a novel or a guide, something. I wish to learn, and I am horrified that I am having this conversation with you at all. I do not want any specifics. I, it is just if you know... of ah... of anything that I could read..." Mrs. Bennet stopped.

Elizabeth thought, *Good, God, I cannot believe I am having such a conversation with my mother*! But she said, "I will... ah... see what I can find, and leave it in your chambers. Will that do, Mother?" Blushing profusely, Elizabeth was determined to change the subject quickly for she did not want to know *anything* of what she *had* heard, but even less, she did not desire to contemplate such concerns of her parents' relationship. But, if she could help... She did know of a book she had in her chambers. She would leave it for her mother.

"Tell me about what you have planned so far for Jane's wedding?" and Elizabeth and her mother spent the rest of the morning chatting.

~~*~*~*

As Elizabeth and her mother were spending the morning in the library, Mr. Bennet was restless and chose to walk the paths surrounding Pemberley house. He had dressed warmly, but as there was not yet snow on the ground, he walked and thought again of the extraordinary discovery of Anne's letter.

She had cared for him. Did that help? Or did it make him more desolate? *I think it helps. I did not imagine that she felt anything for me all those many years ago. It was her family, not her, that was determined she only to marry for connections and wealth.*

But as Tom Bennet continued to contemplate, he could not forget the knowledge that she did choose wealth and connections. *I wonder what our life would have been had we married? Would we have been happy? I most assuredly would not have been the man I am today. I would not have had my five daughters. I imagine she would never have been satisfied to live at Longbourn. Ah, I had never thought of that. She would not have been, would she?*

Tom Bennet ventured toward the small Pemberley Chapel. He saw it in the distance. He put his hands in his pocket and allowed his head to fall in a circle around his neck, attempting to release a bit of the tension that he felt.

Lady Anne would never have been happy at Longbourn. Tom contemplated that neither Longbourn nor Stoke would have been enough. She would have desired the best, and he would have strived to give it to her. Living beyond their means, most likely exactly like his fears of what would have happened if Fanny had known of his wealth. *Amazing! I had never thought about it in this way. Perhaps, just perhaps, my life has been better this way. No pressures from the ton. No attempt to make myself into something I am not. How I would have hated that!*

With that thought, Tom Bennet tentatively smiled. He realized he might have disliked his life even more with a woman who was focused on connections and wealth. He would have spent his life struggling to prove himself, to gain status and connections. His life would not have been his own.

Fanny might be silly at times, but he truly believed she loved him. She had been a good mistress to Longbourn. If only she could have born Tom a son. *But that matters not now, does it. The entail is broken; the estate will be equally divided amongst my daughters at Fanny's passing. Why have I not told Fanny of it? Why do I not relieve her suffering? She has been everything that is proper since Fitzwilliam and Lizzy announced their engagement. I believe I have overlooked and been unfair to her.*

Tom found that he had walked to the chapel, and his feet took him to the small cemetery on the side, the family cemetery. He looked for and approached Anne Darcy's grave. *Did I know this was where I was headed?* He did not know, but he was glad his body had brought him there.

Tom Bennet had been at Anne Darcy's funeral. He stood back in the woods. He did not want to disturb George, did not want to upset the balance his absence from the Darcys' life had brought to them. But he had found he had to be there. Edward had written him of her death and had seen him there that day, but he was the only one. He was far enough away that he did not hear all of the ceremony, but he had wanted to honour her memory. Wanted to see if he could bury his feelings with her body. It had not worked.

He had hoped to be able to spend time at her grave. But it was not to be. George stayed there most of the afternoon, until it was dark; and Tom Bennet had decided he must leave in the soft twilight that day.

But here he was again. He knew he needed to let go. He knew it was time to bury his feelings at long last. They had done him great ill for far too long. So he spoke out loud, "Anne, I cannot thank you enough for that letter you wrote so long ago. You are right. My life would not have been as I would have wanted if we had married. I have always had an idolized view of what that life would have been, only thinking of the fresh feeling of love and passion. You did not feel the same for me. I know you felt something, but not as I felt for you. Not as Fanny feels for me." Tom Bennet stopped and shook his head. Fanny loved him, he was sure of it, a deep and abiding love. And he had rejected that love throughout their marriage.

"I have come to tell you goodbye. To let go of your ghost, a phantom that has haunted me for much too long. Goodbye, Anne, goodbye," and he placed his hand on her gravestone. A lone tear slid down his cheek, and he wiped it away. He was no longer sure whether he cried for the loss of Anne, or for the shame of rejecting his wife.

With those thoughts in his mind, he turned to walk toward the house. Contemplating how he could make amends for his neglect and slight of his wife and family, he returned to Pemberley and his bedchamber.

~~*~*~*

A little later in the day, he found William and Lizzy together in Darcy's study. He told them of the break in the entail, and he and Fitzwilliam had come to an understanding about Stoke. Tom wished for them to have it, so Darcy agreed to take over financial responsibility and property management as well as ownership. It was apparent that it meant a great deal to his daughter and godson, and he selfishly hoped it would assist them in visiting Longbourn more often. He laughed with them, and hoped they were happy with this unique Christmas present!

He found Jane and Mr. Bingley in the front parlour, chatting happily about their new life to come. He had already spoken of Jane's dowry with Mr.

Bingley. As they were alone, he took the opportunity to discuss with them the break of the entail, and how that would affect them.

It was a happy Christmas celebration as dinner came, all assembled sat to partake of a Christmas feast. Presents were exchanged after dinner was complete, and all experienced music and gaiety.

Mr. Bennet ended the day determined to speak to his wife on the morrow, and begin to make restitution for the withdrawal of his admiration. He was resolute in making every effort to nourish the seed of love for his wife, and allow them a chance, as he had never done before.

~~*~*~*

In Fanny's chamber she discovered a book that her daughter, she assumed, had left on her bed. She found, again, that she quite enjoyed expanding her mind by extensive reading. She was studying long into the night.

Chapter 25

In the dawn of early morning, within a huge bed in the Master's Chamber at Pemberley, Lizzy was contemplating the changes and the challenges in her life. So much had changed since her father had found she and her now-husband in an embrace. More importantly, she remembered the precious gift that came with honesty and truth.

William's warm, naked body was spooned against hers, as it had been each night of their wedded bliss as they slept. It was most convenient as they often awoke from their slumber to delight in each other's flesh.

She giggled and William awoke and kissed her bare shoulder. "Lizzy, are you happy, my dearest? What cheery thought awakens you with laughter on this Boxing Day?"

Turning around and looking deeply into his eyes she said, "Oh, I was only meditating on the prodigious good that has come into my life since you followed me into the library at Netherfield."

"I agree with you, my love. We are very lucky to have found the ability to be honest with each other. You know the consequences of lies are not always so positive."

"You are right, of course. But our openness with each other, and ability to tease other into telling the complete truth will serve us quite well throughout our marriage, do you not think?"

"I do, indeed. I believe many marriages could be vastly improved if both parties were willing to be honest with each other. White lies and secrets never bode well in a marriage. I do not think we will have the same problems that many others have. Can you imagine what might have happened had we married after the incident at Netherfield and not been able to openly talk with each other?"

"I would most likely still be terrified of you and marital relations, and would most definitely not be in your arms—bare and exposed to your adoring eyes."

"Yes, my dear, and if I had my preference you would remain unclothed at all times. But speaking of such reminds me..." Darcy's words trailed off as he kissed her languorously, which fanned the flames of their newly discovered intimacy to the point where words were no longer necessary.

~~*~*~*

Boxing Day had started out pleasantly. Over breakfast the entire family met for a scrumptious breakfast, and Elizabeth and Georgiana left to deliver packages to the tenants of Pemberley as the rest of the party sought a variety of entertainments.

"Elizabeth, I cannot tell you what a gift you have given to me. To see my brother so happy is more than I could ever have imagined," Georgiana said to her new sister as they began their journey.

"Georgiana, you are quite kind, but I find it is your brother that has made me more contented than I could ever have anticipated. I am also quite delighted with my new sister. I do not believe I could find a better or a finer woman anywhere," Elizabeth said as she reached over to squeeze Georgiana's hands.

Georgiana dropped her eyes to her lap. "Oh Elizabeth, I fear I am not fine at all. I am so ashamed. I do not know if I can ever make it up to Fitzwilliam. I hurt him so," she said as she trailed off.

"Georgiana, I need you to know that William and I share everything," Elizabeth said quite gently trying to peer down to catch Georgiana's eyes.

"You know," Georgiana whispered as she glanced up into Elizabeth's eyes.

"Yes, dear. I know about you and Mr. Wickham. I have for sometime, and believe me; you do not need to make anything up to William. He blames himself for not taking better care of you, and not trusting you enough to tell you of his history with that man," Elizabeth exclaimed.

Elizabeth continued, "That man was despicable! He sought you out and deceived you only to hurt your brother. He is quite the master of intrigue. You do not know this, but he once deceived me as well. He told me quite a story about your brother, and I believed him. His lies, his horrible lies about your brother! Do not distress yourself any longer, Georgiana. We, your brother and I, hold you in the highest regard. No one other than your cousin Richard knows of this. And no one ever needs to know. If anyone even saw you in Ramsgate and mentions it, you can say that Mr. Wickham was raised at Pemberley and was always like a brother to you."

"But, Elizabeth, he was not like a brother to me then," Georgiana said as she blushed. "I truly did not know myself, I still do not trust myself! How am I to come out into society this coming year?"

"Oh, my dear, you need not worry. Your brother and I will be there for you in all that you do. If you do not wish to be come out this next year, you can always wait another. We will not force you, you know," Elizabeth reassured her.

"Truly, Elizabeth, I can wait if I wish it?" Georgiana smiled as she said it.

"Yes, I will make sure of it. You need not be presented until you feel ready. I will make quite sure of that, my dear sister," Elizabeth said. They proceeded to complete their tasks, chatting about all that was a part of coming out, and whether Georgiana felt up to the task or not. They agreed to continue to talk openly about this subject as well as any that Georgiana supported. The sisters had truly bonded that Boxing Day before they returned to the house.

~~*~*~*

A little later on, Tom Bennet asked his wife if he might speak with her. They moved back to her chambers to talk.

Fanny entered and sat by the fire, and Tom began to pace the floor.

"Fanny, I would like... ah need to... ah talk with you about a number of matters as I know I have not been fair with you these many years," Mr. Bennet spoke.

Fanny's stomach lurched. Somewhere deep within she feared that he might have decided to divorce her. Oh, yes, it would be a disgrace in society. But she did not truly know what he would want to speak to her about. She rung her hands as she worried, but she said, "I am listening, Tom. Please speak to me of whatever you are concerned."

"Fanny, our financial situation is not as you have feared. I have recently discovered that with the death of Mr. Collins, there is no other distant Bennet heir. The entail has been broken with the help of our solicitor. If I should pass this earth before you, you will be allowed to remain at Longbourn until your death, and at both of our deaths the estate will be divided amongst our daughters."

"Truly, Mr. Bennet? I no longer have to be worried about losing my home? Is it really true?" Fanny smiled in delight.

"It is true and that is not all. I began to make investments many years ago with the guidance of George Darcy and Edward Fitzwilliam. We are quite comfortable, my dear," he said as he took her hand. "Our daughters have dowries. I just never informed you that I had provided for you."

"You made investments?" Fanny looked at him with a wrinkled brow. "I do not understand, Tom. Just what is your income?"

"Ah, that has been part of my reticence in telling you, Fanny. You see, I, ah, my income is approximately 20,000 pounds per annum."

Mrs. Bennet's hands went to her cheeks, "Good Lord, Tom, you are more wealthy than Mr. Darcy?"

"Oh no, my love, for your son-in-law's annual income is at least three times what is published. He also owns much more property than I."

Fanny was so flushed for a moment she thought she might faint, but she did not miss that he had said *my love*. "Do you mean that Mr. Darcy has 30,000 pounds a year? Oh, Lord, our Lizzy is quite blessed indeed. But then we are as well," she smiled quite brightly.

Mr. Bennet had been pacing but moved to her. He picked up her hand and kissed the back of it, "Yes, Fanny we are blessed. I have been most unfair to you to hide this. I did not, still do not want my income made public knowledge, Fanny. Do you understand? Can you imagine the mortification Mr. Darcy has felt all these years when upon entering a room, all he has heard is to half the room speaking of him solely based on his annual income? He has told me that he hated it. I did not want any of us, you and I or any of our daughters, solely to be known by our income," Tom said as he turned away toward the window.

Fanny looked at him, and with sudden understanding said, "And you feared that I would be so silly as to share it with the entire neighbourhood. Am I right, Mr. Bennet?"

Tom turned to look at her, and for just a minute he saw a much younger Fanny Gardiner. Her head was slightly cocked to the side, and her eyebrow rose with a quizzical look in her eye. "Yes, Fanny. I am sorry to say that you are right. Can you forgive me?"

Fanny looked at her hands a moment and then up to him, "Oh, Tom, I fear I need your forgiveness as well. I... ah... being back at Pemberley has brought up so many memories. I need you to know that I heard a conversation the day we left here, so many years ago. I know you heard it as well, as I had seen you enter the library. I know why we left here. I know how hurt you were. I know that you were ashamed of me, and had every right to be so. And I... I... I," Fanny stopped. Could she possibly say this next part?

"Fanny, please finish. I had no idea you knew of the reason for our separation. Please tell me," he said gently as he moved back toward her and sat in the seat next to her, looking into her eyes and pleading.

Fanny looked at her lap, "I know you loved Anne, Tom."

Tom looked at the ground. Neither spoke for several minutes.

"Fanny, I had no idea... I am so sorry... But I can tell you... being here, I have finally let go of that ghost," he said as he very tentatively reached toward her, and moved her head up to look into his eyes. Both of their eyes questioned the other. "Fanny, can you ever forgive me for hurting you, for ignoring you for oh, so, long... for building a wall... for allowing my heart to close over? I am so, so sorry!"

They could not continue looking at each other for long. Fanny stood and walked to the window. "Tom, there is more. I hurt so much when we returned from Pemberley, that I chose to close myself off from you. I created the silly, foolish Mrs. Bennet to keep you at arm's length. At the time, I thought it only a white lie. But it became so much more. She really never existed, you know. But the more I played the role, the more I became her. I found if you thought me silly and foolish, it protected me. I could imagine that was the reason you distanced yourself from me, and not because you loved another."

"You need to know I can choose not to be her. I did it for Elizabeth when I knew we would be in the company of the Darcy and Fitzwilliam families for the wedding, and it became easy to be me again. I do not know if you have noticed that I have been somewhat different since Elizabeth's engagement?

"I have noticed. I did not know why you had changed. But I did notice," Tom looked at her, stood, and took a couple steps towards her.

She was looking out the window now. She could not look at him as she said it. "Can you forgive me?"

Tom walked to the window to join her. "I would like to try, Fanny. I would like to think we could try and start again. Would you even want to? Do you even want to try and love this foolish old man? I have been stuck believing in a dream that never existed, Fanny. Anne Darcy was not real. She was a figment of my imagination. I would never have been happy with Anne, Fanny. I am not a man that would have withstood the onslaught of the *ton*. Having all this time to think these last few days, I realize that now. I am grateful for my family, for my lovely daughters, and for my wife," he again lifted her hand to kiss her fingers gently. They both blushed and turned to look out the window.

Out in the garden they saw a couple, walking hand in hand. Their heads close together. They turned to each other and kissed deeply, as they held each other tight. They were truly in love. Their daughter, Elizabeth and his godson, Fitzwilliam were the true picture of besotted love. They continued to watch them as they continued to speak.

"Tom, I wish, oh, how I wish to be them," she said as she smiled at the sight.

They saw below a smiling and laughing husband pick up his bride and swing her around in a circle as she giggled. Then she slid down his body as they kissed and then continued to walk.

"I do not know if we can, Fanny, but I wish it as well. I would like to try and start. Would you allow me to court you, my dear?" Tom turned to her and held out his hand.

"Yes, Tom, I would quite like for you to court me," she said as she smiled a youthful, bright, happy smile at him.

"You look quite lovely today, my dear," Tom said as he looked down to her with a wide smile.

"Tom, you know, I remember we used to read books together. I have a book that I would like to share with you..."

THE END